Divided Interests

NEW YORK TIMES & USA TODAY BESTSELLING AUTHOR

KELLY ELLIOTT

Divided Interests
Book 3 Southern Bride Copyright © 2020 by Kelly Elliott
ISBN PAPERBACK 978-1-943633-63-0

Cover photo by: Shannon Cain
Photography by Shannon Cain
Cover Design by: RBA Designs, www.rbadesigns.com
Interior Design & Formatting by: Elaine York, www.
allusiongraphics.com
Developmental Editor: Elaine York, www.allusiongraphics.com
Content Editor: Cori McCarthy, Yellow Bird Editing
Proofing Editor: AmyRose Capetta, Yellow Bird Editing

This book is a work of fiction. Names, characters, places, and incidents either are products of the author's imagination or are used fictitiously. Any resemblance to actual persons, living or dead, events, or locales is entirely coincidental.

For more information on Kelly and her books, please visit her website www.kellyelliottauthor.com.

Divided Interests

Prologue

Lucas

I STARED AT the old man. There had to have been some sort of mistake. I had heard him wrong. My stomach clenched as I let the words sink in.

"I'm sorry," I said with a bemused chuckle. "I thought I heard you say I was a co-owner of my grandfather's ranch house here in Johnson City."

He nodded. "That is what I said, Lucas."

With a sharp shake of my head, I stated, "This is a mistake, Lou. I'm the only grandchild of William Foster. If granddad didn't leave it to either of my parents, who did he leave it to?"

The old man attempted to hide his smile and failed miserably.

"Fifty percent of the home located at 4547 Ranch Road 175 has been left to one—" I swore he paused for dramatic effect—"Paige Miller."

I closed my eyes, let out a soft groan. "Now I for sure heard you wrong. What name did you just say?"

Without opening my eyes, I could hear the lawyer's humor in his reply. "Paige Miller, formally of Johnson City, moved to Arkansas to attend the University of Arkansas with a degree in International Business with a..."

"Minor in French. I know who Paige is, Lou, and you know I know! *Why* is she named in my grandfather's will?"

The old man, who also happened to be my granddad's best friend, leaned back in his oversized leather chair and gave me a smile. "I'm afraid the only person who knows is your granddad."

I forced a smile. "That doesn't help me any, Lou, when the man was buried three days ago."

His smile faded. "That is true... Where were you again?"

Guilt hit me square in the chest. I'd never forgive myself for missing granddad's funeral. *Fucking Bianca.*

Sighing, I replied, "Fiji."

He snapped his fingers. "That's right. Your momma said you and your girlfriend went there. Heard the girlfriend was expecting a ring. Did you ask her to marry you?"

"No, I did not. Can we please get back to this...mistake?"

"Ms. Miller was in my office two days ago and picked up the keys and a letter your granddad wrote to her." He pulled out an envelope from the file and slid it across his desk. "This is your letter and *your* key." Then he placed a single key on top of the envelope.

I stared at it. If I touched it, I might combust and set the whole damn office on fire.

Then I laughed, rubbed the back of my neck and looked at my granddad's oldest and dearest friend. "This is a joke, right? Granddad pulling one over on me from his grave because he loved his jokes? I know he adored Paige, and always said I needed to get my shit, *er*, stuff together, but he wasn't serious."

He didn't crack a smile at all. He actually looked a bit pissed off. "Trust me when I say this is not a joke. William knew exactly what he was doing. Read the letter, Lucas. All the answers you're looking for start with that letter." He jerked his chin toward the envelope.

I grabbed it and stood. "Half of the house is mine, the other half is Paige's?"

"That's right, as well as the land."

A sinking feeling hit me in the middle of my gut. The land as well. *Mother-freaking-effer.* My first impulse was to sell it. Every time I stepped into that house I thought of her. Of Paige. The woman I now owned it with. Jesus Christ, this was messed up.

"Thank you for your time, Lou."

As I made my way toward the door, he called out, "Welcome back to Johnson City, son."

I placed my hand on the door. A part of me grew angry that my granddad had tried to force my hand. The plan had always been for me to go to college, then come back and work alongside my father and granddad in the family construction company. That all changed the summer after I graduated high school. I didn't want that house or the memories associated with it.

"As soon as I buy Paige out and sell that house, I'm headed back to Austin, Lou."

He frowned. "That's a damn shame. We could use a man of your many talents here in town."

I laughed. The idea that Bianca would even entertain the thought of living in Johnson City was a joke. She was already bitching about staying at the bed and breakfast down the road, which I actually thought was nicer than any expensive hotel we had ever stayed in.

"I won't be staying, but thanks, Lou."

Before the door shut, I swore I heard the old man chuckle and say, "We'll see about that."

Chapter 1

Paige - Three days earlier

"**P**AIGE, SWEETHEART, THANK you so much for coming. William loved you like a granddaughter and missed you so."

I wiped a tear from my cheek and forced a smile as Lynn Foster placed her hands on my upper arms and gave me a onceover. She'd always done this, for as long as I could remember. When I had walked into the home of Lynn and Carl Foster, my heart had been hurting. I had loved Carl's father, William, like he was my own grandfather.

"I had no idea he was sick, or I would have come to visit," I stated. "It's been months since I've seen him."

She shook her head. "Don't you even, young lady. You talked to him every week. You stopped by last Christmas and played dominoes with him and helped him decorate the tree outside the old house. He went on for days about how you decorated that tree."

I smiled warmly at Lynn, but I couldn't ignore the way my chest ached. I had planned on coming home to see my father, brother Tom, and William. I'd used the excuse that I was so busy with work and never made the journey. Coming home to Johnson City always brought with it a blanket of sadness. The memories and lost dreams often made it hard to breathe.

Lynn gazed at me with a loving look. I'd always adored her, and it had nothing to do with the fact that her son, Lucas, had been one of my best friends growing up, along with Milo Elliott and Jen Adams. I had dated Lucas all through high school. He had been my first love. My first real French kiss. Hell, my first with every sexual encounter—until I left Arkansas eleven years ago when I was eighteen.

"I'm going to miss him." I glanced around, looking for her son. I hadn't seen him in a few years. Each time I was in town, he wasn't. And even though we both lived in Austin, we never once ran into each other.

That was a lie. I had stumbled across him a few times, but always managed to slip away before he could see me. Of course, we ran in different circles now. He never did forgive me for going to Arkansas and not to the University of Texas. I had dreams of opening my own business, and Lucas had dreams of staying in Johnson City and taking over his family's business. It wasn't that I didn't love my hometown; I did. But I was young and wanted to see what else was out there besides small-town Texas.

This was the whole reason I chose an international business degree and minored in French. The idea of living in France had always been a dream, one I shared with Lucas a lifetime ago. He had been all for it, but when he found out I didn't want the simple business degree Texas offered, he got upset. A part of me thought maybe he wanted a break; we had dated all through high school, after all. But he gave me an ultimatum and that was the breaking point. If I didn't go to UT with him, we would have to break up because he couldn't do a long-distance relationship. The truth was, he obviously didn't trust me, and that broke my heart in two.

"Paige, before you leave to head back to Austin, would you mind stopping by Lou Howard's office tomorrow? You were named in William's will."

"Me?" I asked, my voice sounding as stunned as I felt.

"You know he loved you. He'd hoped you and Lucas would have found your way back to each other by now."

I forced a smile. A part of me had thought maybe we would, as well. I'd never had feelings for any other man like I had for Lucas. It took me nearly my whole freshman year of college to get over him, and even to this day, my brain tells me he's old news, and my heart argues back.

"Where is Lucas?" I asked, trying to be nonchalant.

Lynn's face went into a scowl. "Fiji."

My eyes widened. "I'm sorry, did you say Fiji?"

For a moment, I thought a growl came from Lynn. She rolled her eyes. "I should say he is on his way back. Once things turned for the worse, and I realized William was not going to get any better, I called Lucas. Bless his soul, no matter how hard he tried to get back in time for the funeral today, it wasn't going to happen. They somehow missed their flight."

Lynn looked around, took my arm and led us both out to the back porch. Fewer people were gathered out there and we could speak more openly. Once we were outside, she leaned in close to me and whispered, "Bianca *conveniently* couldn't find her passport."

I raised a brow.

"Yes. On purpose! Lucas should have left her selfish ass on that island."

The back door flew open and Linda May Hacker strolled out. "Oh Lynn, darling, I'm so sorry to hear about William, and that Lucas couldn't make it back in time."

I covered my smile at Lynn calling her son's girlfriend out like that. I watched as she plastered on a smile and turned to Linda May. I was positive she was still the go-to person in Johnson City for gossip.

"Linda May, thank you so much for coming," Lynn said, as sweet as apple pie.

They hugged, then Linda May looked my way. "Is that little Paige Miller?"

I nodded. No matter how old you were, when you came back to your small hometown in Texas, you were the same little girl who ran around in pigtails. I was still a fan of pigtails, don't get me wrong; I just didn't wear them out in public anymore. Okay, that was a lie,

I did on occasion. When I had an extra pep in my step. I also wore them Friday nights when I changed into my PJs and crawled into bed at eight to watch the latest Netflix obsession. Yes, my life was *that* exciting.

"It is, indeed," I said, giving Linda May a quick hug.

Almost all southern women were huggers. I still hadn't figured that one out yet. There had to be a reason. My momma used to say it was because they wanted to see how much weight you'd gained since the last time they saw you. Or if the rumor about the breast lift was true or not. Regardless, hugging was mandatory as soon as you set foot in this town.

My heart pained as I thought of my momma. She had been gone for four years, and there wasn't a day I didn't miss her or wish I could pick up the phone and ask for a bit of advice.

"Four years," I murmured.

Lynn looked at me with confusion. "Four years, what?"

I waved my hand in front of my face as if I was losing my mind. "I just remembered that's how long it has been since I've seen Lucas. Four years. Momma's funeral."

Lynn tilted her head, as did Linda May. I got that pity look that southern women had perfected down to a freakin' T. Some meant it, some didn't. Currently, I was one for two. Lynn meant it, Linda May didn't. She and my momma had hated each other.

"That's right. I know he was so happy to see you. He often asks about you," Lynn said.

I wanted to laugh. Lucas was anything but happy to see me, and I knew his pride wouldn't allow him to inquire about me. He didn't understand my desire to do something different, to see the world, and I couldn't understand why he didn't want the same things. Moving back to Johnson City was his idea of a dream, and yet my own dreams weren't as valid. When I was younger, I thought about nothing but traveling the world.

And I did travel. I got a job with a large corporation straight out of college and traveled to Europe often. My minor in French came in handy. I'd had amazing opportunities, as well as experiences I would never forget. Regretting my decision never entered my mind, even though the result had been my broken heart. I'd hardly dated at all since Lucas. A few casual dates, one serious relationship which ended recently when I realized that Jeff was not the man I wanted to settle down and raise a family with. Everything had seemed...off lately. I needed a major change.

I had worked for that company for two years, traveling ninety percent of the time as an analyst, before my mother was diagnosed with cancer. I took another job in Austin to be closer to her and my father. She died shortly after I moved back to Texas. My daddy had been so lost without my momma. He was a rancher, fourth generation. Needless to say, my older brother Tom had been a huge help to daddy when our mother was sick. I loved the ranch, but running it was not my dream; it was Tom's. He and his wife Kate were perfect together. Kate loved ranching and was right there alongside my brother when it came to helping Daddy run the ranch. I admired her for so many things. She was a mother to my beautiful niece Callie and nephew Tom Jr. She helped Tom do everything, from plowing fields to castrating a bull. Then she made it back home in time to whip up some fabulous dessert to bring to the PTA meeting that night. She had her shit together and kicked ass at life. That's not jealousy at all; simply me recognizing one badass woman.

As much as my folks wished I had been in Texas more, I had enjoyed traveling the world with my job, and they supported me one-hundred percent. Once I got traveling out of my system, I found myself daydreaming about owning my own little flower shop in Johnson City. It had been a long-term goal, one I'd wanted to do after I got some experience in the business world—another thing Lucas refused to understand.

My mind drifted to the flower shops I'd visited in France. My mother loved flowers and had handed down her passion to me. The longer I worked in corporate America, the more I wanted a simpler life. The life that Lucas had once dreamed for us. The thought made my chest tighten with a dull ache that had never gone away since he'd walked away from me. I had been so angry with him. How could he *make* me choose? Why would he make me choose? Why didn't he trust me? They were all questions I never got answered, and it still hurt as much today as it did back then.

"Paige? You seem lost in thought," I heard Lynn say, pulling me back to our conversation.

With a neutral expression, I asked, "How is Lucas doing, besides traveling to Fiji?"

Lynn forced a smile, and I wasn't sure if it was for her sake or mine.

"He's doing really good. His career has taken off, which I think he's happy about."

Lucas was a CAD engineer and worked for a large construction company in Austin, which I thought was crazy since he had been the one to state that he wanted to live in Johnson City forever and not live in a big city. His plan had always been to work for his father's construction company based out of Johnson City. William had started the business, then passed it down to Carl, Lucas's father. Carl also owned a cattle ranch down the road from my father's. Lucas and I had become friends in elementary school. Way back when, he and Milo were best friends, and me and Jen were. I still kept in touch with Jen. Not as often as I would like, but we always picked up right where we left off, like we'd spoken yesterday. I loved that about Jen.

"He's been traveling a lot with Bianca. She likes to travel," Lynn added.

Ouch. That hurt more than I wanted to admit.

He hadn't been interested in traveling and seeing the world when I had wanted to.

Lynn must have seen the look on my face because she attempted to backpedal. "He hates it, though. Tells me all the time he can't stand the constant vacations."

"I'm happy he's happy," I said, hoping to ease the awkwardness. I truly was happy for him. Okay, that's a lie. Maybe a small part of me somewhere deep in my heart felt hurt that Lucas traveled around the world with his current girlfriend. Maybe that part wasn't small. It was big. Okay, it was huge, and it sucked. I decided I was not going to go down that path again, though, and pushed all thoughts of Lucas and Bianca out of my head.

I couldn't help but notice Lynn's expression fall. Her eyes filled with sadness, and a part of me wanted to ask her if everything was okay. Then I realized her father-in-law had just died. Of course, she wasn't alright.

Lynn took my hands in hers. I couldn't help but notice her cold hands, and I glanced down at them, attempting to rub away the chill. I missed my momma so much.

"Are you happy, Paige? With your life in Austin?"

With a nod, I replied, "*Mmm-hmm.*"

Ugh. That couldn't have sounded any less pathetic.

I basically didn't have a life, and I was tired. Tired of my desk job. Tired of my dull life. A part of me was ready to settle down, get married, and raise a family. I was knocking on thirty's door. I lacked any sort of excitement in any area of my life. Maybe that was my problem. I needed to get out there, date. Go to the clubs when my friends asked me. It wasn't surprising they'd stopped inviting me out. I turned them down ninety percent of the time.

Linda May pulled me out of my thoughts. "Has Lucas asked that model to marry him yet?"

Ah, yes. I could count on Linda May to bring my thoughts back to the happy couple. Bianca Howard. She was beautiful. She was rich. She was *nothing* like me. Lucas had been dating her for the last few years...how many exactly I didn't know because I purposely tried not to keep up with his life.

Fine. That was another lie.

I had found out two years, six days, and a few odd hours ago that the man I thought I would marry someday had found himself the grand prize of a girlfriend.

Like I said, pathetic.

"No, but she was hoping for it on this last trip! I'm afraid William might have spoiled it for her with his passing. Lucas had to cut the trip short."

I internally fist-bumped with William. He couldn't stand Bianca and made it known each time I visited or talk to him on the phone that he wished Lucas and I would find our way back to one another. I had tried, once. When I moved back to Austin, I called Lucas. He hadn't been dating anyone at the time, and we made plans to meet for dinner. But the bastard never showed. He stood me up, and I was pissed. When I sent him a text and asked if it had slipped his mind, he replied back, "I had a change of plans."

Radio silence after that.

My body had pulsed with anger, and I'd vowed to hate Lucas Foster for the rest of my life. Of course, I could never actually hate him. He was my first love. My momma used to tell me that once you open your heart to love, no matter what happens, you always love that person. How could your heart honestly stop loving someone? I believed she was right. It isn't like the feeling fades. It just gets packed away, out of sight and mind. If I wasn't still in love with Lucas, why did hearing about him or thinking about him still hurt?

Why had I never truly moved on? I dated a guy recently for almost a year. For the last few months of our relationship, Jeff had been asking for me to move in with him. He even hinted about maybe getting married. I couldn't do that to him. Especially not after the day I saw Lucas in Whole Foods in Austin, and I hid behind a display to watch him. I knew I wasn't being honest with myself, or Jeff. I went to his place that night and broke up with him. That was almost seven months ago...

I hadn't been on a single date since.

Pathetic. It might as well have been my middle name.

"What about you, sweet little Paige? Are you dating anyone?" Linda asked.

"Not currently. I was, but we broke up."

Lynn gave me a smile that said she was sorry, while Linda May looked me up and down, as if to say maybe it was the five extra pounds I'd packed on that was the breaking point.

Fine, fine. Ten pounds.

"Linda May, if you'll excuse us, I have something *personal* to talk to Paige about."

My eyes widened at the emphasis Lynn had put on personal. Linda May shot Lynn a distasteful look and headed back into the house.

"Like I was saying, I need you to stop by Lou's office before you head back to Austin."

"Okay. I'll do that. Is everything okay?"

Lynn's eyes sparkled with mischief. Something was up, and Lynn wasn't about to fill me in on it.

With a wink, she replied, "It will be."

Chapter 2

Paige - Present day

I STOOD IN front of the old house and smiled. I'd always loved this place. I'd even dreamed of owning it someday, and I was positive I had mentioned that a time or two to William. The fact that he left me the house thrilled me more than I could say.

Well, he left me *half* of the house. The other half belonged to his grandson. My ex.

Lucas.

Looking at the large, two-story white house, I took in the little details. They didn't build houses like this anymore. The large white columns held up the second-floor roof. I remembered sneaking out of the upstairs bedrooms and climbing onto that very roof. Lucas and I would lie out there and look at the stars. It wasn't uncommon for all of us to spend the night at William and May's house. May was Lucas's grandmother. They loved having us kids there. Said it filled the house with love and laughter. Jen and I would stay in one room, while Lucas and Milo stayed in another.

My gaze wandered to the empty front porch. Then Milo's voice interrupted my thoughts. "I can give you an estimate to paint the house and do a few minor repairs. You want to keep it white, right?"

Milo asked, writing in his notebook as we walked up the steps, into the foyer and over to the large living room.

It was a no-brainer to call Milo when I realized the house could use a coat of paint inside and out. I probably should have waited for Lucas, but since I hadn't heard from him after I left him a voicemail asking him to call me, I decided to jump feet first into this project. It had awakened my soul the moment Lou told me I was part-owner. I had to admit, I wasn't surprised when Lou told me William had left the house to both of us. The man had wanted us to get back together something fierce and hadn't been silent on the subject for the last ten years.

"Yes, if we could match the shade of white, that would be amazing. I also found this old picture in one of my photo albums. Do you think you could build me a porch swing? I remember the four of us swinging on it. I was hoping the old one might be on the property somewhere, but I haven't found it yet."

"I can talk to Carl. He'd be the best person to build it, since he probably swung on it too, and might enjoy building it," Milo said with a wide smile, before it faded. "Paige, have you talked to Lucas yet?"

"Nope," I said, popping the *P* and holding up a swatch of paint colors against the wall in the living room.

"Don't you think y'all should decide which half the house is yours and which half is his?"

The humor in his voice wasn't lost on me.

"My plan is to buy Lucas out."

Milo's eyes went wide, and then he laughed. When I didn't laugh, he stopped. "Wait, you're being serious?"

"Of course I am. Lucas doesn't want this house. I'm pretty sure that his girlfriend doesn't want to move to Johnson City. Besides, he has a home in Austin."

"So do you!"

"Not anymore. I put my downtown loft on the market and moved into this farmhouse this morning...right after I quit my job."

He looked around, a stunned expression on his face. "Where's all your stuff?"

"Fresh start, Milo. On everything."

"Okay, but this house belonged to *his* grandfather. You don't think he's going to want to keep it?"

I laughed mockingly. "Please. He'll want to be rid of it simply because I'm a part of it now."

He frowned. "I don't think so, Paige. He has asked about you a number of times in the past. Either to me or Jen."

I stared at him. Jen had never once mentioned Lucas asking about me. I decided to ignore him and keep talking. I'd have to deal with that bit of information later.

"I intend on bringing this house back to its glory days. When William told me he had a storage unit outside of town filled with furniture, I knew he wanted it to be put back the way it was when he was little."

"When did he tell you that?"

With a shrug, I said, "When I would visit him, he would talk about how the house used to be. And, he wrote it in a letter for me, telling me about the storage shed."

Milo looked around the house. "But there is already furniture in this place. And he has a storage shed full of it?"

I nodded. "Maybe his parents' furniture? Things he and May wanted to keep over the years. I haven't made it over there yet to look at it."

"Does Lucas own part of it, as well?"

With a smile that might have been a little snarky, I replied, "Nope. Just me."

Needless to say, when Lou told me William had left me fifty percent of his home here in Johnson City, I thought he was kidding. Then he handed me the letter William had written, and my heart nearly exploded. I felt in my pocket and smiled when I touched the faint outline of the folded-up paper that mentioned the storage shed and its contents being all mine.

"What did he say in the letter?" Milo asked, standing behind me as I stood on the stepladder.

"Just that he knew how much this house meant to me, how I had always dreamed of owning it. He wanted to make that dream come true."

"Okay, so where does Lucas fit in with all of this? Not to mention his hotter-than-fuck girlfriend?"

I rolled my eyes, then stepped off the stepladder, only to have Milo hold onto my hips and look at me with a funny expression.

"Thanks, I'm good," I said. He dropped his hold and took a step back.

"Sorry, force of habit."

I shrugged, not thinking anything of it.

"The way I look at it, William felt obligated to leave Lucas half the house. He is, after all, his grandson. They were very close."

Milo rubbed his chin. "And you think Lucas won't want to move in here?"

This time I laughed for real. "Oh please, Milo. He lives in Austin in a mansion of an apartment with his...what did you call her? Hotter-than-hot girlfriend. I seriously doubt he wants to move her back to the country. I'm positive Bianca doesn't want to live here."

"I said hotter than fuck."

I scowled.

He cleared his throat. "Yeah, I can't see that. Betty said Bianca does nothing but bitch whenever they stay there."

"Why don't they stay at Carl and Lynn's place?"

Milo's cheeks went red. "Well, according to Betty, Bianca is a screamer when they have sex."

I crinkled my nose. "Gross. I didn't need to know that."

He shrugged. "Plus Lynn can't stand Bianca, and she knows it. Lucas told me his mom has slipped a few times and called her Paige."

Gasping, I covered my mouth. "She has not!"

Milo laughed. "She has, and Lucas said she does it on purpose, to piss off Bianca."

With my lips pressed together, I smiled. I always loved Lynn.

It was time to change the subject. "When do you think you can get a crew here to paint?"

"You don't even want to know how much it's going to cost, Paige." He folded up his notebook and slid it into his bag.

"Of course, I do, but I know you're not going to rake me over the coals, right?"

He winked, and I couldn't help but give him one back. Milo had always been good looking. Not as handsome as Lucas, but good looking. It was nice to have a man do something as simple as wink at me. He'd recently divorced the woman he'd met in college. Brought her home to Johnson City and thought she loved it. She loved it alright; she loved screwing the high school's assistant football coach—who happened to be Milo's brother. They were currently living together, which was a huge scandal for the small town of Johnson City.

The divorce was final about six months ago, or at least that was what Jen told me.

We started walking back to the front door. "I'll get you a quote in the next day or two. Once you narrow down the colors for the inside, I'll have a better price."

"What if I helped paint the inside? That would save some money, right?" I asked as Milo stepped onto the front porch.

"Of course, it would. I can buy you the paint at cost, then you can knock out as much of the inside as you can. You've got the time now, especially if you quit your job, which I still can't believe you did."

"Want to help in your free time…off the clock?" I asked, with a hint of flirting in my voice.

He raised a brow and smiled. "Are you flirting with me, Paige Miller?"

I smiled. "If I am, does that mean you'll help me paint the inside and not charge for the labor?"

"Will there be beer and pizza included in this arrangement?"

"Yes, of course. Do you not know me, Milo?"

He laughed. "Consider it done. I don't have much free time, but I'll come over a few nights and help you."

I was about to hug him when a familiar voice stopped me in my tracks.

"Well, isn't this cozy. Ink isn't even dry on the divorce papers, Milo."

Lucas.

Milo turned and let out a laugh. I—on the other hand—shot Lucas a dirty look.

One, because he looked so freaking handsome standing there it was totally unfair. Especially since my body instantly reacted at the sight of him. I let my eyes move down his body and then chuckled when I found fancy dress shoes. Gone were the days of cowboy boots for Lucas Foster. In their place, preppy shoes that looked uncomfortable and so damn out of place on this property *and* in this town. Not to mention the khaki dress pants, which he was filling out quite nicely, if I was being honest. But this look wasn't Lucas. At. All.

"Holy shit, Lucas Foster, the prodigal son has returned."

Lucas's eyes turned from Milo to me. I tried to hide it when my breath hitched. Just the sight of him made my insides quiver. I hated that he still had such a hold on me. He, on the other hand, didn't have a single reaction to seeing me. Well, except for the scowl.

"I'm only in town long enough to settle up a...real estate issue."

My arms folded over my chest as I narrowed my gaze on him. Looks like those ten extra pounds were not helping me in the sexy department because Lucas looked like he was sick simply at the sight of me.

Jerk.

He looked away, totally unaffected. If it didn't hurt so much, I'd ignore him. But I knew how I would handle all of this. Later tonight I'd lie in bed for far too long and analyze every single second, starting with that look. Then I would compare myself to that stupid girlfriend before I finally snapped out of it and realized I may not look like a super model, but I did have a nice body. Even with a few extra pounds on my frame. I could still get guys to flirt with me. Take Milo, for example. Men asked me out at the office all the time. The answer was always *no* because I didn't want to admit I still had feelings for a man who had walked away from me over a decade ago.

God. Again, pathetic. I really needed to dig deep and pull out my inner badass woman. The part of me that said, "Fuck Lucas Foster." I knew what I was worth, and it had been his loss, not mine.

But still, the stupid heart wants what it wants. *Ugh.*

"What are you doing here? Planning a date?" Lucas asked, focusing back on Milo, who shot me a smile that said he wanted to have some fun with Lucas. I was down for that. Milo and Lucas had stayed pretty close, according to Jen.

"Just helping a friend out. I'll give you a call later, Paige," Milo said.

With a wink, I replied, "Thanks, Milo. I appreciate it. Remember, any free night you want to hang out, I'm here."

Lucas and I watched as Milo walked down the old gravel sidewalk to his truck. Behind his truck was a Lexus. Of course; a Lexus to go with the khaki pants and dress shoes.

Once he drove off, awkwardness settled in. I realized I was alone with Lucas. I looked back at the car like a coward, too afraid of my reaction to him. "Where's your girlfriend?"

"Bianca is at the bed and breakfast."

Milo's words about her being a screamer came back, and I hated my jealousy. The idea that she got to be with Lucas was maddening. And that pissed me off. I needed to find a guy to help release some of this built-up sexual energy. It had been a long time and being in Lucas's presence wasn't helping the situation out at all.

Moving my gaze back to Lucas, I found that he was staring at me.

"How much to buy you out?" I finally asked.

Lucas laughed as he walked up the steps. I tried not to let my eyes linger on how his muscular body moved. His stupid khaki pants showcased his thighs. And then there was his chest. Lord, it was as broad and muscular as when he was younger. No, scratch that. He had more muscles. It was official. I truly disliked Bianca.

He walked past me and into the house. His cologne infiltrated my nose. I was pretty sure I moaned a little. It was the same stuff he wore in high school. Damn him. I didn't know why, but it made me happy to know Bianca hadn't changed that about him.

"What makes you think I'm selling my half to you?" he asked.

I shut the door and followed him in, my eyes landing on his perfect ass.

Jesus, Paige. Stop checking him out.

It was definitely time for me to get laid.

"You don't want this place, Lucas. When was the last time you were even here?"

He turned and looked at me, a fire in his eyes. "So, you came and helped Granddad decorate a tree, and called him, and that makes you worthy of this house?"

My brows rose in shock. Was that a hint of something in his voice? Jealousy or anger that I made time for his grandfather when he didn't?

"I was here a few months ago," he said. "Granddad happened to mention you visiting last Christmas. Trying to make sure you kept a hand in things, Paige, for the big payout one day?"

His words cut deep, and I knew he didn't truly mean them. Nonetheless, it hurt. "Lucas, I want to be angry with you right now, but you've always known how much I loved this house, *and more importantly,* William."

He actually looked guilty for a moment, then it was gone in a flash.

"I tried to buy this house from William a few years back, but maybe you don't know that since you rarely came to visit," I stated, wanting to hurt him like he'd hurt me.

He laughed. "Yeah, I remember that. For next to nothing."

My mouth dropped open. "Excuse me, I offered him fair market value, which I'll do the same for you. *Dickwad.*"

That last part I mumbled under my breath.

"What did you just call me?" Lucas asked, taking a few steps toward me. I didn't move back. If he thought he was going to intimidate me, he had another thing coming.

"Obviously you heard it, so why repeat it? Unless you enjoy being called names."

He rolled his eyes. "I'm here to buy you out."

A strangled chuckle came from my throat. "*Ha.* No. I'm not selling. *Especially* after the letter I got from William."

That piqued his interest. "What did your letter say?"

I put on my best pout. "What's wrong? Are you afraid my letter is better than yours?"

Lucas smirked. "I got a letter. I haven't read it yet."

"What?" I said, positive my shock was clear on my face. "Lucas, when did you get it?"

"Earlier today. Lou gave it to me when I went to his office. I wanted to read it here, in his study."

A small part of my cold heart melted because I totally got it. I had done the same thing. After Lou had given me the key, I came to the house and into the study where I sat at William's desk and read his letter, knowing that he'd written it while sitting at this very desk.

I allowed the corners of my mouth to lift slightly. "I did the same thing."

His eyes snapped to meet mine. We stared at one another for longer than we should have before Lucas turned and walked down the hall and turned into his grandfather's study. I jumped when I heard the door slam. What the hell was that about?

I made my way to the kitchen and poured two glasses of tea. I wondered if Lucas still drank tea. I placed them on a tray with a few cookies I had bought at the grocery store in town, and after a few minutes, I walked to the study. I figured it had been enough time for him to read through his letter. Ever the proper hostess, something my mother had taught me to be, I went to the door and knocked lightly before opening it.

When I walked into the study, I stopped. Lucas had his face buried in his hands, elbows rested on the desk. I went to leave, but his voice stopped me.

"Wait. Don't go."

I swallowed hard and readied myself. If Lucas was crying, I couldn't play hardball. No matter how angry or hurt I still was. The sight of him crying would make me crumble.

When I moved closer, he looked up at me, and I frowned. He wasn't crying. Hell, he didn't even look upset. He looked...terrible. He had dark circles around his bloodshot eyes. Maybe he had been crying before I got in here.

"Are you okay?" I asked.

"I'm tired."

I set the tray down and handed him one of the teas. A part of me wanted to be sympathetic, but the girl who was still reeling over my broken heart wanted to be a bitch. It was an internal battle, and I wasn't honestly sure who would win. Oh hell, I knew who would win so I let her come out to play.

Bitch, it was.

"Right, I heard something about your travel *problems* from your momma. Something about a lost passport or some nonsense. For as much as y'all *travel*, I was surprised that you'd misplace a passport." That's right. I had put stress on those words, to get my point across.

Lucas shot me a dirty look, and I smiled politely in reply. Okay, it was a cheap shot with a bit of jealous on the side, but what the hell.

"So. What do we do? How do we resolve this problem?" I asked, taking a seat, then picking up my tea.

Lucas sat back in the chair and rubbed his neck. "What did your letter say?"

"What did your letter say?" I asked with a smug grin.

"I asked you first."

"Well, I'm the one who showed up to the house first, so I win."

He leaned forward, a pinched expression on his face. "You *win*?"

I nodded. "Yeah, I win."

"What the fuck is the game we're playing, Paige? Where someone wins and someone loses?"

"The who-got-to-the-house-first game, Lucas. That counts for something. I care more about this house than you do."

He scoffed. "What makes you think that?"

"If I sell my portion to you, are you moving in?"

"No, don't be ridiculous. I'm selling it."

I nearly choked on my own tongue. "Selling it?"

"Yes. Selling it. I've already got an idea of what to do with it."

My voice was gone. Lost. I couldn't have made a sound if I had wanted to, and believe me, I wanted to.

After a few moments, my mouth moved, and words finally came out. "Lucas, why in the world would you want to sell this house to anyone other than me? To someone who wouldn't cherish this place and would only see it as a moneymaker?"

I saw the conflict in his eyes. There was no way he would sell, or would he?

"Because, Paige. There is *nothing* here for me."

"The memories. All the amazing times we had in this house. *You* had in this house. This house meant something to your grandfather, Lucas."

For a moment, he looked like he was going to smile. "None of that matters anymore. Granddad isn't here, and the dreams I once had for this house died a long time ago, so I have nothing of interest here anymore."

I looked down at my tea. Once upon a time, Lucas had said we would get married here. Raise a family in this house. Make it our home. Then Lucas changed his mind about how he felt about me— and used my choice of college as an excuse to break up. It still made me feel sick to my stomach.

Before I could stop the words, I whispered, "I didn't want to lose that dream either, Lucas. I was simply asking you to put it on hold. You walked away from it."

He stared at me for the longest time. Both of us realizing we shared the same loss. His eyes looked as if he wanted to say something, but when he opened his mouth, the moment was gone.

"Bianca doesn't like the country. Even if I kept my half of this place, I'd never be here."

"Thank, God," I mumbled. Okay, the inner bitch was back. The idea of that woman sharing a house with me made me want to gag.

"What's that supposed to mean?"

I shrugged. "Rumor has it she's a screamer. And sound carries in the country. Might be awkward with me living here. Don't you think?"

"You can't live here, *Paige*. You live in Austin. You work in Austin. Are you really going to make that drive every day?"

I took a slow, deep breath and exhaled just as slowly. I could tell he was waiting for my response.

"First off, *Lucas*. I can do whatever the fuck I want to do."

"Nice language."

"Thanks. Second, *dickhead*, if it's any of your business. I quit my job and moved into the house this morning."

He coughed and hit his chest. "Wait, you did what?"

"Which part of that are you asking me about? The job or the house?"

He grunted. "You quit your job and moved into the house already?"

"Yes. And yes." I took another sip of tea and watched as his face grew redder by the second.

"You moved in. To the house. This is still my house."

"Half of it is, and half is mine. I left you the main master downstairs that was William's room. I took the guest room with the bathroom upstairs. I always did like being on top."

He stared in disbelief as I snapped my mouth shut. I wanted to punch myself for making that sound so sexual. *What in the hell is the matter with me?*

"I mean, I always liked the bedroom upstairs. That bedroom. That particular bedroom. Not that I want to be upstairs all the time, of course. The kitchen and everything is down here, so that would be ridiculous."

The corners of his mouth twitched ever so slightly. "Are you done yet?"

I pressed my mouth into a tight line. Lucas looked at his tea, and I could tell he was fighting a smile.

Then he let out a long sigh. "You need to just sell me your half, Paige."

"No, you need to sell me yours."

"I'm not selling you mine," he stated.

"I'm not selling you mine."

With a frustrated groan, he stood. "Then what the fuck are we going to do because I can't own a house with you."

"Then let me buy you out."

"No!"

I gave him a half shrug as I remained seated. "Then it looks like you own half a house and twenty-five acres of land. Oh wait, I know what we can do!"

His eyes lit up. "What, do you have an idea?"

"Yes! I'll take the house and ten acres of the land and you can keep the rest and sell it to whoever the hell you want."

I could practically see the steam coming from his ears. "I want it all."

I lifted a brow and smirked. "I see some things never change."

I stood and took the tray. Turning away, I made my way to the door.

"Still walking away from me. You certainly have that down, don't you?"

Stopping, I slowly turned back. "I wasn't the one who walked away, or did you forget that, Lucas?"

He looked as if he might be sorry for his decision all those years ago, then a cold expression moved over his face. "And look how well we've done for ourselves, all the *places* we've seen?"

I didn't want that jab to make me feel the way it did. A part of me wasn't even sure how I felt. Sad, angry, jealous? It all mixed together in one flash.

"Fuck you, Lucas."

He smirked. "You wish you could."

I forced a smile. "Why would I wish that when I've got Milo?"

Lucas's smug expression instantly faded, and I walked out of the room without another glance.

Shit. Shit. Shit. Shit.

What had I done? Milo was going to kill me for dragging him into this. Maybe, if I was lucky, he'd be in the mood for a bit of fun.

Who was I kidding? He'd add this inconvenience onto the bill for painting the house, and I had a feeling the price of that *upgrade* was going to be a steep one.

Chapter 3

Lucas

I DIDN'T WANT to admit how hard her words hit me, sending pain through my chest. Even though I had thrown out hurtful words at her, I hadn't expected her to toss them back. I sat down at the desk and scrubbed my hands over my face. Seeing Paige had thrown me into a swarm of emotions. She was so goddamn beautiful, even more so now, and it took everything I had not to show any sort of reaction. When she was about to hug Milo, I nearly bolted up the steps to beat the shit out of him. I had no right, none whatsoever.

I groaned—I couldn't get that moment out of my head. I pulled out my phone and hit Milo's phone number to type a text.

Me: Are you sleeping with Paige?

His reply was instant.

Milo: Are you high or something?

Then another text came through.

Milo: Dude, why do you care? You're with Bianca.

That response bothered me more than I wanted to admit.

Me: I don't care.

Milo: Good, then it's none of your business. When are you leaving? Bunch of us guys are going out for beer tonight. Guys' night out. You in?

Staring at his text, I got even more pissed off. What did he mean it was none of my business? Paige was mine; that made her my business.

I scrubbed my hands down my face as I realized what I had just thought. Paige *wasn't* mine. She hadn't been since we were almost nineteen years old. When I had made the biggest freaking mistake of my life. After I had broken up with her, I spent nearly two years alone, only hooking up a few times for meaningless sex. By the time Bianca came into my life I was so fucking numb I wondered if my heart could feel anything for anyone other than the woman I now owned half a damn house with.

"Fuck."

This woman was going to drive me mad. Moving around the desk, I made my way through the house until I found Paige. She was looking at her phone, probably telling Milo to play along with her bullshit game.

"What are you doing?"

She jumped and screamed. I didn't bother to hide my smile.

"For fuck's sake, you jerk! You scared the piss out of me."

"Wow, your mouth has gotten colorful these last few years. Who are you texting?"

Paige looked at me like I was insane. I was pretty sure I was on my way there where she was concerned.

"I'm not texting anyone, if it's any of your business. I'm looking at fabric samples for curtains."

When she flipped the phone over to show off the fabric, I instantly smelled my grandmother's oatmeal cookies.

"Those look like the curtains grandma had in here."

She smiled. "Yeah, I know. I've been looking everywhere for this fabric. I'm going to order it and make some curtains."

"*You're* making the curtains?" I asked with a laugh.

Paige almost looked hurt, and I hated myself for it. Like I hadn't already hurt her enough and had to keep taking jabs.

"Why? Do you think I'm incapable of making curtains?"

With a shrug, I answered honestly. "I don't know what you're capable of anymore."

She swallowed hard and looked back at her phone. I was an asshole. Yep. Grade-A fucking asshole.

I shrugged off my dickhead behavior and went for brute honesty. "Are you dating Milo?"

Her eyes met mine. "No."

"So you're just randomly going to hook up with him for sex?"

Something in her eyes changed. "Maybe," she said evenly.

"You can't. He's my best friend, and you're not that type of girl, Paige."

Her eyes widened, not from shock but anger. I took a step back as she moved closer to me.

"You don't know what kind of *woman* I am, and by your own admission only moments ago, you don't know what I'm capable of, Lucas."

My eyes roamed openly down her body. Yeah, Paige wasn't a girl anymore. Fuck me, she still had a body that would make any guy's cock come to attention, and I remembered feeling that way many times when we were dating. She had an incredible body in high school, but now she was all womanly curves. Curves that would bring a man to his knees. Paige had the kind of body guys broke their necks to get a second look at. In a word, perfect.

And I was a total bastard.

You have a girlfriend, you asshole.

I looked back at her eyes, my face still neutral so she couldn't see how my body reacted to hers. "You're right, Paige. I don't."

For moment, she looked like she might tear up. The urge to pull her into my arms was so strong that it instantly freaked me the hell out.

She cleared her throat. "I'm going to put up new curtains on all the windows. I'm going to head to the storage unit to see what's in there. I'm assuming you would want to sell all of the contents of that, but lucky me, that one is all mine."

"What storage unit?" I asked, drawing in my brows.

Paige looked confused. "William didn't tell you about the storage unit that has a lot of furniture in it?"

My granddad hadn't mentioned anything about a storage unit. When I opened his letter in the study, I had expected there to be an explanation for why he left the house to both me and Paige. There wasn't. All that was inside was two items: a picture of me and Paige the night of our senior prom and a key. The letter simply said, *"To my beloved grandson, Lucas. Find the chest and you'll find the answers. Always follow your heart, son. It will lead you home."*

I wasn't in the fucking mood to play games. I needed to buy Paige out before Bianca got wind of all of this. She was not going to handle the news well about Paige co-owning this house with me. For Bianca, Paige was a sore subject. It probably had to do with the fact that I had accidentally called her Paige *once*...while having sex. Yeah. Not one of my finer moments. And my mother purposefully slipped up every now and then and called her Paige. Didn't help that my parents didn't really care for Bianca. Hell, if I was being honest with myself, even I was at the point where I didn't care for her.

That thought made me pause for a moment. I'd almost broken up with her before this stupid trip.

"No, he didn't mention that in his letter."

"Really?" she honestly looked confused.

"What was in your letter?"

Paige pulled out a folded piece of paper from her back pocket and stared at it. She chewed on her lip, then handed it to me.

"You can read it."

I looked down at it. The fact that Paige carried my granddad's letter in her pocket made my chest tighten. I knew how much she loved him, and he loved her. In the last few years, their relationship had grown, while mine had faltered. Regret and guilt felt like they were swallowing me whole. Bianca had hated coming to Johnson City, so I had made the trip less and less. My voice cracked slightly as I asked, "Are you sure?"

She nodded.

My hands shook as I reached for the letter. I wasn't sure why I was nervous. Was it because I didn't want to be upset that Granddad had left Paige a better letter than me? Maybe it was because I was an asshole and was checking out her body when I had a freaking girlfriend back at the bed and breakfast. Or was it simply because this was Paige, the woman I had wanted to marry and raise a family within this very house? We hadn't wanted the same things, and I had been too stubborn to listen to her reasons. I pushed all that aside; I couldn't go back and change the past. Our past.

Truth be told, I wasn't angry at Paige for following her own dreams, I was pissed that I had forced her to pick. Her life, or mine. And when she did pick, it wasn't the choice I wanted to hear. I was hurt she hadn't picked me. Why should she have, though? I had acted like a stupid fool. I was jealous. Scared to death she'd meet someone who would offer her more. I was angry she didn't want to start the life we had talked about as quickly as I did. Over the years, I realized what a fool I had been. It wouldn't have hurt us to spend time together before moving back home. All the times I had seen her posts on Instagram, in a distant country, exploring it by herself, I realized I should have been with her. Maybe I had truly feared that she would end up loving her career more than me.

Opening the letter, I dragged in a breath and started to read it. Out loud.

> *"My Dearest Paige,*
>
> *You are probably wondering what in the world I was thinking when I gave you fifty percent of the house you have always loved. Well, that is part of the reason, because you love it and it is part of who you are. I'm sure you know by now that Lucas owns the other half.*
>
> *I have a storage unit at 4547 Ranch Road 175, that is solely yours to do with as you please. Once my beloved passed away, I put all of her furniture in there. It was too painful to look at. The pieces were all professionally stored, and the unit is climate controlled. There are a few other things in there, as well, for you. It is all yours, Paige. Do with it as you see fit.*
>
> *As for everything else, you'll figure it out, but destiny*

is a funny thing. She tends to take us down some very big detours, but she eventually gets you back to where you belong.

Now, I give you this house for you to find the answers. You can't find the answers without the key, and Lucas holds it.

Love always,
William.

P.S. Paige, please remember to follow your heart. It is the most important rule of the game."

Glancing back up at Paige, I said, "Game?"

She shrugged. "I don't know if by *key* he means metaphorically or literally a key. And what answers is he talking about?"

I handed her the letter back and then took the key out of my pocket. "I think he means this key, which he left to me in my letter."

Paige narrowed her eyes on it. "Looks old."

"He said I have to find a chest, and I'll find the answers. Hopefully it's an updated will giving me the whole house."

"Ha ha," she snapped. "Lucas, how is this going to work? I'm not selling you my portion of the house."

"I'm not selling you mine."

She let out a sigh.

My phone buzzed, and I pulled it out to see it was Bianca calling. Perfect.

"Hey, babe." I cringed when Paige looked away at my words. *Yep. Fucking asshole.*

"Okay, enough is enough, Lucas. I want to go home," Bianca said.

I walked out of the room and into the hallway.

"Like I said before, you're more than welcome to go back home."

"Why do you insist on staying in this dreadful little town?"

"My family is here, and my granddad just died. I'm pretty sure my mother would be pissed if I left. I did miss my grandfather's funeral, if you remember, because of your conveniently misplaced passport."

31

She sighed, overlooking my anger. "What did you get from your granddad? That house? Are we selling it? We could put the money into this cute little house I saw on Lake Travis. We would be downsizing to only eight-thousand square feet, but I think it would feel cozy. Maybe get someone in the mood of popping the Big Question."

"*We?*" I asked.

"What?"

"You asked if 'we' were selling it. Who told you about Paige?"

The silence on the other end of the line made me realize she was talking about her and me, *not* me and Paige. So stupid. Why would that mean Paige? *Good Lord. I'm not good at this game, and I don't want to be.*

"Paige? What about *Paige*? Is that little tramp in town? Is she trying to put the moves on you?"

"What?" I said, a little too loudly. "Why in the hell would you call her a tramp?"

"Come back to this hell hole now, Lucas. We obviously need to talk."

Instead of telling Bianca my plans over the phone, I decided it needed to be done in person.

"I'm finishing up a meeting, then I'll head that way."

"Is she in the meeting?"

I rolled my eyes. "Yes."

More silence.

"Right, I'll be there soon."

Before she could say anything, I hung up.

When I turned around, Paige was standing there.

"Did she really call me a tramp?"

"Did you really stand there and listen to my phone call?"

She smiled. "I really did. She sounds like a real winner. Good job, Lucas."

Paige started to walk away, so I followed. "You don't know anything about her, Paige."

"She obviously has been told lies about me if she thinks I'm a tramp, and she appears to have you wrapped around her little finger, not to mention she caused you to miss your grandfather's funeral. So yeah, I know plenty about her, and that's just what I've learned in the past couple of days."

Paige turned back to face me, causing me to bump right into her. My hands reached out to steady her. I quickly let her go when I felt the zap of electricity rush between us.

"Did I miss anything that would give someone a different impression of exactly the type of woman she is?" she asked, a smug smile on her beautiful face.

"You missed a lot. She's a really nice person who does a lot of things for different charities."

Did I really just say that?

Her brows raised. "With or without camera crews?"

"Excuse me?"

She rolled her eyes like I had said the stupidest thing. "These charities...are there camera crews around when she helps them?"

I thought about it for a moment. "As a matter of fact, there are."

She smirked. "Then she's doing it for PR. Doesn't count, sorry."

Spinning on her heels, she walked away, and I balled my fists up and followed her into the kitchen.

"I need to leave, so I need you to tell me the magical number that will get you out of here, Paige. You name it, I'll pay it."

Her head tilted as she regarded me. Finally, we were getting somewhere. If I had known all it was going to take was money, I'd have done this when I first walked in.

"Let me get this straight, I can throw any number out at you, and you'll agree to pay me if I sign over my half?"

"Yes! If I knew money was your driving motive, Paige, we could have done this without all the drama."

Something in her eyes flashed. Either she was angry, or she was coming up with a number. I decided to help her.

"One-point-one million for you to walk away from this house."

Holy hell, why did I throw that number out there? I didn't have that kind of money. Bianca did, but I didn't.

Her chin wobbled, and I felt like the biggest asshole on the planet. She wasn't interested in money. That wasn't who Paige was.

It was like she said when I first got here. Her motivation for wanting to live in this house was the memories.

Paige looked away for a moment, then cleared her throat.

"I don't want your money." Her voice shook. "None of it. I'm not selling. And if you honestly think you can throw some crazy number out there and I'll bite, then you never knew me at all, Lucas."

"Paige, wait."

She pushed past me and grabbed her purse. "Lock *our* door when you leave."

"Wait, Paige. Please stop."

I could hardly keep up with her as she rushed through the house and walked out the front door.

Pulling the door shut, I quickly pulled out the house key and locked it.

"Wait a freaking second! You set me up for that."

I watched as she climbed into a Toyota 4-Runner. That made me pause. I had initially wondered who that car belonged to, but it never crossed my mind it was Paige's. I knew she had a successful job, she made six figures and lived in a swanky downtown loft in Austin, which wasn't cheap. Not that I stalked her or anything. I may have asked Jen, who was more than happy to fill me in on what Paige was up to in her life. I had figured she would be in a little sports car. But then, that wasn't Paige Miller.

Shit, I had messed all of this up from the get-go.

Paige peeled out down the driveway, kicking up dirt and rocks in her wake.

I groaned and dropped my head back, staring at the sky. "Good going, Lucas. You're watching her leave one more time."

Chapter 4

Lucas

AFTER LEAVING GRANDDAD'S house, I went to my parents' and spent some time with them. I needed the sense of normalcy that my family gave me before I faced Bianca.

My father wasn't handling his dad's death very well, and it broke my heart. They had been so close. They ran Foster Construction full-time together, at least up until a few years ago when Granddad finally retired.

When I walked out to the car, my mother took my hand. "Lucas, I hope you can stay a few days. Your father mentioned something about going fishing, and I know he could use some help here on the ranch."

I smiled. "I'd like that."

"Does that mean you'll stay? When I talked to Bianca earlier today, she said you were leaving after your meeting."

Anger pulsed through my veins. "Did you call her?"

"No, she called before you got here and asked if Paige was in town, which I thought was strange. She didn't have very nice things to say about Paige, and truth be told, I told her not to speak about someone she clearly didn't know. She didn't appreciate my tone, I don't think."

I rubbed the back of my neck. "They've not met, and they never will."

Her brows rose. "Well, she sure doesn't like her for someone who doesn't know her."

"It's because I dated Paige, and Bianca found a ring once, thought I bought it for her and I had to explain it had been for Paige. So, yeah, she's a bit of a sore subject."

My mother's eyes lit up. "You bought Paige a ring? When?"

"I was going to give it to her Christmas of our freshman year of college, but we all know how that turned out."

"Lucas."

"Mom, please. Not now. I've had a really shitty day, and I'm dealing with two very different women who are pissed off at me for two very different reasons."

She nodded. "Please don't let her talk you into leaving."

I kissed her forehead. "I won't. I'm going to tell Bianca to head back to Austin. She'll understand my need to stay. Actually I'm not going to be giving her a choice."

My mother smiled but attempted to hide it. "Will you be staying here after Bianca leaves?"

With a smile on my face, I shook my head. "No, I'll be staying at Granddad's place."

The second I walked into the large suite at the bed and breakfast, Bianca was all over my ass.

"What is going on, Lucas? Why is Paige involved with your granddad's house? Did you see her? Speak to her?"

"Jesus, Bianca, can I at least get in the door and make myself a drink before you hit me with a million questions?"

"Well, I need answers. I've been down at the pool all afternoon waiting for you to meet with the lawyer, then you don't come back for hours."

"I went over to my folks' house. You knew I was going over there, remember? I asked you to come and pay your respects to them?"

She sighed and wrapped her arms around me. "I'm sorry, baby, but you know how much your mother dislikes me."

I stared at her in disbelief.

With a purr in her voice, she said, "Let me make it up to you."

Her hand moved down my chest and rubbed against my dick. She actually expected me to get hard after the day I'd had, and I was limp as a fucking noodle.

With a frown, she stepped back. "Okay, you're stressed. Let's talk about what happened."

This was not going to be fun. "My granddad left me the house and property, but he only left me fifty percent of it."

Her brows drew in tight. "Okay, well buy your parents out of the other half so we can sell it and be done with this place."

"He didn't leave it to them, and there is no *we* on this."

Why it was taking her so long to put two and two together was beyond me.

"Just buy out the other person, Lucas," she said, frustrated.

"She doesn't want to sell."

A fire burned in her eyes. The light bulb finally clicking on.

"He left the house to *her*? To your ex-girlfriend?"

"Yes."

"Why?"

I walked into the bathroom and turned the shower on, pushing it all the way to hot.

"I don't know."

"And she is refusing to sell?"

"She's always loved the house, and my granddad knew that. He wanted her to have it because she mentioned to him a few times about how she'd love the opportunity to restore it."

"That little bitch. She worked her way in."

I sighed. "Paige isn't that way, Bianca."

"How do you know how she is? The last time you saw her was how many years ago?"

The irony of this conversation wasn't lost on me.

"Four years ago, her mother's funeral. Bianca, I offered her a large sum of money to buy her out, she didn't want it. She wants the house."

Bianca sighed. "Okay, I'll get my best lawyer, and we'll contest the will. Say that you're blood and your grandfather was clearly manipulated. We can make her look like a gold digger."

Facing her, I laughed. "I'm not doing that."

"Why not?" Her perfect eyebrow went up. Were those even real, or had she had them painted on or something? Why was I just noticing how fake they looked? "Do you still care for this girl?"

I gave her a humorless laugh. "I'm not doing that because I'm not going to make it look like my Granddad lost his mind in the end. He wanted Paige to have the house, so I have to figure out a way to make Paige not want the house."

Her hands went to her hips. "No. I am not moving into that dumpy little house."

"It's not a dumpy little house, Bianca."

"Whatever, I'm not living here in the middle of bum-fucking-Egypt."

"I'm not asking you to move here. I'm moving in with her."

Her face dropped, then she started to laugh. "That's rich, Lucas. You really had me there for a minute."

Stripping out of my clothes, I stepped into the hot water. "I'm not kidding. I'm going to move in and make her life miserable. Maybe I can hire someone to make her think the house is haunted or something."

When I didn't hear Bianca, I pulled the shower curtain back. She was no longer in the bathroom. I breathed a sigh of relief. Leaning my hand against the tile, I pulled in a deep breath. What was going on here?

I wanted to be away from Bianca. Truth be told, I had known long before Granddad's death that this needed to end. I just hadn't wanted to see another relationship fail. The last nail was hammered when she pretended to lose her passport. She hadn't cared about me or my family. She never had.

"This isn't working," I whispered, closing my eyes.

I shut off the shower and wrapped a towel around my waist and headed into the other room.

"George, I don't know this little tramp's name. Paige Mustard? No, Mulligan? No. Listen I'll find it out, and I want you to dig up as much dirt on her as you...*hey!*"

I grabbed the phone out of her hand, and hit the end button.

"What in the hell are you doing?" I asked.

She grinned. "I'm hiring my best private detective to dig up some dirt on Paige. Now, sweetie, what's her last name? I'll take care of this little witch for you."

I shook my head. "Bianca, you're not going to hire someone to pull up dirt on anyone, especially Paige."

Her hands went to her hips. "If you think for one minute I'm going to let you stay in the same house as her, you are insane. You are my boyfriend, soon to be fiancé, and you're not staying with her."

I reached for my jeans and pulled them on. Then I grabbed the first T-shirt I could find. I went into the bathroom, grabbed all my shit and tossed it into my bag.

"What are you doing?" she asked.

"I'm packing up my stuff."

"Thank God. We're going home!" She practically bounced into the bathroom and started packing up the hundreds of bath products she had hauled with us to Fiji.

I set down the keys to the rental car.

"Bianca."

"I honestly thought you were losing your damn mind there for a second. I was actually feeling a small sweat coming on. You know how much I hate to sweat."

"Bianca."

"My lawyers will handle everything. Don't you worry, baby."

"Bianca!" I shouted, causing her to freeze and look at me.

"Jesus! What?"

"I'm leaving you."

A short laugh slipped from her lips. "I'm sorry. What are you saying?"

"This isn't working. You want something I can't give you."

"Excuse me?"

I shook my head. "I'm not ever going to ask you to marry me because I don't love you. I think you've known for some time. I can't do this anymore, I'm sorry."

Her face twisted up into an evil expression. "Are you breaking up with me?"

"Yes, and I should have done it back in Fiji and left your ass there so I could make it back in time for Granddad's funeral. Hell, I should have done it a long time ago."

Her mouth worked open and shut a few times. "Is this because of her?"

"This is because you and I are nothing alike, and I've only been pretending. I'm not happy, and I really can't believe you're happy with me either. If you were, you wouldn't be trying to change me all the time to fit your idea of what a perfect boyfriend should be."

"I only tried to change you for the better!" she spat out.

I sighed. "Enjoy your life, Bianca. I'll send someone to Austin to pick up my clothes. Everything else, you can keep."

I didn't own a car, since we lived near downtown Austin. Leaving behind the place we lived in wasn't a big deal at all. It was all in Bianca's name, and I didn't want a single thing. Bianca had picked out everything in our apartment. Nothing was mine. I actually hated the fucking place. It had never dawned on me how much I hated it until this very moment.

"If you walk out that door, Lucas, don't ever come back to me."

I grabbed my two bags and headed to the door.

"I'm being serious. I don't need you. You were the one who needed me to get over that little whore."

I glanced back at her and smiled. "Paige is ten times the woman you could ever dream of being."

I walked out the door and headed down to Betty's private residence. After knocking on the door once, it opened.

"Hey, is there any way John can give me a ride? Bianca is taking the rental car."

Betty looked at my bags and smiled. "Please tell me you finally left her."

"I left her."

Her eyes went up and she said, "Thank you, Heavenly Father."

Chapter 5

Paige

"**I**F YOU EAT any more ice cream, you're going to be upset that I didn't plan an intervention."

With a sigh, I let the spoon fall back into the tub and pushed it away from me.

"Thanks, Jen. I needed that."

Jen and I were celebrating my big move. I think she was even more excited than my father when I told him I was moving back to Johnson City.

"Do you feel any better?" Jen asked.

"No. Only bloated."

She chuckled. "That boy always did get you fired up."

I dropped back into the chair. "That boy is not a boy. It's so unfair. He's better looking now."

"Oh, I know. I saw him next to his Barbie doll in some magazine article. Honestly, I think this chick keeps him by her side because he's so pretty."

I laughed and then groaned. "He's a Class-A jerk. I mean, how long is he going to punish me for following my own dream? I didn't want to break up. He was the one who broke up with me. If anyone should be pissed off, it should be me because I loved him, and it took me forever to get over him. A part of me will never get over him."

"You two were always good together, the perfect couple," she said with a sigh, adding, "Men are idiots."

"But you found a good one."

She smiled. "I did. There are a few exceptions to the rule, but even Gene can be an idiot at times. It's in their DNA."

"I think you may be right. I'd better get back. I need to measure the windows. I might have time to drive into Dripping Springs and get some blinds. It's kind of creepy being in the house without blinds. This being my first night sleeping there, I need some sense of privacy."

Jen reached for my hand. "Paige, what if he won't sell you his half? I hate seeing you put all your hard-earned money into that house."

I gave her a warm smile. "I'm not wasting it. Part of it is still my house." I looked down at the floor and then back at her. "He offered me over a million dollars for it today."

Her eyes went wide. "What?"

With a nod, I replied, "I turned him down. He now knows I'm serious. I'm not leaving. I think it's a pride thing now. He'll go back to Austin, wait a few days, then make a deal with me to buy him out. I'm sure of it."

Jen nodded. "I think you're right. He was probably butthurt his granddaddy left you half the house. Once he gets back to Austin, and it's out of his mind, he'll sell you his half."

I had to admit, I was feeling confident about the situation.

"If you need anything, let me know."

I hugged her. "I will. Thanks so much."

"Of course. I'm just tickled pink you're back in JC!"

"Me, too." I waved goodbye and headed back to the ranch house to measure the windows. In my mind, I went over everything that needed to be done. The costliest project would be the kitchen. I wanted the rest of the house to be exactly as it was when William and his wife May had lived there. But the kitchen was going to be state-of-the-art fabulous. My dream kitchen. If I budgeted right, I could make it happen. Especially if Milo gave me a break on the painting.

As I drove down the old gravel driveway, I couldn't help but think back to earlier. It had hurt so much when Lucas tossed out a number, expecting me to bite. He was used to dealing with his precious Bianca. Well, no amount of money was going to make me leave. As a matter of fact, nothing would make me leave this house. Ever.

As I got closer to the house, I saw someone on the front porch sitting in one of the rocking chairs. I parked and sat there, staring at him. What in the hell was Lucas doing, sitting on the front porch? He was dressed in a green T-shirt that would undoubtedly showcase his eyes; they'd be almost mesmerizing up close.

He stood and moved closer to the steps. I quickly looked around for Bianca and saw no sign of her. If she was in my house, er, *our* house, I was going to throttle Lucas.

A low moan slipped from between my lips. "*No.* Dear God, no. Why? Why are you punishing me with this man's looks?!"

Lucas had changed. He now wore jeans, cowboy boots, and had put on his cowboy hat. The same one he wore all the time in high school. I swallowed hard. So, that was the game he was going to play.

Fine. Game on.

I threw open the door to my SUV and glared at him as I stomped up the steps. If he thought he could dress up like the old Lucas and still convince me to leave, he had another thing coming. I may have caved to this Lucas once upon a time, but no more.

Nope. Not happening. I am stronger now.

"Hey, roomie."

My heart fell to my stomach and a lump formed in my throat, making it hard to speak. That word froze me in my angry tracks.

"Wh-what?"

He walked closer and looked down into my eyes. The way his hazel eyes were sparking told me I was fixin' to be in some serious trouble.

"Congratulations. You got your wish. I'm not selling the place. Instead, I moved in. We're housemates."

My eyes flew past his shoulder and through the screen door. "Bianca?"

My voice sounded scared to death, which pissed me off. There was no way I could live in this house with her. That would be cruel, even for Lucas.

"She's decided to go back to Austin. It's just me."

Standing up taller, I forced myself to smile.

Do not show the beast fear. You are a strong, confident woman, Paige Miller. Show this asshole who is boss.

"Sounds great. Now I've got an extra set of hands to help me remodel and paint."

To Lucas's credit, he didn't waver. That made me nervous. He shouldn't want to be roommates. This should be awkward. Then it hit me. This was probably Bianca's plan. She wanted her greedy little hands on my portion of the house.

Steeling my resolve, I decided that whatever this man threw at me, I was ready for it.

He lifted his hands and winked. "In case you don't remember, I'm good with my hands."

My knees wobbled because I *did* remember. Boy, did I ever remember. Every. Moment. I'd spent many nights with my dildo lost in those memories.

I shook the memory away. *No, no, no! The man has a girlfriend. Stow the dirty thoughts, Paige.*

I gave him a humorless laugh. "You have clearly lied to your girlfriend and told her you were staying at your parents'."

He shook his head. "I haven't."

"She's okay with you living here, without her?"

"No, she's not okay with it at all."

"Then why are you here if it makes your girlfriend upset, Lucas?"

He smiled. It wasn't a forced smile. No, it was the kind of smile that said Lucas was keeping score. Lucas, one. Paige, zero.

"Shit," I whispered. When his eyes roamed down my body, I tried not to let him see me shiver.

Please don't say what I think you're fixin' to say.

"Bianca and I broke up."

Oh God, there it was.

"You broke up? Just like that?"

He nodded. "Truth be told, it had been a long time coming. Her calling you a tramp was the last straw."

I narrowed my eyes at him, then snarled. "That was not the reason."

He laughed. "No, it wasn't. But it was long overdue. I'm going to need to borrow your car tomorrow to head into Austin. Looks like I need to buy myself a truck."

"A truck?"

I was positive I sounded like a freaking idiot.

"Yeah. A guy who owns a ranch needs a truck."

Slowly, I shook my head, walked back to my car.

"Hey! Roomie, where are you going? I thought we could go over the paint samples. I'm not so sure about some of these colors."

My fists balled at my sides as I practically ran to the car. I got in and headed down the driveway. When I got to where I was out of sight, I stopped, pulled my phone out and called Jen.

"Hey, you made it home safely."

"Yep, and there was a package of sorts on the front porch. Waiting for me."

"Oh, what did you order?"

My head dropped to the steering wheel. "Well, I can for sure tell you I didn't order a six-foot, dark-haired, hazel-eyed man I used to know very intimately."

"I'm confused."

"So am I. Lucas just informed me he's moving in with me. Moving into the house. Living here."

"Wow. So he's going to go that route. Okay, well, the model won't let that happen for too long, so you just need to buck it up until he folds."

"It's game on, Jen. It's game on, and that bastard is already one point ahead."

"Why?" she asked, nervousness in her voice.

With a groan, I answered, "He broke up with Bianca."

"Oh. No. Hell no. Code freaking red! I'm on my way to your place with the ice cream and movies."

Jen and I sat in the living room, in our pajamas with the TV turned up. *Top Gun* was playing, and we squealed like school girls when the volleyball scene came on. Lucas came walking into the room. His hand raked through his hair, clearly pissed we had woken him up.

My eyes nearly bugged out of my head as he focused on the TV, wearing practically no clothes. "It's one in the morning. Are you two serious right now? *Top Gun?*"

Jen placed her finger on my chin and closed my gaping mouth. I had a good excuse for it. Lucas had come out of his room dressed in nothing but thin sweats that left *nothing* to the imagination as far as his package was concerned. And his chest was exposed. Void of any shirt, leaving his impressive chest on display.

"Wow," Jen whispered; I nodded. Lucas Foster had a body to die for. I found myself hating Bianca all over again for getting to sleep next to him for years. Touch him. Run her tongue over his body. Scream out his name. *Bitch.*

Lucas noticed both of us staring. My eyes wandered down to his crotch. Instead of letting out a moan like I wanted to, I went in the opposite direction. I scrunched up my nose and said, "Huh." Then I flicked my eyes back up at him.

He glared at me. "What's that supposed to mean?"

I shrugged, glancing at his crotch again. "Nothing."

He walked closer to us. "You just looked at my junk and scrunched up your nose, Paige. Why?"

Jen cleared her throat and stood. "Okay, so this is awkward. I'm going to go to the little girl's room while you two...roommates...work this out."

Once Jen was out of the room, Lucas reached down and adjusted himself. I wanted to die, but I sat there, not a single emotion on my face. He'd done it on purpose, and if he thought I was going to give him any sort of reaction, he was insane.

"It's nothing, Lucas. I just remembered you differently."

His eyebrow rose. "Differently?"

"Yeah," I said with in a half shrug. "I guess because I was so young and naïve, it seemed..."

I laughed and purposely didn't finish my sentence.

"Are you saying you think I'm *small*?"

My eyes drifted to his very impressive bulge. His growing bulge. Oh my goodness, why was he getting hard? Was that from me looking at him? Or was it from talking about it? A man's penis was a weird and complex thing.

"I'm saying at the time I thought you were impressive, but you know." I winked.

Frustration clouded his face, and it was hard not to smile. "No, Paige. I don't know."

I sighed and looked up at him. "I've seen other cocks since then and you're...average."

The look of pure shock almost made me burst out laughing. I looked around him and back at the TV.

"Average? You're saying you think my cock is average?"

I waved him off. "I'm missing the movie, Lucas."

He stepped in front of me, his midsection right at eye level. "You think I'm average?"

"Okay," I said, standing, because let's be honest, a girl cannot have a way-above-average dick at eye level and not want to play with it. Lucas's or not. Especially if that girl hasn't had sex in forever.

"Lucas, this is silly. I'm sure you're sporting a nice little package."

"You just said *little*."

I rolled my eyes. "What do you want me to say?"

He smiled.

I frowned and folded my arms across my chest, noticing how he quickly took a peek at my breasts before meeting my gaze again.

"You need an ego boost that bad, huh? What's the matter, did your girlfriend not compliment your dick enough? Maybe she had a reason not to," I said with a shrug.

His smile faded. "You are not a nice person, Paige."

"Then move out."

"*Never*. Oh, and in case you forgot, the house is haunted."

I laughed. "It is not."

He lifted a brow. "Don't say I didn't warn you."

He turned, and I couldn't help but look at his perfect ass as he retreated. I bit my teeth into my lip and forced myself not to moan by digging my nails into my palms.

"Stop looking at my ass," Lucas called as he rounded the corner.

"You're an asshole, and I wasn't looking at your ass!" I cried out.

"Beg to differ, you were totally checking out that ass," Jen said as she walked back into the room.

"He drives me mad," I said, dropping back on the sofa.

"Yeah, he's something else. I give it three weeks." Jen grabbed her pillow and headed for the stairs.

Following her lead, I turned off the TV. "Three weeks for what?"

She remained silent until we walked into my room. Jen flopped onto the bed, hugged her pillow and closed her eyes. "Three weeks and the two of you are going to be bumping uglies."

I laughed. "Not a chance."

She peeked her eyes open. "Tell me, what was the first thing you thought of when he walked into that living room half naked, hair messy, his impressive cock on display in those thin pants? I'm married and even I had a dirty thought...or three."

I opened my mouth to answer, then shut it quickly.

Jen smiled. "It's okay to think about it but keep your head in the game. If he realizes his body makes you go all goofy, he'll use your weakness to his advantage."

She closed her eyes like she was about to go to sleep, then shot up quickly, scaring the crap out of me.

"What? What's wrong?"

Jen turned to me, looked me up and down, then smiled.

"I don't like that smile."

"It's time to kick it up a notch, Paige. And I know exactly how to do it."

Chapter 6

Lucas

COFFEE. GOOD GRIEF, nothing ever smelled better.

Rolling over, I stretched and let the memories of yesterday crash over me, remembering where I was.

"Paige," I grumbled as I sat up. I needed to come up with a plan to get her to move out of the house. I was going with the ghost theory. If Jen hadn't spent the night, I would have put my plan into action right away. As I stumbled to the bathroom, I thought about Jen. Why the hell was she even here last night?

While brushing my teeth, I had a thought. Had Paige needed someone around so she didn't have to be alone with me?

I had to admit, the idea made me smile, and made my dick jump in my pants. Paige was afraid to be alone with me. I needed to capitalize on this, literally. I'd seen the way Paige was wearing frumpy pajamas, covering herself from head to toe last night. She acted like me being here meant nothing to her, but she was more uncomfortable than she wanted to admit. And the way she looked at my junk. Average, *my ass*. I knew exactly what I needed to do to get under her skin.

I laughed. "Oh hell, this is going to be easy."

After getting changed into jeans and a pull-over shirt, I headed into the kitchen and came to an abrupt stop. I'd just come up with new rules for this game, and in a flash, Paige had changed them all.

She was leaning over as she looked into the oven, dressed in nothing but short silk pajama shorts and a matching top. Her perfectly round ass was playing peek-a-boo with me, and I fought to keep my other brain from jumping into overdrive. Then she turned around and the whole fucking room felt like it tilted.

My eyes swept over her body. The spaghetti strap top was so thin I could see her nipples pressing against the fabric. When I managed to pull my eyes off her tits, I had to grab the chair to keep my knees from giving out.

When my gaze moved further up, I was positive I would pass out from all the blood leaving my brain and making the journey to my already hardening cock. Paige stood before me, her hair in pigtails. It was the cutest and hottest damn thing I'd ever seen. She didn't have an ounce of makeup on, unlike Bianca who would get up every morning to load up on makeup. Not Paige. This, this right here was the girl I remembered. The girl who used to drive me insane with her innocent beauty. Nothing had changed. She was still the most beautiful woman I'd ever laid my eyes on.

She grinned. "Lucas, I thought you were gone."

I willed my mouth to speak, but it suddenly felt dry.

"What...?"

Her head tilted. "Cat got your tongue?"

I swallowed a few times, licked my dry lips and managed to speak. "What the fuck are you wearing?"

She glanced down at herself, then back up at me. "Pajamas."

I shook my head. "Those are not pajamas, Paige. This is not... this..." I moved my hand up and down as I motioned at her body. "This is not okay."

She frowned. "Why not?"

I laughed. "Why not? You're practically naked. I mean, I saw your ass. I can see your..."

With a smirk, she asked, "My what?"

Glaring, I shouted, "Your nipples! Paige, I see your nipples. This whole innocent, sexy girl thing is a hard *no*."

Paige set a tray full of blueberry muffins on a cooling rack.

Then she took off the oven mitts, which strangely enough, made her look even sexier, and dropped them into a drawer.

She reached into another drawer, took out a knife, and proceeded to use it to take out a muffin and set it on a small plate.

"I thought you were gone. These are my normal pajamas. If I'd known you were still here, I'd have changed or worn my robe."

"No," I said, shaking my head. "The ones you had on last night. Those were normal."

She let out a careless laugh. "My yoga pants? I'm not wearing my yoga pants to bed, Lucas. Sorry."

I pointed to her again, waving my hands in the air indicating her body. "Well, you can't wear that."

She smiled. "So you really think I'm sexy? I've got about seven, maybe a bit more, extra pounds on me." She looked down and frowned. "I guess I need to start running again to lose them."

"No!" I shouted, then closed my eyes. Holy fuck. I was losing my mind. I opened them and took a deep breath as I tried to focus on her face. Even that was hard to do. Why did her look scream, *I want you to bend me over the counter right now and fuck me hard, Lucas?*

"You look fine, Paige. You don't need to lose anything."

Chewing on her lip, she looked away, her cheeks pink with embarrassment. Then she spoke and I couldn't believe what she said. It stunned me into an even deeper stupor.

"Well, *fine* is a lot different than sexy. Maybe it was just a slip of your tongue. I'm sure your super model ex-girlfriend had a much better body than mine, and I doubt she ever ate blueberry muffins." She shook her head as if she hadn't meant to say that out loud. Then she shrugged. "Help yourself, by the way, or I'll end up eating them all."

My gut ached as she walked by me. I wanted to reach out and stop her. Tell her that wasn't what I meant, and that her body was ten times sexier than Bianca's. But I didn't. I let her walk by, eyes filled with something that looked a little like sadness and a lot like unshed tears.

Holy hell. I'd managed to hurt her once again.

"Fuck," I mumbled as I rubbed my hand over my chin stubble.

After I stood there for far too long trying to decide if I should go up to her room and tell her I didn't mean fine as in just *okay*, or if I needed to let her think I wasn't attracted to her... Damnit, I was! When I saw her and Milo yesterday, jealousy ripped through my body like an old, familiar friend. It was the same feeling I had when she said she wanted to go to a different school and I told her that guys would be all over her if I wasn't around. When her eyes met mine a few moments ago, I had a hard time catching my breath. I did everything in my damn power to act like seeing her wasn't playing havoc on my body and my heart.

I walked over and poured a cup of coffee and stared at the blueberry muffins.

Reaching across the table, I used the knife Paige had used to take one out. The moment I bit into it, an explosion of flavor assaulted my senses.

"Oh Jesus, this is amazing. Damn."

Bianca never allowed food like this in the house. I couldn't remember the last time I had a muffin, or anything sweet, for that matter. I needed to find out the brand and buy some for the future.

Just then, I heard Paige walk down the steps and out the front door. I quickly made my way through the house and caught her as she was getting into her car.

"Paige, where are you going?"

She looked back at me. "Home Depot, if you must know."

"Can I come? I need to grab some stuff."

The look on her face said I was the last person she wanted to be in a car with. I wanted to think that was a good thing, that my plan was working, but all it did was make the middle of my chest ache.

"Please?" I said with a half-smile, half-pout.

"Yeah, that doesn't work on me, Lucas. You of all people should know that."

Her voice was cold and distant, and I deserved every ounce of her condescension.

"Okay, I'll see if Dad can swing by and pick me up to get what I need."

She let out a frustrated sigh, then shook her head. "Fine. I'm leaving now though."

"Great! Let me run and get my wallet and the house key. Don't leave."

After rushing around and nearly tripping and breaking my ankle, I finally climbed into her SUV, winded.

"What are you getting at Home Depot?" I asked when she pulled out onto the highway.

"Blinds."

"For your room?"

"Yes."

I looked out the window. Clearly she wasn't in the mood for small talk. We drove in silence the entire way to Dripping Springs. It was a long twenty-five minutes. Once Paige parked her car, she walked into the store as fast as she could. The only problem was, I could walk just as fast, even faster. She was trying to lose me and that tickled me for some reason.

"Do you want to split up, or should we stick together?"

She looked up, shock registering, and for a moment I was transported back to the day I had asked her almost that exact question. She must have been thinking the same thing.

"Do you want to stay with me in Texas? Or are we splitting up?"

"It will probably be faster if you grab what you need while I order the blinds."

Disappointment rushed through me, but I quickly pushed it away. "Okay."

I watched her walk away and couldn't ignore the way I had wanted to touch her cheek softly and tell her how beautiful she was.

Jesus, Foster. Get your head in the game.

Before I turned to head off to the tools, I saw Paige look over her shoulder before facing forward again. I ignored the way that made my heart jump a bit.

After picking up a few tools, I made my way back to the specialty blinds area. Paige was sitting in a chair, smiling at something the associate had said. I hated that she didn't smile like that when I talked to her. Of course, maybe if I wasn't such a dick she would. If I hadn't broken her heart by acting like a complete asshole when we were younger, she might not look at me like it hurt to breathe around me.

"How's it going over here?" I asked, winking at Paige and then giving the guy a nod. His smile faded but he reached for my hand. I knew the type of impression I was giving him, and so did Paige. He instantly thought we were together. Paige didn't look the least bit happy.

"It's going good. We've just about got your blinds ordered for your room."

"It's not *our* room. It's *my* room," Paige said with a sweet smile directed at the guy.

"Well, it's *our* house," I added.

The guy's eyes bounced from me to Paige then back to his computer.

"Okay, looks like we are all set. Did you want us to install them?"

"No, I can do it," I said quickly.

Paige shot me a dirty look. "I can manage to hang them myself, thank you."

"Ah, a resourceful woman," the employee douche said.

She giggled, and I jerked my head back in surprise. Was she falling for this guy's lame attempt at flirting? And why the hell was he flirting with her when I was standing here? As far as he knew, we could very well be together. As a couple. Having sex. Lots of sex with me grabbing onto her hips and....

I shook my head to clear my wayward thoughts. She needed to take those pigtails down. The sooner the better.

He pulled out a card and wrote a number. "Here is my card. I went ahead and put my cell phone on there, just in case."

"Thank you, Doug. I appreciate all of your help," Paige said with a sticky sweetness to her voice that made my stomach feel like I had just eaten an entire jar of my mother's peach jam.

I didn't like the way he was looking at her.

"Ready to go, Paige?" I asked, breaking the weird little connection they had going on.

Paige gave Doug another flirty smile. "I'll be back to order more soon."

He waved. "Looking forward to it. Make sure you ask for me, so I can give you the concierge treatment, Paige."

When he looked at me, my expression clearly said *back the fuck off*. His smile vanished in an instant.

Asshole.

As we walked to the counter, I chuckled. "Seriously, Paige? The Home Depot guy?"

"What was wrong with him?"

I looked back toward the area we had come from. "For starters, he's for sure married."

She laughed. "And what drew you to that conclusion, Detective Lucas?"

"He had a tan line from a ring on his left hand."

"He's divorced. Recently."

Well, shit.

"Oh."

"What else is wrong with him? He works at Home Depot and not some big fancy company in Austin? Is that what I'm supposed to look for? A guy with money? Security?"

"Well, a guy who makes good money isn't a bad thing. And neither is security."

"Well, I'd much rather have happiness than money."

"What about security?"

She looked up at me. "You can have that without money."

"Aw, so you believe that happiness *can* buy you everything."

Her eyes filled with sadness again, and when she spoke, her voice shook slightly. "No, I'm not that naïve."

We checked out in silence. The only words spoken were to the cashier to say thank you and have a nice day.

After I put my purchases in the back of her 4-Runner, I slid into the passenger seat. This time I wasn't going to sit for nearly thirty minutes and not talk.

"Do you want to go across the street and get a frozen yogurt?"

"What, are we friends now, Lucas? Because that's what friends do, and you've made it quite clear that that isn't the case," she reminded me, her voice cold again.

"I'd like to think so. Haven't we always been friends?"

"Didn't seem that way when you stood me up for dinner."

"Is that what this is about? You're pissed at me for something that happened a few years ago?"

She looked at me with a stunned expression. "Are you for real right now? Pot meet kettle."

"So is that a no on the yogurt?" I asked in agitation.

With a roll of her eyes, she put her signal on to head into the plaza across the street that had a frozen yogurt place.

When we walked in, I said, "My treat."

"No, thanks. I don't want any."

I looked at her like she'd lost her mind. "You're seriously turning down frozen yogurt? I thought it was your favorite."

"Not anymore."

"Oh." I rubbed the back of my neck and motioned for her to head back out the door. "We can go ahead and leave then."

She looked confused. "I thought you wanted yogurt?"

"Nah, I just thought maybe you'd like some. I remembered you used to love it anytime we came across it."

She studied my face before she shook her head. Her expression lost some tightness, and she lifted the corners of her mouth a little. "I don't eat it anymore but thank you."

Before we got back to her car, I took her by the wrist and made her stop.

"You look more than fine, Paige."

Her face screwed up in confusion. "What?"

"Earlier, in the kitchen. You asked if I thought you looked sexy and I said you looked fine. I didn't mean it that way. You are a beautiful woman with an even more beautiful body, and any guy would consider himself damn lucky to be yours. Honestly, you looked fucking hot this morning. That's all I'm trying to say."

Her eyes widened in surprise, and she worked her mouth open and closed a few times before finally speaking.

"Thank you. And you look...*fine*, too." She winked, and I loved that her cheeks turned pink. I also loved that she seemed to warm a little. It had been my comment to her in the kitchen that made her upset. I hated myself for making her feel that way. Paige hadn't ever been the type of girl who worried about her looks or her body. But something told me that this Paige, the older Paige, the one whose heart I had broken, was more sensitive. I needed to keep that in the back of my mind. Especially since she had compared herself to Bianca. Which was laughable. Bianca couldn't hold a candle to Paige.

I laughed. "And just to set the record straight some more, he's not average."

"If you say so," she said, unlocking the car doors.

"I can show you, if you want."

"No, thanks. I've seen my fair share," she replied with a smile.

And there it was. The smile she had given the douche at Home Depot. I fist pumped internally. I had a feeling chasing Paige out of this house was going to end up being more fun than I thought. Seeing that smile reminded me that a small part of me didn't want her to leave. Yeah, I was losing my mind for sure.

Chapter 7

Paige

THE LOUD NOISE caused me to bolt up in my bed. I sat perfectly still as I tried with all my might to hear where it was coming from.

Tap. Tap. Tap.

My eyes went to the window.

I squeezed them shut and whispered, "It's a tree branch, that's all."

Tap. Tap. Tap.

Snapping my eyes open, I flew out of bed. Picking up the small baseball bat my brother had given me for self-defense, I walked over to the window and pulled the makeshift curtain back.

I was ready to scream, but laughed instead. "Well, who are you?" I asked, opening the window and letting a black and white cat in. She rubbed against my legs, looked up at me and meowed. Then she jumped on my bed and made herself comfortable, turning in three circles.

"Okay. Welcome home Oreo."

The cat opened her eyes and meowed. "Is that your name? Oreo?"

I decided if this cat was going to invade my home, I had the right to name it.

"We'll take you to the vet in the morning and see if anyone has lost you, sweet girl."

Clink. Clink. Clink.

I froze.

That was *not* the window. This sound was coming from downstairs.

With my trusted bat still in hand, I slowly made my way down the steps. Oreo ran ahead of me. Clearly, she knew the layout of this house, and I wondered if she might have belonged to William.

Another noise came from the kitchen. Where in the hell was Lucas? Why wasn't he investigating? Then I remembered his stupid comment about the house being haunted. I smiled. Was he really going this far? I chuckled to myself, but still kept the bat firmly in my hands.

Slowly I made my way into the kitchen. There was a shadow in the corner and I froze. It looked like a woman. A younger woman. Oreo walked right over to the shadow and it disappeared. Goosebumps instantly raced over my body, and I began to shake.

A creaking sound came from behind me. Oh my goodness. The ghost was coming for me! I turned and swung the bat, making contact with something hard.

"Ouch! What in the fuck!"

I dropped the bat, stunned. That wasn't a woman's voice. "Lucas?" I said, desperately trying to find the light switch. When I flicked it on, Lucas was bent over, moaning in pain.

"Oh my God! Oh my God! I hit you with the bat! I'm so sorry! Are you bleeding?"

He stood up, his expression dazed and confused. "What's going on?"

"Wait, did I hit you?"

"No, a cat scratched the living shit out of my chest when you hit the damn doorframe. By the way, you just missed hitting me with that thing, you freak."

From behind me there was a *meow*. I turned to find Oreo sitting on the table, cleaning herself. She looked up, and I swore she smirked at Lucas. I was going to really like this cat, I had decided, and hoped she didn't belong to anyone.

"The cat jumped on you?"

He sighed as he rubbed his chest.

"Yes. You probably scared her."

His voice sounded like he was talking slower. Like it took him a bit of concentration to speak.

"Why are you walking around in the dark with a baseball bat, Paige?"

"I heard a noise. When I came down here, I saw a shadow in the corner right there. It's okay, though. I think it was just Mary."

"Mary? Who the hell is Mary?"

"Mary, the ghost."

He blinked at me, repeatedly. A blank look on his face. "Wait, you really think the house is haunted?"

I laughed. "I don't think, I know. William told me it was. Apparently, there was a family who lived in a cabin that was almost in the same exact spot as the house. Their youngest daughter Mary was riding on her horse and tried to jump a small fence. She fell and got hurt. She laid in her room for weeks, not able to wake up. Then she caught a fever and died. William said she can't cross over because she's waiting for her fiancé to come back home for her."

Lucas shook his head and then leaned against the counter, almost like he was exhausted. Then he scrubbed his hands down his face and mumbled something about things not going to be easy now.

"Wait a minute, where were you coming from when the cat clawed you? Did you go out?"

"Yeah. Milo invited me out with a few guys. We were supposed to go out last night but ended up doing it tonight. We grabbed some beer at the brewery and just hung out and talked. Back to the more pressing details, you're not afraid of the house being haunted?"

I laughed. "No. Why, are you?"

He glared at me. "No."

His response was quick and sharp. Then he let his gaze wander down my body like he had this morning.

"Son-of-a-bitch, you're wearing those pajamas again."

With a quick look down at my clothes, I smiled before peeking back up at him. "Yes, because they are my pajamas, and it's the middle of the night."

His eyes looked down my body greedily this time, and it instantly gave me goosebumps. This time I wasn't scared; I was turned on. The way he was looking at me warmed all the important parts.

I felt my nipples tighten as his gaze heated up. He licked his lips and then smirked as he said, "What about me? Are you afraid of me?"

With a scoff, I replied, "Why would I be afraid of you, Lucas?"

He took a few steps toward me. I took a few away until I was backed up against the counter.

When he stopped in front of me, I smelled a hint of alcohol. His eyes looked clear, but he was certainly acting a bit tipsy.

"How much did you have to drink?" I asked, assuming that's why he'd been talking slowly a few moments ago.

He smiled, and it made my stomach dip. It was his sexy, carefree smile. The one he didn't give often, but when he did, it made my insides clench with anticipation. The silky fabric of my shirt rubbed against my hard nipples and I had to force myself not to move.

"A lot."

"Really?" I asked. But he must have, because sober Lucas wouldn't be looking at me like this. Sober Lucas wanted me gone, like yesterday.

He looked down at my mouth and licked his lips once again. I swallowed hard and went to speak, but he spoke first. And what he said nearly made my knees give out.

"I want to touch you."

"*Um...*"

Yes. That was my response. *Um.*

What in the living hell?

Then I heard my response, and instantly wanted to swallow myself whole and disappear. "Where?"

Dear Lord. Where? Paige, you are so out of practice. Now is the time to stop this nonsense. He is drunk and probably thinks you're Bianca.

"Is that a yes?" he asked, his words ever-so-slightly slurred. Was he drunk from alcohol or desire? I couldn't deny I wanted it to be from desire.

Say no. Say no. He thinks you are someone else, and he is clearly drunk.

When I didn't say anything, Lucas rubbed his thumb over my hardened nipple. I gasped, then pressed my mouth in a tight line.

"Christ, Paige. You're so fucking sexy."

Sooo, clearly he knows it's me and not his ex. Okay. Now, I really need to stop this.

"Thank you?"

I closed my eyes and groaned inwardly. It had come out like a damn question. I had meant to say, *'Lucas, stop touching me. You're drunk. Go to bed.'* Instead, when he pinched my nipple, I moaned in utter delight because it felt damn good. And I was horny. And Lucas was standing in front of me looking utterly delicious, and my mind couldn't think straight around him.

"You like that?" he asked before dipping his head down and pressing his mouth to mine.

For a moment, I stood there, shocked. Lucas was kissing me... while pinching my nipple. And sweet mother of God, it felt really good. Really, really good.

I put my hands on his chest and tried to will myself to push him away. Instead, I grabbed at his shirt and pulled him closer. He groaned and grabbed my leg, pulling it up so he could push his hard dick into my core.

Gasping at the feel of him *there*, I slid my hands up his chest and pushed them into his hair. God, I'd forgotten what an amazing kisser he was. How lost in him I could get.

He moved his hips, and I could confirm that he was indeed, not average. He pushed harder against me, and I snapped back to reality because sober Lucas would not be doing this. I knew that much. There was no way in hell. He acted like he couldn't stand to be around me most of the time. I needed to stop this before things went too far. Drunk regrets are the worst kind of regrets.

I broke the kiss, but he was still pushing against my core. Even in the darkness, I could see the desire in his eyes. Yeah, he was drunk.

"Stop," I whispered.

Lucas instantly stopped. He looked into my eyes and didn't say a word. Stumbling back, he stared at the ground.

"You've been drinking, Lucas, and don't know what you're doing. If you were sober, you wouldn't even have looked twice at me as you headed to your bedroom."

He brought his gaze back to meet mine. I wanted to be able to read his expression, but his eyes were void of all emotion, a drunken haze covering their usual luster. He swayed from side to side.

"You should go to bed," I said, looking down the hall that led to the master bedroom.

"Is that what you want?" he asked. Suddenly he seemed perfectly fine.

I nodded, but didn't speak, because it wasn't what I wanted. I wanted to feel his hands on my body again. His tongue dancing with mine. His hard dick inside me.

My hand came up to my mouth to stop me from saying anything more, and for a moment, he looked like he was going to speak. Then something on his face changed. He almost looked...mad?

He laughed. "Damn, well, okay then. Goodnight."

I watched as he made his way down the hall. After steadying my breathing, I took a quick look around the kitchen and made sure all the windows and doors were locked. I heard a loud crash from Lucas's room. With him drunk, I couldn't just walk away and ignore it. I made my way to his bedroom. A random thought occurred. Had he driven his dad's old truck while he had been drinking? I was totally going to lay into him for driving while drinking. I knocked on the door to his bedroom.

"Lucas?"

His bedroom door hadn't been shut all the way, and it pushed open just enough for me to walk inside. I stepped into the bedroom and quietly called his name. I didn't want to scare the hell out of him if the sound I heard was nothing. The shower was going and the door to the bathroom was wide open. All I could see was steam coming out of the doorway.

"Shoot, what if he freaking fell?" I whispered. Part of me wanted to leave him there for what he had just done to me. The other part, the part that still cared slightly for him, knew I couldn't. He hadn't seemed all that drunk, but he had always been able to handle alcohol much better than me.

I tiptoed to the bathroom and was about to call out his name when I heard moaning. I froze. My heart instantly hammered in my chest.

"Oh God. Yeah, faster."

I looked behind me and then around the room like an idiot. Had he brought a girl home and was having sex with her in the shower? How in the world had I missed a woman coming into my own house?

What an asshole! He was just coming on to me! Ugh! Men.

I turned to leave, then froze when I heard my name.

"Paige."

My heart dropped. He had said it in such a desperate, wanting manner. I swallowed hard and looked back into the bathroom.

"That's it, baby. Faster."

After picking my jaw off the floor, I peeked farther into the bathroom. Since the door was open, the mirror wasn't fogged yet, and I had the perfect view of Lucas standing in the glass shower, one hand on the wall, the other jacking himself off.

"Fuck. Faster. Paige, I'm going to come, baby."

My mind was telling me to turn and leave. This was wrong. I was invading Lucas's privacy. But holy hell, he was calling out *my name* as he made himself come. In the shower. Drunk or not, it was hot, and my heart almost hammered out of my chest. My hands covered my mouth as I watched him fall over the edge. It was the hottest thing I'd ever seen, and I couldn't tear my eyes from him.

His body trembled as he came down from his orgasm. Then he let out a frustrated groan, pounded his fist against the tile wall and said, "That woman is going to fucking be the death of me."

I turned and rushed out of his room, down the hall, and then raced up the steps as quietly as I could. Oreo was hot on my trail.

Once I got into my room, I shut and locked the door, then turned and leaned against it. I was completely out of breath and my pulse was racing. I'd never in my life felt my heart beat so hard in my chest. It drummed so loudly in my ears that it scared me for a quick moment.

The vision of Lucas making himself come while saying my name replayed over and over in my mind. It wasn't Bianca he was fantasizing about. It was me.

Me! Holy mother of Jesus. How drunk had he been?

I looked at my new cat. "I don't know what to do with this information, Oreo."

She meowed.

"What? What are you saying to me?"

Another meow.

"No. No. He was drunk. That's all. He can't even stand to be around me. Or, at least that was the case yesterday. He's been so nice today, but I know it's all a game. He's playing me to get me out of the house. And tonight, he was drinking. He saw me in my skimpy PJs, and he acted like any man would. That's it. That explains it. Men are...men. Plain and simple. He got turned on, played with my nipple and kissed me. Then I said no, he needed to release his...horniness or whatever, and that's it. Simple as that. Doesn't mean anything."

Oreo stared at me. "You agree, right?"

This time she decided to keep her thoughts to herself.

I rolled my eyes and decided I needed to push this out of my head and deal with it tomorrow. "Whatever. I'll talk to Jen about it in the morning."

Pushing away tonight's turn of events was easier said than done, and it wasn't until four in the morning when I finally felt myself drift off to sleep.

Jen stared at me, her mouth gaping, eyes wide. She went to speak, then snapped her mouth shut. Then tried again.

Oreo rubbed my legs as I stood in the kitchen, patiently waiting for my friend to figure out how to use her words. The same kitchen that Lucas had touched me and kissed me in. By the time I had gotten up and come down this morning, Lucas had left. He'd left a note on the table saying he was going into Austin for work and would be back in a few hours. I had silently thanked God I didn't see him because I had no idea how in the hell I would face him after last night. Did he remember anything? Remember touching me? Kissing me? Asking me if I was sure I wanted him to stop? Did he remember the shower? Him coming while he called out my name?

Lord, I'm in a pickle. A freaking gigantic pickle.

"He...nipple?"

I nodded as I chewed on my lip.

"Kissed you?"

"Yep."

"Then the shower?"

Another nod. "Do you see why I'm freaking out here? This is all your fault!"

"My fault!" she gasped.

"Yes! You told me to wear my sexiest pajamas. 'Put your hair in pigtails! It will drive him nuts' you said."

She covered her mouth and had the nerve to laugh.

"Well, to be fair, it appears it did drive him nuts because he came on to you."

"When he was drunk! That doesn't count."

"It doesn't sound like he was that drunk if he could take care of business in the shower."

I sighed.

Jen took a drink of her sweet tea and then took in a deep breath. "Okay, so what are you going to do about it?"

"Nothing."

Her eyes widened. "Nothing? You're going to pretend it didn't happen? What if he remembers it?"

I shrugged. "If he feels like he needs to talk about what happened, then he can approach me."

With narrowed eyes, she tilted her head to regard me. "You said you pushed him away when he kissed you."

"That's right. I did." I felt rather proud of myself. Lord knows my body wanted to be ravaged by the man in that moment, but I had stayed strong.

"But he asked you if you were sure you wanted him to go to bed. How long after the kiss did you push him away?"

I swallowed hard, then hoped like hell I was hiding my instant guilt.

"Does it matter?"

She leaned in closer and stared into my eyes. "Oh my gawd! You kissed him back!"

I didn't say anything.

When she jumped up and down, I rolled my eyes. "You totally kissed him back. You didn't tell me the whole truth. Spill it, Paige. Right now!"

I sighed. "Ugh! Fine! When he kissed me, I placed my hands on his chest to push him away, but I sort of pulled him closer."

She gasped and sat down. Placing her chin in her hand, she said, "You whore! Go on!"

I smiled slightly. "Well, I might have gotten caught up in the kiss because I slid my hands up to his hair."

She wiggled her brows. "Then what happened?"

"Nothing."

"Liar."

I buried my face in my hands and moaned. "Shit! Fine! He lifted my leg and sort of, you know."

She smirked. "No, I don't know. You're going to have to explain this one to me, Paige. Heck, here's a napkin and a pen, draw me a picture if you have to."

With a roll of my eyes, I exhaled, then told her. "Fine, he started grinding against me."

"Holy shit! Was he hard?"

My face heated. "Yes. But it was for like thirty seconds and I came to my senses. I told him to stop, and he instantly did."

Jen held up her hands. "Wait. He stopped like right that instant, the moment you said stop."

I nodded. "Yes."

Her mouth dropped open and something in her eyes lit on fire. "He wasn't drunk."

I laughed. "Yes, he was."

She shook her head. "No, he wasn't."

"Jen, I watched him stumble. He smelled like alcohol. He swayed on his feet after we broke apart. A sober Lucas would not have said he wanted to touch me, then proceed to grind himself against me."

A knowing smile appeared on her face. "Then why did he leave at the crack ass of dawn? If he had been that drunk, he'd have dragged his ass out of bed and sat in here with aspirin and a cup of coffee. Instead, he gets up early and jets off to Austin? I'm not buying it."

"So just because he stopped when I told him to, it means he wasn't drunk? Even drunk, I think Lucas would still respect when a woman tells him to stop."

"Sure, he would, after he nipped on your neck, or placed kisses along your jaw line, asking you if you were really sure you wanted him to stop. But you said stop, and he instantly stopped. He used the alcohol as an excuse to touch you, Paige."

I gulped down the breath that seemed to be stuck in my throat.

"But...but he even admitted to drinking."

"So? Did he drive home last night? You and I both know Lucas wouldn't have driven if he didn't have his wits about him. Milo wouldn't let him."

"His eyes looked glassy," I said weakly.

"From lust. He immediately went to his shower and jacked off, with you as the fantasy playing in his head. He wants you." She said the last three words seductively.

I rolled my eyes again. "No way. I'm not buying it."

The front door opened, and Jen and I both froze.

"He's home!" I whisper-shouted.

"Act normal," Jen advised, whispering herself.

"So, I told Gene about your window problem. He can totally recommend someone."

Confusion swirled in my head. "What?" I asked, staring at my friend like she'd lost her mind.

Her eyes widened in frustration. It only took a nano of a second to realize what she was doing.

"What a great guy," I quickly said. "You really lucked out with that one."

She smiled. "I know. I think we're going to go watch a local band tonight. Want to come?"

Lucas walked into the kitchen. His eyes met mine, and when he didn't look away, a sinking feeling hit me.

He didn't remember last night.

"What window problem?" Lucas asked.

"Hello to you too, Lucas," Jen said.

Glancing at Jen, Lucas smiled, then leaned down and gave her a kiss on the cheek. I was instantly jealous. "Jen, how are you doing? Here to watch another movie with shirtless men on a beach?"

She smiled. "No sleepover tonight. I've got plans with the hubby. I was just inviting Paige along. Gene knows the lead singer in a band. He's single, hot, and I'm pretty sure you would get along with him, Paige."

That made Lucas pause for a moment as he looked at Jen, then me, then back to Jen.

"I'd love to come. I need a night out. It's been forever."

Lucas opened the refrigerator and put in a six pack of beer. Then pulled one out and opened it. He leaned against the counter and took a drink. I tried not to look at him, but I could feel his eyes on me. I quickly glanced his way.

Yep. He was staring at me.

"Didn't get enough to drink last night?" I asked.

He smiled, and I instantly felt my cheeks heat. Jen cleared her throat and stood.

"I'm going to take off. I've got to get to the post office before they close. Great seeing you again, Lucas."

"You don't have to run off on my account, Jen," Lucas said.

"I really have to get going," she said with a smile that said she knew something we didn't.

Facing her, I gave her pleading eyes that begged her not to leave. She simply winked, grabbed her purse and called out as she walked away, "Let me know if you want to meet us there or have us pick you up! It's at the Pecan Street Bar! They go on at eight!"

When I heard the front door shut, I took in a deep breath and turned back around. I made my way over to the sink and started to clean the glasses from our tea.

"Sorry if I woke you up last night when I got home. I honestly don't even remember coming in."

Sadness washed over my body, and I was positive my shoulders sagged slightly. Damn it all to hell. The last thing I wanted was for Lucas to think I was upset about something.

"I was already awake. You didn't drive drunk, did you?" I asked, focusing on washing the glasses. I moved slowly and washed one of the glasses at least four times before rinsing it.

"No, Milo's friend Chuck was the designated driver. He brought us all home."

Nodding, I rinsed the other glass and reached for the dish towel. When I looked at Lucas, he was still staring at me.

"Good. Hope you had a nice time."

He nodded. "I did. Was good hanging out with our old friends. Bianca never did much like my friends from JC."

I forced a smile. "I'd imagine she didn't have much in common with them."

Lucas didn't say anything, but the way he watched me made me uneasy. I dried off the glasses and moved around him to put them in the cabinet.

The smell of his cologne filled the air, causing me to hold my breath. The last thing I wanted to do was smell him. Even his stupid smell made my body ache for his touch.

"If you'll excuse me, Lucas, I've got to go get ready. I have a meeting with someone."

He pushed off the counter and blocked my way. The way he looked at me almost made me feel like he was willing me to say something.

"Did you need something?" I asked, staring up into his green eyes.

"I don't normally come home drunk, just so you know. It won't happen again."

I wanted to ask him what part wouldn't happen again. Him coming home after drinking or him coming on to me? Maybe him jerking off in the shower and calling out my name? But I didn't ask any of that. With a shrug, I gave him a slight smile. "What you do is your business. Not mine."

He nodded, then smiled. "I didn't wake you at all?"

I swallowed hard. The fact that he had no memory of what happened between us hurt more than I wanted to admit. I had been right last night. Sober Lucas would not have wanted to touch me. Or kiss me. Or ravage me in the middle of the kitchen in the house we both owned.

But he hadn't seemed *that* drunk. Not drunk enough to not remember. Unless Jen was right. He was using it as an excuse. Since I wasn't mentioning what happened, he was going to pretend he didn't remember.

"No. Not at all."

For a moment, there was a cat and mouse look on his face—something in his eyes. But it was gone as quickly as it came. "Good. Give any more thought to me buying you out?"

I let out a frustrated groan and pushed past him. As I headed to the stairs, I called out, "I'm not selling my half to you!"

Oreo raced up the stairs and into my room. I slammed the door shut and walked over to my bed. When I sat down, I took in a deep, slow breath, then let it out. Pulling my phone out of my pocket, I sent Jen a text.

Me: He doesn't remember, so I played it off. He asked if he woke me up when he came home last night.

I hated that I felt so let down by the fact that Lucas hadn't remembered anything. Jen texted back almost immediately.

Jen: I call bullshit. He remembers. He's playing a game. You have to outplay him.

I fell back onto the bed. Jen had always been a hopeless romantic. I knew she had hoped that Lucas and I would end up back together. It was clear that was never going to happen. Even if I didn't want to admit to myself how much I had wanted that, too. And I was already growing tired of this game. Why had William done this? Thrown us together with unrealistic expectations? The only good thing that had come out of this was that Lucas had broken up with Bianca. Not that it had benefitted me any. Okay, last night it had for the briefest of moments, but I needed to forget that anything had ever happened. If Lucas didn't want to admit to it, I sure as hell wouldn't either.

I resolved that from here on out I would attempt to move on. Put my past—including Lucas—exactly where it belonged.

Chapter 8

Lucas

MILO RUBBED THE back of his neck as he stared at me. I couldn't tell if he was pissed, or just unsure of what to say.

"Why did you pretend to not remember what happened?"

I laughed. "She wasn't going to acknowledge it, so why should I?"

He narrowed his eyes. "Dude, you came on to her, pretended to be drunk, then acted like it never happened. Even for you, that's a dick thing to do."

"She told me to stop. I stopped. She rejected me. Do you really think I want to have her rub that shit in my face? We both know she would."

"What's with the games, Lucas? This was never your MO. And do you really think Paige would bring that sort of shit up? The Paige I knew wouldn't."

I knew he was right, but didn't want to admit it to him, let alone myself. "I had too much to drink, she was dressed in those fucking sexy pajamas, and I simply wasn't thinking straight. It was a mistake, a mistake that is best forgotten. Clearly, she realizes that, too. Why make things awkward?"

"Dude, you didn't have that much to drink, and you lied to her about driving home. You came in your dad's truck and left in it after what, two beers?"

"It doesn't matter. She'll forget it soon enough."

He nodded. "Can you forget it though?"

I scoffed. "I was horny, that's all. It didn't mean anything."

I hated the way Milo was looking at me, as if he could see my truths flashing on a bright neon sign over my head. That kiss meant a fuck ton. I hadn't been able to sleep last night because all I kept doing was replaying the way her hands slid up my chest and into my hair. The way she moaned when I pinched her nipple. The way her heat felt against my hard cock.

Fuck. Fuck. Fuck.

Then the asshole laughed. "Dude, if you want to lie to yourself, go for it. We may not have hung out together the last few years, but I know you. You wanted something to happen."

I rolled my neck, popping a few spots where the tension had been building. He was right. About everything. I had wanted something to happen. The moment I saw Paige in the kitchen, dressed in those fucking pajamas, hair pulled back into pigtails, my cock had gone hard.

"Well, it's a good thing she said no. I had a moment of insanity. I need to get my head back into the game and figure out a way to get Paige to sell me her half of the house. That's all this is about. Her walking away from what is rightfully mine."

"She's never going to sell. Just cut your losses, Lucas, you don't need the money. And the fact that you even want to sell your granddaddy's house makes me question just how much you've changed. You loved that place, man. You dreamed of raising your family there."

I huffed. "Yeah, with the woman who currently owns half it." I sighed. "And I have no intentions of selling it. That was just me pissed off. I would never do that to Granddad."

He raised a brow. "Work something out with her, Lucas. This isn't you. You know how much that house means to Paige. How much it meant to William."

Glancing around the office of Milo's shop, I sighed. "I think I'm going to head on back to the house. If I'm going to find a solution to this problem, I need to start looking for the damn chest Granddad was talking about."

Milo wore a look of disappointment. "I'll be by the house tomorrow. Paige needed help painting. I told her I'd cut her a deal on the interior if she helped do most of it."

I tried to ignore the zip of jealousy that raced over my body. "You don't need to help her. I've got it. I'll help her paint the inside of the house."

He simply nodded. "If that's what you want."

Standing, I forced myself to smile. "That's what I want."

Milo followed my lead and stood. "She isn't yours anymore, Lucas, unless you're making a claim on her."

"A claim?" I asked with a laugh. "Wait one damn minute." I glared at the man who had been my best friend since we were old enough to figure out girls made us a little crazy. "Milo, are you interested in Paige?"

He shrugged. "Maybe."

I balled my fists at my side. "You're fucking interested in my girl?"

Expecting him to back down, or tell me he was kidding, I crossed my arms over my chest. He didn't do either of those things. "She isn't yours anymore, Lucas. Unless…"

He let his voice trail off. I stared at him with a hard look. He either was trying to make a point, or he really was interested in Paige. Either way, it pissed me off.

"You don't need to help her paint this weekend. I'll help her. It's half my house, after all. And don't forget the goddamn bro code. You don't go after your friend's old girlfriend."

He raised a brow and smirked. "Especially when he's still very much interested in said old girlfriend."

My jaw ached from how tight I was holding it. I walked out of his office, slamming his office door behind me. I hated that the asshole was a hundred percent right.

All I heard as I stormed away was his annoying-as-fuck laughter through his office door.

The moment I walked into the house, I came to a stop. Paige was walking down the steps, Oreo, her newfound friend, running ahead of her.

I shut the door and stared at her. She looked me right in the eyes and smiled. "Hey."

"Hey," I said, the anger from earlier with Milo still evident in my voice.

"You sound mad. Everything okay?"

"No. I need to find that fucking chest and get this bullshit over with."

She stopped at the bottom of the stairs, and I couldn't help but let my eyes take in every inch of her. Her brown hair was pulled up into a neat bun on top of her head. A few strands of hair encased her beautiful face in soft brown curls. Her makeup was light but gave just a hint that she was wearing some. Her lips were painted with a pale pink, and I ached to kiss them. My eyes lingered a little too long on those lips. The memory of my mouth on hers last night hit me hard. Why in the hell was she pretending last night didn't happen? The more I thought about it, the more pissed off I got.

I looked away. Maybe she hadn't wanted it to happen. Lord knows I did. I couldn't get to the shower fast enough and jerk off, images of Paige riding on top of me fueling my release.

"What bullshit?" she asked.

With a long, drawn-out sigh, I motioned between us. "This."

One eyebrow arched perfectly as she repeated the word in the form of a question. "This?"

"Yes, Paige. This. You and me, living under one roof."

"That's your fault, Lucas. You're the one who moved in here. I'm perfectly fine if you'd like to move back to Austin."

I felt my jaw twitch as I clenched in frustration. All I wanted to do was pull her into my arms and kiss the living shit out of her. That would shut her up.

"You're wearing that?" I heard myself bark out. It had come out harsher than I had intended.

Paige looked down at her light blue dress. It hugged her body in all the right ways. Her toned legs were capped off with black high heels. For a night out in Austin, it would have been perfect, but for a night out in Johnson City, it was probably more than the boys here could handle. She'd be having guys stare at her all night, and that idea bothered the hell out of me. There was no way she could wear that dress.

"What's wrong with what I'm wearing?" she asked.

"This is Johnson City, Paige. Not Austin."

Her eyes filled with hurt. I hated myself for even saying anything. I needed to soften my words and tell her she looked beautiful, because she did, but if she went out in that dress, every man in the damn bar would be staring at her.

"Right," she said, turning and walking back up the steps.

"Paige, wait."

"No, you're right, Lucas. I should change, heaven forbid I look out of place." She gave me a forced smile over her shoulder and started back up.

"Goddamnit, will you wait a second, Paige."

Not paying any attention to me, she kept walking.

"Paige!"

"It's fine, Lucas. You made your point."

I rushed up the steps after her.

"You look beautiful. I just meant, maybe you might want to tone it down."

She turned to face me. Her face contorted with confusion. "I look *beautiful*? Are you afraid you hurt my feelings and now you're trying to make me feel better? Well, please, don't let your guilt eat away at you."

"That's not it at all," I said, reaching for her arm.

"Let me go, Lucas. I need to go dress down apparently."

I closed my eyes. "I told you I didn't mean it that way."

She pulled her arm, trying to get away from me. I let her go, then stood in front of her door, blocking her from going in.

"All I meant was every guy in the damn bar will be staring at you, Paige. Is that what you want? A bunch of men undressing you with their eyes? Because that is what will happen if you show up dressed like that."

Paige lifted her chin. "Maybe that is exactly what I want, Lucas. A man's attention. His hands on my body, making me feel things I haven't felt in a very, *very* long time."

My body heated, and I took a step toward her. I couldn't have stopped myself if I tried. Hearing her say she wanted a man's hands on her, that she hadn't felt that in a long time? Yeah, those words were my kryptonite. "Is that what you want, Paige? A man to touch you?"

She swallowed hard but kept her expression void of anything. "And more. I could use a good orgasm from a man who actually wants to touch me and will remember it the next day."

That made my stomach lurch, and my heart drop. "A man like... Milo?"

Paige shrugged. "If he was interested, yes."

Full-on rage pulsed through my veins as I took another step toward her, making her back up against the wall opposite her bedroom door.

"You're playing with fire, Paige."

She let out a humorless laugh. "How so? I'm a single, young woman who hasn't had sex in a very long time. If I want to have some fun, why shouldn't I? Men can have one-night stands, why can't a woman?"

"You forgot attractive."

Her eyebrows pulled in tight. "What?"

"You're a single, young, and very attractive woman."

Her mouth opened to say something, then she quickly closed it.

"So, you want a one-night stand."

"Maybe," she softly said.

"Anyone in particular? Maybe Milo? My best friend?"

"Your old *high school* best friend? Is there some sort of law against that?"

"As a matter of fact, yes, there is."

She laughed and went to push past me when I caged her against the wall with my arms.

My eyes searched her face and fell to her mouth, and she pressed those luscious lips into a tight line.

"Do you want me to touch you, Paige? Give you that long-overdue orgasm?"

"Wh-what?"

"It's a simple question. And the answer involves you, me, and an orgasm...or three. I can help you with that, you know."

Her eyes flashed with something I hadn't seen in a long time. Determination. Pure fucking determination. I just wasn't sure what in the hell she was determined to get, and I instantly worried I was pushing her away.

"Please move, Lucas. I need to change. As you pointed out, I'm not dressed appropriately."

My eyes dropped to the exposed area of her breasts. Her body had had the starring role in a number of my dreams over the years. Even when I had been with Bianca, it was frequently Paige. A fact which at the time had filled me with guilt. Dreaming of another woman when one was sleeping next to you was a douche move indeed. But I couldn't forget this woman no matter how hard I tried.

I pulled in a quick breath as I ran my finger along the edge of her dress, lightly touching her skin. Paige's breath hitched at the touch, as well.

"Did you also hear me say you look beautiful?"

Her eyes watched as my fingers moved over her skin, and it only made my dick grow harder. Hell on wheels, this woman could always make my cock rock solid just by watching me touch her. It was one of the hottest things I'd ever experienced with a woman. I moved my hand down the side of her dress, feeling every sexy curve on her body until I touched the bare skin of her upper leg.

Paige opened her mouth and drew in a shaky voice as she asked, "What are you doing, Lucas?"

"I know what you like. I know how to make you come within seconds. Do you remember that?"

Her tongue darted out to lick her lips. My hand moved under her dress, and I loved that I could feel her body tremble. I loved it even more that she wasn't pushing me away.

"Are you drunk again, Lucas?"

I smiled. "No, I'm very sober."

Pushing her dress up, I looked down to see she was wearing black lace panties. I moaned. I would bet my half of the house it was a black lace thong.

"How long has it been, Paige, since you've had a man make you come?"

Before she had a chance to answer, I moved closer and slipped my hand into her panties. When she sucked in a breath, memories of the first time I ever made her come with my hand flooded my mind. The sweet moans she made as I pumped my fingers inside her. The way she ran her fingers through my hair, begging me to finish her off. I had nearly blown my load in my own pants when she finally let herself tumble over the edge. Watching Paige have an orgasm had been one of my all-time favorite things to do.

I didn't even have to touch her to know she was soaking wet. I could practically smell her arousal.

Dipping my head down, I buried my face into her neck and lifted her leg, then slipped a finger inside her. When she moaned, I let out a primal growl. There was no fucking way any other man would be touching her tonight. Paige Miller was mine. She'd always be mine.

I moved slowly at first, then slipped another finger inside her.

"Lucas," she gasped, jerking her hips, silently begging me for more as she grabbed onto my shirt to steady herself.

Drawing back, I smiled when I saw her head leaning against the wall, a slight O formed on her lips, her eyes closed tightly.

"Do you want more, baby? Tell me you want more. Do you want me to stop this time?"

Her eyes opened, and our gaze met. She opened her mouth to speak, then quickly shut it. Her hands went to my chest and she pushed me away hard. A look of pure anger swept over her face.

"You fucking asshole. You do remember last night!"

I stared at her, not saying a word.

"Last night. You touching me, kissing me. You remember it, don't you?"

Rubbing the back of my neck, I looked away, trying to figure out how to explain.

"Why did you act like you didn't remember?" she asked while pulling her dress back down.

"Why did you act like you didn't care?" I asked.

She looked mad as hell. "I asked you first!"

"I...didn't want to make it awkward."

Her eyes turned black as night.

Clearly that had not been the right answer.

Chapter 9

Paige

I STOOD THERE, staring at him. I had never been so angry in my entire life.

"You didn't want to make it *awkward*? Do you do that often, Lucas? Feel up a woman and then pretend like you don't remember?"

He let out a gruff laugh. "Don't be silly. I've been with Bianca for..."

He stopped talking when he saw me draw in a slow, angry breath.

Stupid, stupid, stupid! I let him do it to me again. This time I let him go farther and Lord knows how far it would have gone.

"I can't believe how stupid I am," I said in a disbelieving voice.

"What? Why would you say that?" He honestly looked confused.

"You don't want me, Lucas. You only want this house and will stop at nothing to make that happen."

He shook his head, staring with a befuddled expression.

"Is that your game plan? Get me to fall for you again so you can sweet talk me right out of my half of the house?"

"Paige." He looked at me like I had lost my mind, and maybe I had. When it came to this man, I wasn't sure which way was up and which way was down, and I didn't need him using that to his advantage.

Poking him in the chest, I walked toward him, causing him to walk backward.

"From this point on, you do not touch me. I don't want you to make any comments about my clothes, how I'm dressed, who I go out with, nothing. None of it is your business. And if I want to have a one-night stand, I'll have one. And I couldn't give two shits if it's with one of your friends or not. I do not belong to you. You made sure of that when you broke up with me and walked away like our relationship was meaningless. Now if you'll excuse me, I'm late."

Turning, I headed down the steps. I could feel his eyes, and it took more willpower than I knew I had to keep putting one foot in front of the other.

When I reached the front door, his voice stopped me in my tracks.

"I'm sorry."

I took a shaky breath. I wasn't sure if I wanted to know what he was sorry for. If he told me that touching me like that had been a ploy, I wasn't sure what I'd do. My ego had been taking shots from this man for the last few days, and I wasn't sure how much more I could take.

"I would never take advantage of you like that, Paige. I thought you knew me better than that."

With a quick look back over my shoulder, I let out a humorless laugh. "I stopped knowing who you were a long time ago, Lucas."

Once I opened the front door and stepped outside, I slammed it. My heart raced and the intense throbbing between my legs hadn't eased with my anger.

"Damn him!" I mumbled as I made my way to my car and slipped inside. I pulled out my phone and texted Jen.

Me: What are you wearing?

It didn't take her long to reply with a picture of her dolled up in a dress. It didn't look all that different from mine, and she had on high-heeled shoes as well. I glared back up at the house.

Jen: Felt like dressing a little sexy. Hoping Gene will decide to take advantage of me tonight.

I smiled.

Me: Lucas remembers last night.

My phone rang, Jen's name flashing across the screen.

"Hey," I said, still sitting in my car parked in the driveway.

"I knew it! I told you he remembered. And I bet you anything he wasn't that drunk. How did you find out?"

Chewing my lip, I replied, "Well, it's a long story. Let's just say he was going for a repeat and slipped when he told me not to stop him this time. Honestly, I think I slipped first."

"Holy crap. Did he kiss you again?"

I crinkled up my face. "Well..."

"He touched your nipple again!"

"Not exactly."

"Then what exactly happened?"

Dropping my head on the steering wheel, I sighed. "Dear God, when it comes to this man I'm weak. So very weak."

"Oh my God! You had sex with him!"

"What? No!"

"Okay, well, I'm waiting, and I'm going to guess this is not something we can talk about at the bar."

Laughing sadly, I leaned my head back against the headrest. "No. I don't even remember how we got on the subject of me possibly having a one-night stand, but I said something about needing a man's touch. Somehow poor Milo got dragged into the conversation, and before I knew it, his hand was in my panties, my leg hiked up, and he was on his way to giving me what I know would have been a mind-blowing orgasm."

Silence filled the line.

"Jen?"

"I'm here. I had to walk into my bathroom. Gene was in the bedroom, and I didn't want to pass out in front of him. Wow. Okay, y'all are really getting after it. You let him finger you, Paige?"

I crinkled my nose. Somehow hearing her say it made me feel dirty.

"I told you! I'm weak. He was talking so seductively, and I could tell the idea of me sleeping with Milo drove him mad. Everything just happened. I think the dress is to blame."

"The light blue one I told you to wear?"

"Yep. He told me I was overdressed for this town."

She laughed. "He told you that because he knew every man in the bar would be staring at you and that didn't make him very happy."

I started the car and waited for it to connect to Bluetooth before I drove off down the driveway and out onto the county road.

"He's confusing me, Jen. One minute he acts like he can't stand me, the next he is telling me he knows how I like to be touched."

A loud gasp came through the speakers. "Bastard! We need to figure out what game he's up to."

My heart felt as if it stopped beating. A game. That was all this was. Lucas wanted me out of his granddad's house and it looked like he would do anything to make it happen.

I turned the car around and headed back to the house. "I've changed my mind, Jen. I'm not coming tonight."

"What! Why not? Are you going back to kick his ass? Please tell me you're not going back in hopes of finishing off that orgasm."

With a frustrated laugh, I said, "I need to figure out what William meant for us to find in the house. I love this place, and I don't want to lose it. I'm not going to find anything out by sitting in a bar."

"Paige, you also need to have a life."

I scoffed. "I will, once this is all taken care of. Listen, have fun tonight, and I'm sorry. To be honest, I'm not much in the mood for it anyway."

Jen sighed. "I could kick his ass if you want."

I pulled back down the driveway. Once I got to the house, I frowned at the sight of a light coming from behind the house.

"I'm back. Have fun tonight, and I hope you get lucky with Gene."

She giggled. "Trust me, I will once he gets a look at how good my boobs look in this dress!"

"At least one of us will be having fun tonight."

Jen sighed yet again. "You could still come. Save the treasure hunt for tomorrow."

Walking up the front steps, I unlocked the door. "Nah. I'll give you a call tomorrow."

"Okay. Good luck tonight, and remember, keep your distance from him."

With a firm nod, I replied, "Consider it done." Even though every word of that was a lie.

Oreo sat at the bottom of the steps and looked at me as I shut the front door. Then she meowed.

"Oh right, like you knew I'd be back."

She rushed up the steps and waited by my bedroom door.

After changing and putting on baggy sweats and an oversized T-shirt, I threw my hair into a ponytail and slipped on my sneakers.

"Let's go see what he's up to, Oreo."

With a flashlight and my phone in hand, I made my way through the house and out the back door. Through the trees I could see the light better. Lucas was in the old greenhouse.

I had yet to explore that disarray. Mainly because the memory of me and Lucas standing in there years ago, talking about getting married, made my head and heart hurt.

As I made my way down the path, I thought back to William's letter.

I give you this house for you to find the answers. You can't find the answers, though, without the key.

One thing was obvious. William had wanted me and Lucas in this house together. And he wanted us looking for something that a stupid key fit into.

The path opened up, and I could see the greenhouse. The light shining inside cast the most beautiful glow in the trees. It took my breath away.

I walked to the glass door and quietly attempted to open it. I failed. A loud creak made Lucas turn and look at me.

"What are you doing here? I thought you went out," he asked.

"Turns out my mood was ruined. I figured I would come back to the house and start looking for this chest or whatever. Why are you out here?"

Lucas stared at me for the longest time. He looked conflicted about something. Maybe he had been up to something and had been caught red-handed. Or maybe he had been hoping he'd have the place to himself.

"Okay, fine," I said. "You can go ahead and stay out here by yourself, I'll head back to the house."

"No, wait. Don't leave."

Lucas closed the distance between us and handed me a small, old leather notebook. "I found this in Granddad's room. Actually, in the closet that was Gram's. Oreo had been sitting on an old chest of drawers in the room and knocked something off the back. When I moved it, I found this."

I ran my fingers over the old leather book. Lucas's grandmother's name was carved into the leather.

May.

"This was May's?" I asked, meeting his gaze.

"Yes, I think so."

"You haven't opened it yet?" I asked.

He shook his head. "After reading the first few words of her journal, I decided to come out here and read it."

I opened the book and read the first page, understanding why he needed to be in the greenhouse when I read the opening line.

Tonight I sat in the glass house, alone in my thoughts. I'm not sure how I will ever be able to forgive him, but I know I must. I know I will, for I love him so. He has hurt me beyond all I could ever imagine. My heart feels as if it might stop beating altogether. All I had wanted was for us to share in this. For it to be ours. Both of ours, and he took that away.

My head jerked up. "May wrote this?"

He shrugged. "It's her journal, so I'm thinking yes."

I shook my head in confusion. "Who is she talking about? William?"

"I think so. By the date on the journal, she would have been twenty-six when she wrote it."

Glancing down, I ran my finger over the date. "And it was in her closet?"

He nodded. "Granddad had never emptied it. Everything looks exactly how it was when she died."

My heart ached. "Do you want me to read more out loud?"

"I'm almost afraid to. What if my granddad cheated on Grams? I'm not sure how I would feel about that."

I swallowed hard and turned the page. The handwriting continued on.

The babe would be one today. My heart still suffers the pain of that dreadful day. The day God took my baby from me. My anger toward him is slowly ebbing. Maybe William and I will have another babe. Our baby, to share together.

My eyes lifted to Lucas. He had turned his back and was looking around the greenhouse.

"I think she's talking about God."

He spun back around. "What?"

"May, she lost a baby, I guess, after she had your father. She's talking about forgiving God, not William."

Relief washed over Lucas's face, and he closed his eyes. "That would have really sucked if Granddad had turned out to be a jerk."

I smiled slightly, then walked farther into the greenhouse. "It's just like I remember it."

A grin spread over his face. "Do you remember afternoon tea in here with Grams?"

"Yes!" I said with a light chuckle. "I loved afternoon tea, and you hated it."

"I was sixteen at the time. What sixteen-year-old boy wants to sit in a greenhouse with his grandmother and girlfriend and drink tea?"

"What else did you want to do?" I asked as I ran my finger along one of the glass windows.

"I'm sure you probably know what I wanted to do, Paige."

Heat rushed to my cheeks, and I quickly looked away. We walked around the greenhouse in silence. I wasn't sure what we were looking for. It was empty. Completely empty save for one chair and small table that sat in the middle of the glass room.

When I walked up to one of the windows, I pushed it open and smiled when the cool night breeze hit me in the face. Fall was finally here, my favorite time of year. And although we wouldn't see cooler temperatures for another month or two, I still loved this season. It reminded me of sitting in the bleachers, watching Lucas and his friends play football. Sitting around a campfire while we all drank alcohol we'd smuggled from our folks' houses.

Warmth moved through my body as I took in a slow, deep breath and let it out. This building had been a place where I thought all my dreams would come true. Now, I wasn't sure what it represented because my life and my heart were in complete turmoil.

I opened my eyes and saw the reflection of the chair in the window. "We said we'd get married in here," I said, almost in a whisper, but loud enough for Lucas to hear. "Just you and me with our families."

When he didn't say anything, I turned to look at him. He was at the end of the greenhouse, his hands in his pockets, staring into the darkness beyond the glass windows. Did he have any idea how much I had wanted to marry him? How much I had truly loved him? Glancing down at the ground, I forced myself not to let the tears spring free.

How much I still love him.

Chapter 10

Lucas

HER WORDS RATTLED around in my head, hitting from side to side, instantly forming a headache. Or maybe my head was trying to take on the pain my chest felt when she mentioned the dream we once shared.

I wanted to turn and face her. I could feel her eyes on me. Hell, I was almost certain I could hear her heart beating. Or maybe that was mine.

"I'm going to see if Milo knows someone who can take a look at the greenhouse, make sure it is still safe," I said, doing my best to change the subject.

"You don't think it's safe?"

With a shrug, I finally looked at her. It had been a dick move not to acknowledge her comment about the wedding, but I couldn't bring myself to admit how badly I had messed up.

"The damn thing is over a hundred years old. It needs to be looked at."

Paige pressed her lips together tightly, then nodded. She walked over to the chair my grandmother had sat in so many times. Her hand traced along the back of it.

"It would make a lovely greenhouse again. Or even an office."

That caught my attention. "An office for who?"

When her soft brown eyes met mine, I tried not to let my breath catch. Jesus, she was stunning. The moon had risen and cast the perfect amount of light into the greenhouse. The lantern also added to her glow. I needed to look away, or the urge to walk across the room and kiss her would win over all sense.

"It was just a thought."

I nodded. "Paige, how are you affording to not work?"

She smiled. "If you think I won't be able to pay for the taxes, you're wrong. I've got a nice little nest egg built up over the years. I live a simple life, so I put a lot of money away, invested it early on."

The corners of my mouth rose slightly. Paige was nothing like Bianca, and I knew that was why I had even showed interest in Bianca in the first place, to take my mind off of what I'd lost. She didn't remind me of the sweet, down-to-earth girl I had fallen in love with at such a young age. Bianca was also someone I would never have the desire to marry. Ever. How could I when I had given my heart to the woman sharing the air around me at this very moment.

"I'm not surprised. You always were one to save," I replied with a wink.

I wanted to ask if she still had the account in her bank that was for her wedding. She had opened it when she was twelve and had informed her parents it was her wedding fund money. I wanted to ask, but I didn't. She most likely had used it for college, or traveling.

Paige kicked at nothing on the ground, then looked back at me. "I had a meeting today with Virgil, from the bank in town. There is a little bit of storefront on highway 290. I was thinking of maybe opening a flower shop."

This time I did smile. A full-on smile, and I felt my chest fill slightly with pride. "You always did love flowers, just like your mamma. You talked about owning a flower shop."

"It's always been the long-term plan, learn the business world and then settle back here." Her voice trailed off toward the end.

That felt like a kick in the stomach. I hadn't given Paige the chance to tell me what she wanted in this life. I had only focused on what I wanted. Once I'd broken up with Paige, the idea of moving back to Johnson City became a distant memory. Every trip I went on with Bianca made me feel like that much more of an asshole. The woman I had loved, planned on spending the rest of my life with, had asked me to follow her plan, just for a bit, and I wouldn't do it. How did it make her feel to know I traveled all over the world with another woman, lived in Austin, so close to her? I'd seen her from time to time, and always hidden. I'd watch her, laughing with a friend at dinner, trying to pick the perfect cantaloupe at the Whole Foods on Sixth Street. From afar, I'd study her. I'd wonder if she was happy, who she was dating, if she'd found love again. All the while I lived a life I despised. A life that didn't include her, and it gutted me.

"Will you be renting or purchasing the space?"

"Well, I have either option. Long-term-investment wise, it would be smart to purchase it."

"I agree."

She gave me a weak smile. "I was going to talk to my dad and Tom about it. Then maybe have Carl swing by and give me a bid on what it would take to renovate and redo the store front. Milo said he'd help with painting, to keep the costs down."

Anger boiled up all over again at Milo and his fucking *paintbrush*, but I tried to hide it. The sound of his name off her lips would forever drive me mad. I knew for a fact neither one of them were interested in each other, but it still boiled my blood.

"Paige, I'm sorry about earlier. I shouldn't have…"

She held up a hand. "Please, can we just forget it happened?"

Hell no, I'd never forget her desire for me because it was for *me*. Not for Milo or some other guy she might have wanted to hook up with. It was entirely for me, even if she didn't want to admit it. I made her feel that way, moan that way…

"Did I ruin your evening?"

She gave me a sexy smirk. "Yes. You did."

My hand rubbed at the back of my neck. "I'm sorry."

"So you said. Now, we need to figure out why William wanted us in this house together. What did he want us to find?"

Paige sat down on the old chair with a frustrated sigh.

"I don't think he was trying to play matchmaker. It was something else." She went on, leaning back in the chair in deep thought. That's when I saw it. A paper sticking out of the bottom of the chair, maybe?

"There's something on the chair."

With a scream, she leaped to her feet. Paige ran over and jumped into my arms. She scared me so bad with her sudden movements that I didn't have time to laugh.

"Get it off me!" she yelled, shaking her hair and letting out small yelps.

"Paige! I didn't mean a bug!" I said, trying not to double over with laughter, setting her down on her feet. "I meant there was something sticking out of the chair, like paper."

She stopped jumping around. It was adorable as fuck to watch her toss her hands in the air and swipe at bugs that weren't even there. The way her ponytail swung around inspired amazing dirty thoughts.

"Jesus, you nearly gave me a heart attack," she said.

"Just so you know, that's not how I want to gain your half of the house."

She snarled at me then looked back over to the chair. I pulled the seat cushion up and gently tugged on the piece of paper sticking out.

"What is it?" Paige asked, hitting me on the side of my arm. She always had been impatient.

Giving her a look that told her to settle down, I carefully unfolded it and read it out loud.

M, will you do me the honor of having dinner with me? I have a very important question to ask you.

Yours truly, William

Paige and I lifted our gaze from the paper to each other. We both smiled.

"What do you think he asked May? To marry him?" Paige asked.

"I don't know. The date on the note doesn't make much sense. I didn't think they were engaged that long."

I looked back down at the paper, then at the chair. "We need to take that seat off."

"You'll ruin the chair, Lucas."

Without paying any attention to her, I leaned down and pulled at the chair bottom.

"Lucas!" she protested, but stopped when it popped off and revealed a little chest.

"Is that *the* chest?" she whispered.

I shook my head as I reached for it. "No, the chest we're looking for has a lock. Remember, the key?"

"That's right," Paige said, reaching over and gently touching the chest. "What is this?"

"Maybe a jewelry box?" I said, slowly turning the latch and opening the box.

"It's empty," Paige said, disappointment laced in her voice.

With a wide grin, I lifted on the little tab sticking up on the inside of the box, and it revealed another folded-up paper.

"It's another letter!" Paige screamed right into my ear.

Jerking, I glared at her. "Yes, and now I've lost all hearing in that ear, so thank you."

She shot me a dirty look. "Open it, Lucas! See what it says before I do more damage to you!"

I handed the small box to Paige and unfolded the paper. It was old and brittle.

"My Dearest M, you have forever saved my broken soul. You were brought into my life when I thought all hope was lost. I give you this conservatory to do with as you wish. It is my wedding gift to you.

Yours truly, William"

One quick glance at Paige, and I couldn't help but smile and shake my head. "The old man was a romantic."

"Stop it! Keep reading."

When I looked back at the paper, my smile faded, and a lump formed in my throat.

"What's wrong?" Paige asked.

"The date is wrong."

"What do you mean, the date is wrong?"

"The wedding date. It's earlier than Granddad and Gram's wedding."

"Maybe they changed the date, got married later than they had first intended."

I shrugged. "Maybe. That's weird, though. They didn't get married for almost another year after the date on this letter."

A strange feeling came over me. An uneasiness I wasn't sure how to respond to. It felt like I had stumbled upon a secret, one that I wasn't supposed to find.

"Lucas, is everything okay?"

I looked at Paige. "Yeah, it's fine. Maybe it's like you said, they just had a long engagement. But Granddad used to talk about their rush to get married because they couldn't wait."

Paige chewed on her lip and I knew we were thinking the same thing. Granddad had always said his relationship with Grams had been a whirlwind. They married quickly, for reasons beyond their control.

"Are you thinking what I'm thinking? About the stories of their..."

"Whirlwind romance? The quick wedding?"

Paige didn't answer; she simply looked at the box, then back up at me.

With a sigh, I said, "We need to find that goddamn chest, and now."

Chapter 11

Paige

L UCAS RUSHED OUT of the greenhouse and down the path, back to the house.

"Lucas! Wait! Where are you going?" I called out as I attempted to follow him without tripping over a rock or stick.

"The attic. It has to be in the attic. It's nowhere in his room; I've been looking," Lucas called out.

Once we got back into the house, I rushed ahead and stepped in front of him, blocking him from going up the stairs.

"Stop for one second, please."

"Why? I figured you were ready to get all of this over and done with. The only way we are going to get any answers is to find the chest."

I walked up two steps backwards, then placed my hands on his shoulders to keep him from moving.

"Trying to search in the attic in the dark isn't going to help. We need to do it in the morning."

He shook his head. "We need—"

"To calm down. Lucas, these letters were written before your grandmother and grandfather were even together. You're reading into this and getting all the wrong ideas about their relationship. Take a breath and think for a moment."

He looked down to the floor and sighed. "I just don't understand what's happening. What is he wanting us to find, Paige? And does it have anything to do with us?"

"It has to! Why would he give us *both* this house? We can't overthink it. They had a long engagement, or maybe they broke up for a while. Or they did get married, and that's all that mattered in the end."

His eyes jerked back up. "They broke up?"

"I don't know. But we know they got married, they were happy, so let's just take a moment and not freak out. We'll find the answers, Lucas. I know we will."

He nodded. "You're right. I guess I felt, hell, I don't know what I feel anymore."

I squeezed his shoulders. "We'll figure it out, Lucas. First thing in the morning we can tackle the attic."

"This would be a hell of a lot easier if you just sold me your half."

I shook my head, then folded my arms across my chest. "Wasting your breath, Lucas. Why are you ready to sell this house? What are you afraid of? I know you well enough to know that money cannot be the driving force behind why you want…"

My voice trailed off, then my eyes widened.

Lucas looked directly at me, and I could see the truth, threatening to spill out.

"Are you doing this because you're still angry with me?"

He looked away. "You're right. We need to take this up again in the morning. I'm exhausted and ready for bed."

He turned to leave, but I grabbed his arm. "Lucas, please tell me you're not selling your family's home as a way to punish me and rid yourself of the guilt of walking away."

When he didn't respond, I had my answer. I covered my mouth with my hand, and I nearly stumbled on the steps.

"You would be that cruel, that insensitive to sell this place because you know how much I love it?"

"It's late, Paige. I'm tired, and right now is probably not the right time to talk about this."

I let out a harsh laugh. "You broke up with me. You were the one who left me standing there while you turned your back and left. You walked away from us! It wasn't the other way around."

He looked pissed. *Very* pissed, but I didn't get the feeling it was at me. More at himself because he knew I was right. I swallowed hard as I took a step backward, up another step.

I should have stopped, but the more I thought about it, the more ticked off I got.

"If anyone should be pissed off, it should be me!"

He laughed. "Enlighten me on your reasoning, Paige."

Heat flashed over my body. *This impossible man.* "You didn't want to travel, remember?"

His face turned white as a ghost.

"You needed to be here, in Texas. With your daddy and William, helping them with the business. I believe those were the words you used when I told you I wanted to study international business. Travel and see the world a bit before we settled down. I wasn't asking you to do it forever. Just long enough to learn about the business world so I could follow my dream of opening the flower shop. In Johnson City. You didn't give me a chance to even tell you all of the details of my plan. All you heard was I wanted to leave you. You were stupidly jealous and didn't trust me. Do you know what it was like for me to hear your momma or William talk about you when I would come back to visit? Your mother told me you and Bianca, your new girlfriend, had gone to Europe on a three-week tour. How you'd come back from California only a few weeks before that and were jetting off for her...*job*."

He closed his eyes, regret evident.

"Do you have any idea what it was like to open a paper and see a picture of you and Bianca in New York City, or London? Or Paris? Let's not forget the trips to Paris. You didn't want that with me, but you certainly wanted it with her and followed her wherever she wanted to go."

His eyes opened, and he shook his head. If I hadn't known better, I would swear I saw tears building in his eyes.

I felt my own slip free, and I quickly brushed them away. "Do you have any idea how that made me feel? Years later, how much that still hurts?"

"Paige."

"Don't you dare *Paige* me. You're on some damn vendetta to hurt me. Well, newsflash, Lucas Foster, I will *never* feel the type of pain I felt that day you walked away from me. From us. And I'll never forget how painful it was to see you with..." A sob escaped, and I wanted to scream. "To see you with her, looking at her like she was your..."

"Don't say it because that isn't true. You know that's not true."

"Shut up!" I yelled, more tears threatening to spill. "I hate you for making me feel this way. I hate that you made me question our entire relationship. Why I wasn't good enough, but she was."

He shook his head harder, but I kept going.

"I know I'm not the beauty she is. You don't have to remind me with your stupid comments that I'm not a supermodel."

With that, he came to life. "What in the fuck are you talking about?" he asked, his brows pulled in confusion.

I lifted my chin and folded my arms over my chest. "I knew you were angry with me, but I honestly never dreamed you'd want to hurt me...again."

"Hurt you? You have it all wrong."

"Do I?" I asked, letting out a bark of laughter. "You might as well put your fighting gloves on because no matter what we find in this house, or whatever game William wants us to play, I'm in it to win. I will *never* let go of this house, Lucas. Never."

I spun on my heels and marched up the steps. A part of me wanted him to come after me. Explain why he was doing this, tell me that everything I was thinking was wrong. But he didn't. When I shut the door to my bedroom, I let out a shaky breath and dropped down to the floor. With my hands covering my mouth to keep quiet, I finally let my tears fall free.

The morning light shone through the window. It felt like I had only fallen asleep an hour ago. I groaned when I looked at the clock. I *had* fallen asleep only an hour ago. Fabulous. That'd make for a wonderful morning look.

I pulled the pillow over my head and groaned. Now I'd have to face Lucas after I spilled all that out last night.

Just as I decided to roll back over and get some more sleep, not ready to face any part of this day, a knock on my bedroom door made me sit up fast. Almost too fast. A wave of dizziness hit me. Was it Lucas? A part of me hoped and prayed it was. The other part, not so much. But who else would it be?

"Yes?"

"Are you still sleeping?"

"Milo?" I asked, climbing out of bed and rushing to the door. Thank God. I opened it and found him standing there, a cup of coffee in one hand, paint samples in another.

"What are you doing here?" I asked, confused.

He laughed. "You told me to come over this morning, even though Lucas told me not to. You never sent over the colors you wanted, so I brought paint samples for the living room, the bathrooms, and the study."

I closed my eyes. Holy hell, it had slipped my mind.

"Shoot, I forgot. Sorry, things got a bit...crazy last night."

He looked past me into the room. "Hot date?"

I laughed. "Ha! Not that crazy."

He lifted a brow as if to say he didn't believe me. I stepped aside. "Take a look for yourself. The only other soul in this room is my newfound cat."

"I believe you."

His face didn't agree with him. "Seriously, I'm alone. Look!"

Milo chuckled and took a quick step into the room, "Paige, you don't need to explain yourself to me. You're a grown woman.

Although, I was thinking you and Lucas would have finally worked your shit out by now."

I didn't bother responding.

Oreo meowed, and Milo walked over to pet her. "Please tell me you're not going to turn into a cat lady. You're much too hot for that and way too young."

His cheeks turned bright red, and he rubbed the back of his neck.

"I didn't mean it like that. That was not me trying to come on to you before you'd even had your coffee, I swear."

I smiled. "You're a good friend, Milo. Let me get dressed, and I'll meet you in the living room."

"Sounds good. However, I'm at least hoping you had fun last night."

As Milo stepped out of my bedroom, Lucas appeared. He must have come down the hallway from the attic. He looked at Milo, then me, then back to Milo. His eyes turned dark with anger.

"You look like shit," Milo said to Lucas.

"I didn't get much sleep last night." He shot his gaze at me, and if I hadn't known better, I would have sworn I saw hurt in his eyes. Surely not.

"I just got here. I was supposed to meet with Paige this morning to pick out paint samples." He lifted the wheel of paint samples to show Lucas. Maybe Milo had realized, just like I had, how it looked for him to be stepping out of the bedroom, me still in my pajamas. Thank goodness they weren't the sexy ones, but my oversized comfy pants and shirt. Not that Lucas would care, but I understood how Milo felt, with him being friends with the stupid jerk standing in the hallway.

"I told you we didn't need your help painting."

That caught me off-guard. When had he told Milo that?

"I called Paige yesterday when she hadn't gotten back to me about colors. She asked to meet with me this morning to pick out some."

Lucas glared at Milo. "Did you think I'd want to be a part of this little *meeting*?" Lucas said, his words dripping with ice as he looked at Milo, then me.

"Give me five minutes to change, and I'll meet you both in the living room," I said, trying my best to smile and not act like my heart was thundering in my chest. I had no idea why I was suddenly in a panicked state.

Lucas walked past Milo and down the steps. Milo raised his brows and pursed his lips.

"He never was a morning person," I said in a joking manner. Lucas grunted, and Milo laughed.

"See ya in a few," Milo said, following Lucas down the steps.

Rushing into the bathroom, I quickly brushed my teeth and looked at my hair. It was a mess. Pigtails today.

I changed into jeans, a T-shirt, and slipped on a pair of pink Keds. I made my way downstairs. I could hear muffled voices, but they didn't sound like they were coming from the living room. I followed them and stopped outside William's study, which Lucas had made into his home office.

"I don't understand the problem, Lucas."

A loud bang made me jump. "You know the goddamn problem, Milo."

"No, I honestly don't. And to be frank, I don't know you anymore, man. I don't think you know either. Why are you here, dude? If you don't want the house, just give it to her. Let her have it, let her rent your part from you. Why are you so desperate to sell this place? Once upon a time you wanted to live in this house."

"With her!" Lucas shouted.

Milo sighed.

"I don't want to sell the fucking house anymore. I already told you that."

My hand covered my mouth.

"Lucas, calm down, dude. You know I would never do that to you. Nothing happened. I knocked on the front door and no one answered. It wasn't closed all the way, so I walked in. I figured she was still asleep."

Lucas made a noise and then said, "I don't give a shit anymore. If you want to ask her out, ask her out."

My heart dropped, and I dug my teeth into my lower lip to keep the instant flood of emotions at bay.

"I'm not asking her out, Lucas. Anyone with two eyes can see you're still crazy about her."

Before I could hear Lucas's response, I decided I was done eavesdropping. Probably because I was scared to death what his response would be. I knocked on the door.

"Come in," Lucas barked.

With a wide smile, I walked into the room. "Thought y'all would be in the living room, but if you want to repaint this room, we can certainly pick a color. The cost to paint it will fall on you, though, Lucas. Since you've claimed this room."

Milo smirked, and Lucas stared at me. He gave me a once over before he stood, grabbed his keys and wallet, then quickly walked out of the room.

"I don't give two shits what color you paint any of the rooms. I'm leaving."

I watched him storm past us like a five-year-old. "Will you be coming back, or have you decided to sell me your half of the house?"

Lucas stopped abruptly and walked back over to me. He leaned down, let his eyes search my face, then let out a long breath. Through gritted teeth, he slowly said, "Will you *please* stop wearing the pigtails. For the love of God and all that is holy, just stop with the pigtails!"

Then he stormed out again, leaving me stunned into silence with Milo holding onto his side, laughing his ass off.

I faced Milo and shook my head. "What in the world was that about?"

Lifting both hands, Milo said, "I'm staying out of this."

Chapter 12

Lucas

I PULLED THE saddle down and made my way out of the tack room. When I rounded the corner, I smiled.

"Morning, Dad."

My father stood before me, wearing his worn-out favorite Stetson hat, work gloves in hand, and a smile on his face.

"You have no idea how good it is to see you in this barn, son." His eyes swept over me. "And dressed like a goddamn man for once."

I chuckled. "It's good to be here, Dad. You need me to do anything? I need some hard labor."

He laughed. "That's a loaded question. This ranch always needs something done. I need to head into town later for a meeting with the city council."

After I tossed the saddle onto my favorite horse, Ranger, I looked at him. "The city council? What's going on?"

"They want to look at restoring some of the store fronts on the square. I offered to give them some numbers to crunch."

I nodded. "Paige is looking at buying or renting a place to open a flower shop."

"Lou told me."

My heart stopped at the mention of granddad's best friend. For a moment, I debated going there, but my curiosity won out. "Dad, did Grams ever date Lou before granddaddy?"

Putting on his work gloves, he reached for a bale of hay. I walked over and helped him.

"Not that I know of. They were thick as thieves, the three of them."

"Did Granddad and Grams ever break up?"

He laughed. "I'm sure in the beginning they had their arguments, just like any couple."

We tossed the hay bale onto the back of the ATV.

"Did Grams and Granddad ever date other people?"

He looked at me with an expression I couldn't read, but then it was gone.

"Yes."

I looked at him with a shocked expression.

"Don't look so surprised, your grandmother was a beautiful woman. There were other young men who had their eyes on her, not just your granddad."

I rubbed the back of my neck and grinned. "She was beautiful, no doubt about it."

He stopped what he was doing and faced me. "Why are you asking?"

With a sigh, I leaned against the barn wall. "This whole thing with Paige... Granddad leaving her half of his house and me the other half. He has us on some sort of treasure hunt, if you will. I guess the reason he did it is in some chest or something."

My father laughed. "Sounds like your granddad. He adored Paige and knew how much she loved that house. I'm sure he would be upset if he knew you wanted to sell it."

The guilt in my chest made me look away.

"You want to talk about that? You once loved that house, son. Talked about raising a family there."

"Yeah, everyone keeps reminding me of that."

"So, why the sudden urge to sell it?"

"I thought I wanted to sell it. Guess I was having a moment."

He lifted a brow. "And now?"

I pushed off the wall and walked back to Ranger, who was patiently waiting on me to finish saddling him up.

"Now, I don't know what in the heck I want. I will admit my reasons for wanting to sell it might have been wrong."

"Wrong? How so?"

I tightened the saddle, adjusted the reins, and walked Ranger out of the barn, my father walking next to me.

"Paige. It all comes back to Paige. I was angry, mostly at myself. For giving up on us, for my damn foolish pride. For hurting her. For her hurting me. Hell, I don't know. A part of it was knowing Bianca would have an absolute fit, I know that."

"And now, do you still want to sell it?"

I looked at him. "No, Dad. I would never sell that house, just like I would never sell the ranch."

"Then why keep this charade up?"

With a grin, I replied, "Well, now it's just fun, getting Paige all worked up. Seeing her get angry every time I mention buying her out. She's not going to give up her half, I know that. That woman is more stubborn than a damn mule."

"She always was a stubborn girl. Gets that from her daddy. Her brother Tom is just as stubborn, and a word to the wise: her daddy is pretty pissed off at you. Tom as well."

With a nod, I replied, "I'm sure they are. They both think I'm trying to take away the house from Paige. I'll stop by the Millers' ranch in the next few days and talk to them."

"Something else is on your mind, son."

"I don't know what to think anymore, Dad. Seeing Paige in that house, being around her again... I knew things with Bianca had been over for a while, and I didn't want to admit defeat, but this whole chain of events gave me a good excuse to break up with her."

"What excuse is that, son?"

I looked around the barnyard and swept my hand across it. "This. Home. The life I once wanted. I love my job in Austin, but damn, I've missed being me. Missed this place. Missed my family."

"You have no idea how happy that makes me to hear you say that. I know your momma has been tickled pink since you, uh, broke up with Bianca."

This time I laughed. "I know y'all didn't like her."

"It wasn't that we didn't like her. We just knew she wasn't the girl for you. Hell, everyone in town could see you were only dating her because she was the polar opposite of Paige."

"I won't disagree with you on that, sir."

"Figured as much. Now, let's get back to the real reason you're here. Is it Paige? The house? Your job?"

I faced him. "All of the above. Mostly Paige, I guess. She said some things last night that hit a little too close to home. I was up all night, thinking about it. She has this crazy notion that I'm comparing her to Bianca. That I don't like her and that I'm only wanting to sell the house to hurt her."

"There is a bit of truth in that one statement. You did want to sell it to hurt her."

Swallowing hard, I had to look away from him.

"I raised you to be a gentleman, so I know you're not comparing her to Bianca. I see the way your eyes light up when Paige is mentioned, so I know you don't hate her. That leads me to think she's spot on about the house, and she figured it out, which I'm guessing hurt her just as much as you're hurting now, son."

Shame bubbled inside, and I couldn't look at him. "I guess, at first I wanted to sell it because of Paige, but not to hurt her. It was to erase the past. To erase my mistakes."

He scoffed, then climbed into the ATV. "You of all people know you can't change the past, Lucas. You can grow from it, be hurt by it, heal from it, but nah, you can't change it. The mistakes we make in our past shape us for the future. The way you two handled things with each other was back asswards. You have the chance to fix it. So it's up to you. Do you want to fix it? Or move on?"

I shrugged.

"Did you ever stop for five minutes and think that maybe, just maybe, your journey was bringing you right back to the beginning?"

"The beginning, sir?" I asked.

My father smiled and started up the utility vehicle. "It's your journey, Lucas. Only you can decide which way to go."

I rolled my eyes. "Did you and granddad get together and decide to teach me some sort of lesson with all this cryptic bullshit?"

Tossing his head back, my father let out a roar of laughter. "Hell, I'm sure Daddy is up there laughing his ass off right now. Enjoy your ride, and if you happen to take a wander down the fence line over in the west pasture, see if those damn kids have cut into it again to ride their 4-wheelers. I'm gonna tan their behinds if I ever catch 'em."

"Will do," I said as I climbed onto my horse. I was ready to be alone with my thoughts.

As Ranger started toward the trail that led from the barn, I exhaled deeply and let the feel of being alone with my horse, on this ranch, in my hometown, settle into my soul.

"I have no damn clue about anything anymore, Ranger. Not a damn clue."

The horse let out a nicker and started into a trot as we headed to open pasture. I could feel his body tremble with the need to run. He wasn't the only one who needed to feel the wind on his face and to get lost for a bit.

Once we were in the open pasture, I gave him a squeeze with my legs. "Let's go, Ranger."

I stepped into the kitchen and inhaled deeply. "Jesus, what is that delicious smell?"

My mother swatted at me with the dish towel. "Lucas Foster, do not use that language."

Moving out of her way, I removed my cowboy hat and leaned down to kiss her on the forehead. "Whatever it is, it smells amazing."

"It's chicken pot pie."

I groaned. "I have missed your cooking, Mom."

"You could stand to gain a few pounds. That woman only had you eating salad and tofu."

With a laugh, I took the bowl of salad from her hands and placed it on the table. "As you hand me a salad, how ironic."

"That's not the same thing. I'm also giving you meat and vegetables."

"Bianca wasn't all that bad."

She snarled, then gave me a sweet smile. "I'm glad you finally saw the light."

I inhaled a deep intake of air, then quickly let it out. "I think I saw the light a few months in. Took me awhile, but it feels good to be on my own again."

As she moved about the kitchen, I could tell something was on her mind. "Say it, Mom. You were never one to keep your thoughts in for long."

Shrugging, she faced me. "I'm just curious if you're going to be staying in Johnson City or moving back to Austin. I mean, how long will they let you work from Johnson City?"

I popped a cherry tomato into my mouth. "I can work from anywhere. As long as I get my projects done on time, they don't care if I'm in Alaska or Australia."

My mother leaned against the counter and gave me a serious look. "Have you thought about coming and working alongside your father?"

"Yes, as a matter of fact, I have."

A look of pure happiness crossed her face.

"If I decide to make JC my home again, I can help Dad with the ranch and the construction business."

She smiled. "If you *decide*? Does that mean you and Paige will be permanent roommates?"

I rolled my eyes and reached for a biscuit. "I'm not sure how that is going to turn out, to be honest with you."

"Lucas, you can't be serious. *Selling* the house? It's been in your father's family for over a hundred years. How could you do that?"

"Not you too, Mom. Please."

"Well, I just can't believe someone who once loved everything about that house could be so eager to sell it."

Clearly, she hadn't talked to Dad yet.

"Do you think I should sell my half to Paige? If I did that, the family would still be losing it."

Without answering, she reached into the oven and pulled out a casserole dish. After placing it on the wire rack, she waved her hands above it to smell her masterpiece.

"Whatever you decide to do, Lucas, your father and I will support you. I have to admit, I'm curious as all get out to know what you'll find in this mysterious chest."

"Me, too. I tried to get into the attic this morning, but it's locked. You don't happen to know where Granddad would have kept the key?"

The back door opened, and my father walked in.

"I don't, but I bet he does," Mom said, pointing to my father.

"I do what?" Dad asked, removing his hat and setting it on the counter before pulling my mother into his arms and kissing her. I couldn't help but smile.

"You're all sweaty, Carl. Go clean up. Lunch is ready."

He nuzzled his face into her neck, causing her to giggle. I had missed this. Missed being around my family. Seeing the love my parents had for one another. A part of me avoided it because I didn't want to be reminded of everything I had given up.

"Go, before lunch gets cold!" my mother said, pushing my father out of the kitchen.

With a wide smile on her face, she turned back to me. Tilting her head, she regarded me for a moment. "Are you okay, sweetheart?"

I cleared my throat and forced myself to give her a small grin. "I'm fine, Mom. Just a bit tired. I've missed being with y'all. Being home."

"We've missed you, too. I do hope you will think of staying in JC, Lucas. I cannot even begin to tell you how much better you look in your cowboy boots over those stupid city slicker shoes."

With a laugh, I pulled my mother into a hug. "It's good to be home, Mom. Really good to be home."

My phone rang, and a part of me hoped like hell it was Paige. When I pulled it out from my back pocket, I was instantly disappointed.

"Goodness, is it a bill collector?" my mother asked with a laugh. "You almost look afraid to answer it."

I sighed. "It's Bianca."

My mother rolled her eyes.

"Better take it, I guess."

"Of course," my mother said, her voice void of any emotion. That was her typical demeanor anytime she spoke about Bianca.

"Hello?" I said as I stepped out onto the back porch.

"Lucas, darling. I've been waiting for you."

I rubbed the sudden ache in the back of my neck. "Why would you be waiting, Bianca?"

"For you to come to your damn senses, that's why."

"When I said it was over, I meant it was over."

"Because that little tramp showed back up?"

"I've already told you not to call her that, and I meant it the first time."

She huffed. "So, I see your distaste for her has faded away. Have you fucked her?"

With a frustrated sigh, I shook my head. "Is there anything you need, or are you just calling to give me a headache?"

"You still have stuff here at the house. I thought maybe you might want to get it, or I could bring it to you. See the little house you got from your grandfather."

"I already told you, I don't want anything. I've got my clothes, that's all I need."

"So that's really it? You're going to leave me. You clearly have lost your fucking mind. Her? Really? You've got a woman like me on your arm and you want a nobody from your hometown."

My body tensed as my heartrate sped. "Let me tell you something, Bianca. Paige is ten times the woman you could hope to be. She's beautiful, kind, loving, and nothing like you. And yes, I've really left you. Erase my number from your phone as I'll be blocking yours. We have nothing left to say to each other."

I hit End and let out a breath. With a long look out over my folks' ranch, I let it all settle in. This was my new life. A new beginning. A second chance. Smiling, I pulled my phone back out and sent Paige a text.

Me: Are you free tonight?

I waited a minute or two, hoping she would reply.

Paige: Depends on why you're asking.

Me: I want to start over, Paige. I'm tired of fighting. Can we call a truce? Have dinner with me. I'll even cook.

Paige: Have you fallen and hit your head? Wait, is this really Lucas? He lost his phone, didn't he?

With a chuckle, I typed my reply.

Me: I have not fallen or hit my head. It's really me. I need to talk to you, Paige. Please.

Paige: I don't have any plans other than painting.

Me: Perfect, I'll be there in a bit to help. Then we can eat around six or so. I'm at my folks' place for lunch.

Paige: I'll see you in a bit then.

Hope bubbled in the middle of my chest. I walked back into the kitchen only to find my folks getting ready to sit down for lunch. What was I doing? I needed to get over to the house and talk to Paige now. I was done wasting time.

"Sorry, Mom. I need to leave."

A low growl came from the back of her throat. "That woman is bound and determined to keep you from eating!"

Laughing, I kissed her on the forehead. "Bianca has nothing to do with this. I'm heading back over to Granddad's place to help Paige."

A light twinkled in my mother's eyes. "Oh, do you want to bring her some chicken pot pie?"

One look at the heavenly dish and my stomach growled. "Considering I just offered to cook her dinner, and I have no idea what I'll cook, I better bring a back-up plan."

My mother jumped up and grabbed a container for the chicken pot pie and one for the salad.

"I hope the two of you can work through things," Mom said as she handed me the plastic bag plus two slices of her pecan pie.

With a quick kiss on the cheek, and a nod to my father, I replied, "It will all work out."

I headed out to my truck—the same old truck I drove when I was in high school. She was still a good ride, so I was in no hurry to run and buy a new one.

I had sounded more convinced than I felt when I told my folks it would all work out. I had no idea how Paige and I would handle this ownership of the house. I had to believe that somewhere in that house, Granddad had left us the answers we were both looking for.

It hit me that I had forgotten to ask my father about the key to the attic. I'd call him when I got back to the house. The key had to be somewhere. Paige and I needed in that attic. I knew that was where we'd find the answers.

At least, I hoped like hell we would.

Chapter 13

Paige

I STOOD IN the middle of the living room, staring at Lucas's text. My chest felt lighter than it had in a long time, while my hands shook slightly as I held the phone.

"What in the world is wrong with me?" I whispered. Oreo sat on the windowsill, cleaning herself. She offered a single meow as answer to my predicament.

"I'm not scared."

She looked at me, then meowed again.

I snarled at her. "Fine. Nervous, but not scared. Definitely not scared."

Oreo looked as if she rolled her eyes. If cats could do that she most definitely was.

"Oh, what do you know?" I said, blowing at a piece of hair that dangled in front of my eyes.

My gaze swept over the living room. I'd pulled all the furniture out from the wall and covered it. Milo had one of his guys drop off the light-colored greyish blue paint only an hour ago. I couldn't wait to get started. I had only gotten one wall done before Lucas texted. Now my mind was swirling.

"He feels guilty, that's what this is about," I said as I rolled the paint roller in the tray and started painting the next wall.

Oreo moved positions on the windowsill.

"Last night, I broke down and shared too much, and he now feels guilty. Great. The last thing I need is his pity."

A long meow came from Oreo. I stopped rolling and looked at her. "You don't think so? Oh, I do. I called him out on a few things, namely him trying to sell the house to hurt me. I know Lucas, if that was his motive for selling the house, it was done purely out of anger. He'd never really do it. I brought it to his attention and the decent side of him, the side I know is still somewhere in there, feels guilty. Well, we need to be strong tonight, Oreo. No letting him sweet talk us or say sexy things. If he even tries to compliment me, I'll know it's the guilt speaking, and not him."

Oreo jumped off the windowsill and made her way over to sit next to me. She stared up at the roller moving on the wall.

"If you jump on this wall, you're going outside."

She looked up at me.

"What? Are you offended now?"

She turned, whipped her tail a few times and made her way out of the living room.

"Don't even act like that! You know you thought about it!"

"Who in the hell are you talking to?"

Screaming, I dropped the roller, jumped back and instantly knew I'd made a huge mistake.

"Shit!" I called out as I looked down at my foot, in the paint tray, covered in grey blue. "Damnit all to freaking hell."

"Since when did you start swearing so much?" Lucas asked, grabbing the box of rags and making his way over to me.

"Since life started being an asshole to me."

He laughed and bent down. "Hold onto my shoulder and lift up your foot."

I did as he asked. He pulled out a bunch of rags and wrapped them around my shoe, carefully pulling it off my foot.

"I hope you didn't like these shoes."

I pouted as I looked down at my pink Keds. "I did. They were one of my favorite pairs."

When I moved my gaze to Lucas, he was looking up at me, a smile on his face.

"What?" I asked.

He shook his head. "Nothing. This is just refreshing, that's all."

I drew my brows in. "What's refreshing? Me stepping in paint? Because I beg to differ that it's not the least bit refreshing."

With a laugh, he stood, holding onto me so I wouldn't lose my balance. "Seeing you smile. By the way, do you need help getting out of your pants?"

Narrowing my eyes, I held my tongue. "No."

His brow lifted. "You're going to track paint everywhere."

With a quick look down, I knew he was right.

"Stay here, I can go grab you something."

Lucas set off to my bedroom.

"Get me my yoga pants! They're in the basket folded!"

"You mean the movie-watching pajamas?" he called out.

Ugh. I wasn't sure if I wanted to punch him or laugh. "Yes!" I called out, trying not to smile.

Oreo walked back into the living room. Sat right in the middle and bathed herself while sneaking glances my way.

"I'm not smiling because he makes me happy. What he said was funny, is all." I was whispering these replies...to a cat.

She rubbed her paw over her face, then meowed.

"You think you know it all, but you don't." Still whispering.

"Have you taken up talking to the cat, Paige? Maybe we should go out to dinner. Get you around people. Out in society and all."

"Ha ha. Let me have my pants. Can you grab a garbage bag from the kitchen for me to put my jeans in?"

He nodded. "Sure."

When he took a step back, Oreo was at his feet. He tripped, spun, and tried to keep his balance by reaching for me. Needless to say, I had been trying to keep my own balance as I held up one leg.

"Lucas!" I cried as we both went down. The tray full of paint somehow flipped up in the air and landed directly onto Lucas's head.

He sat there with paint running down his face. My hand came up to my mouth in an attempt not to laugh.

"Holy shit," I said, smirking. "I couldn't have planned that better if I had wanted to!"

Glancing at Oreo, I said, "Well done, kitty."

She flicked her tail and meowed as she walked out of the room.

With a look of pure anger, he faced me. I pressed my lips together tightly. Then I lost it. And laughed so hard, tears streamed down my face. It didn't take Lucas long to join in. He reached up and wiped paint off his head, then grabbed me and smeared it all over my face.

"You asshole!" I cried, trying to crawl away from him, only to have him grab my shoeless foot and pull me back over. With a brush in his hand, he got to work throwing paint all over me. Thank God I'd covered the furniture, because it was now an all-out war.

Lucas leaned over to get more paint on the brush, and I grabbed the roller and went straight up his back. He spun around, grabbed me, threw me over his shoulder then started walking. When I looked back over my shoulder, I saw where he was heading.

Oh. No. The paint can.

"Lucas. Do not do it!" I shouted. Then kicked and slapped him in an attempt to get him to put me down.

"What is it you think I'm going to do, Paige?"

I watched him pick up the can. "Something with the can of paint. Expensive paint, I might add, and I'm on a budget."

"I'm not the least bit worried about that," he said, sliding me slowly down his body as he grabbed me with one arm and pressed me firmly against his chest. I'd forgotten how crazy strong the man was.

My eyes met his as I gazed up at him. "You wouldn't."

Then he smiled, and my heart felt like it exploded in my chest.

Oh hell. I was still crazy in love with him.

"Lucas," I whispered.

"Paige," he whispered back, then tipped the can over my head.

As I laughed harder than I had in years, I used my fingers to wipe away the paint that now ran down my entire body.

Lucas wore a wide smile.

"You did it."

He winked. "Did you doubt me, sweetheart?"

My smile faded. It felt like his green eyes were looking right into my heart. The last thing I wanted him to know was how I still felt about him. Not now. Maybe not ever, because I had no idea how he felt about me.

He reached up and cupped my face. My heart slammed against my chest. Using his thumb, he wiped the paint from my mouth.

I was just about to reach up on my toes and press my mouth to his, when a throat cleared behind Lucas.

"Am I interrupting something?"

Lucas closed his eyes while I peeked around at Milo.

"If I had known it was going to be like the food fights in high school, I'd have brought more people to this painting party."

Lucas shook his head and backed away from me.

When I looked at Lucas, he was smiling, and I couldn't help but smile back.

Milo took one look around the trashed living room and laughed. "You two always did know how to have fun." He slapped his hands together. "I brought you over some more paint, glad I did."

"Thanks, Milo." I said. "Want to stay and help clean up?"

He laughed. "No, thanks. I have a date tonight."

Lucas quickly turned to Milo. "A date? With who?"

Milo grinned from ear to ear. "She just moved to town and is working at the courthouse. Her name is Rachel Greene."

"As in *Friends*?" I asked with a chuckle.

"Yeah, can you believe it? I teased her a bit about it and finally worked up the nerve to ask her out."

Lucas smiled at Milo, and it was sincere. "That's awesome, dude. I'm glad to see you getting out there and dating."

Milo lifted a brow. "Right. Well, I'm going to slowly back out of here before you two drag me into this little war." He looked at Lucas, then me. "But from what I just saw, I'd say y'all were fixin' to call a truce."

My cheeks heated, and Lucas cleared his throat.

"Enjoy your date, Milo. I hope y'all have fun," I said.

He took the hint and waved goodbye. "Talk later. Have fun... painting."

Once Milo was out the door, Lucas turned back to me. "We need to start locking the fucking front door. It creeps me out how often he walks in."

I giggled, then looked around the room. "Oh my gosh, we made an absolute mess in here."

Lucas pulled his T-shirt off and wiped his face. My knees felt weak when I looked at his perfectly toned body.

Look away, Paige. Look. Away. No, don't lick your lips and wonder what it would be like to trace each ab muscle with your tongue.

"Paige?" Lucas's voice pulled me from my dirty thoughts.

"*Mmm?*" I asked, tearing my gaze from his abs to his stunningly beautiful green eyes.

"Do you want me to carry you up the steps to your room?"

Yes. Yes. Yes.

"No, it's okay."

I watched as he reached down and started to take off his cowboy boots, then his jeans.

"Um, what are you doing?"

He looked at me with a blank expression. "I don't want to track paint everywhere."

"So you're stripping in front of me?"

Lucas laughed. "I'm not stripping," he said, pushing his jeans down and exposing his boxer briefs. And one impressive bulge.

God help me.

"I'll grab some bags for us to put our clothes in."

"Our clothes?"

He looked back at me. "You're not walking up the steps dripping in paint. We'll never get it off the wood floors."

"You want me to get undressed?" I asked, a tremble very evident in my voice.

With a roll of his eyes, he walked backwards. "Paige, I've seen you naked before."

"Yeah, years ago. When I had an eighteen-year-old body. Now I have a twenty-nine-year-old body with a few extra curves."

He frowned. "If you're trying to say your body isn't as hot as it was when we were eighteen, you need someone to smack you. You're perfect."

Aw, there was the guilt speaking. I knew it had to be just under that layer of paint somewhere.

"Lucas, you don't have to feed me a line because of what I said last night."

Something flashed across his face. It wasn't anger, and it wasn't regret. His eyes gleamed with something only for me. It was the same as when he used to tell me he loved me. Honest, and so pure it would leave me breathless sometimes. "I'm not feeding you anything. Why can't you believe I still think you're attractive, Paige?"

An uneasy feeling hit me in the middle of my stomach. I hated that I felt so unsure of myself with this man. That I had compared myself to his stupid stick-thin girlfriend for the last two years.

"It's just... I mean... I don't think I'm ugly or anything," I said with a chuckle. "I'm just not..."

My voice trailed off.

Lucas stared at me, not saying a word. It was as if his mind was also racing. Both of us trying to say the right thing so we didn't start another argument, or maybe he feared he'd hurt my feelings. I hated that I made him feel like he had to tiptoe around me. I hated that I felt this way.

"I'm not a supermodel and I'm perfectly fine with that. I'm being stupid and acting like a silly girl." I pulled the shirt over my head and then quickly slipped off my other pink and now paint-splattered Ked. I unbuttoned my jeans and slipped them down. I was silently thanking God I had on matching panties and bra. And thankful I hadn't grabbed a thong.

Lucas swallowed hard, as he let his gaze move over my body. Goosebumps erupted everywhere. The way he was looking at me was exactly how he looked at me the first time we ever made love. I could see the desire in his eyes right now, and everything he'd said over the last few days seemed to be ripped from my memory. All I needed was this. A man to look at me like he wanted me. Needed me. Craved me like I was an addiction.

I reached down and grabbed my T-shirt, wrapping it around my head to hopefully keep the paint from dripping on the floor. Then I gathered up my jeans and shoes and tossed them into the paint tray. It was all trash now.

When I looked back at Lucas, my eyes instantly went to his now very hard bulge in his boxer briefs.

My teeth dug into my lip and I had to bite hard to keep from smiling. "I'm going to go get cleaned up. Meet you back down here to take care of this mess?"

Lucas opened his mouth to speak but nothing came out. Then he nodded. I made my way through the living room, up the stairs and into my bathroom. I shut the door, then placed my hands on the sink, dragging in one deep breath after another. Memories of Lucas in his shower the other night, making himself come while calling my name flashed through my mind. I jerked my head up and looked into the mirror.

"Holy fuck," I whispered. "You're so stupid. Paige, you're so stupid."

I threw open my bathroom door, ran over and shut the bedroom door. William still had a land line, so I rushed to the desk and picked it up. Luckily, Jen hadn't changed her phone number since high school. I dialed and carried the cordless phone into the bathroom before I got paint anywhere.

"I'm not buying," Jen said when she answered the phone.

"It's me! Paige."

"Where are you calling me from?" she asked.

"The landline at William's house. Something big has happened. A few big things. Okay, huge things."

I heard a door shut. "I'm alone and ready to decipher his actions. Go. Leave out nothing."

"Jen, I think he pretended to be drunk that night because he was worried I'd turn him down."

"Um, hello, I already deduced that."

I sighed. "Fine, you did. Then, the next day, when I thought he was insulting me by comparing me to Bianca, he wasn't. As a matter of fact, I don't think he was trying to do that at all."

"Okay, you've lost me there."

"Then the pigtails... He was agitated because when he sees me in pigtails, it turns him on."

She laughed. "He always was on the verge of kinky, wasn't he?"

"Focus! Jen, I think Lucas still wants me."

Silence loomed over the line. Oh God, maybe I had read it all wrong.

"I mean, we just had a paint war in the living room, and he stripped down and then I stripped down, and he had a hard-on after looking at me. And his eyes looked like they were on fire. Seriously, on fire. Am I reading into this?"

Then came the laughter. A lot of laughter.

I groaned in frustration and waited for her to get it all out.

"Done yet?" I asked as I turned on the shower water. I needed to get this paint out of my hair.

"Yes, sorry. Oh my gosh, Paige, you're just now figuring this all out. I knew the moment he walked into that living room and saw you watching *Top Gun* he wanted you. Everything that man has done has screamed he wants you."

"Then why did he try to sell the house I love? Why did he want to buy me out, make me give up something he knows I love?"

"I think that was his initial reaction because it makes him think of what y'all lost. What you both used to dream about. Paige, I never truly thought Lucas Foster stopped loving you. He picked a girl who was the complete opposite of you. Then, when you walked back into the picture, he broke up with her the same day. Sure, maybe he had been wanting to end things anyway, but you gave him the reason. You. It was your name he was jacking off to in the shower."

I let out a breath and leaned against the bathroom door.

"He said he wanted to talk tonight. Asked me to let him make me dinner. He wants a truce."

My head felt like it was spinning. What did this mean for us?

"Are you having dinner with him?"

"I think so. I mean, yes. Crap, I need to get this paint off and go clean up the living room. We made a mess."

Jen chuckled. "Lord, I cannot wait to hear how this night goes. Call me if anything major happens. Don't give him the woohoo tonight. Make him earn it."

I rolled my eyes. "I'm hanging up now."

"Wait! I'm ser—"

Hitting End, I let out a deep breath, put the phone on the counter and pulled the T-shirt off my head. I needed a hot shower and then I would think about Lucas—and my woohoo—and how desperately it wanted him.

Chapter 14

Lucas

I COULDN'T GET the image of Paige in her panties and bra out of my head. I stood in the shower, my cock in my hand, jacking off. She was upstairs, in her own shower. Naked.

"Fuck," I groaned as I pumped harder. It was a new record for me. My cum was hitting the shower wall only a minute or two after I started.

"I'm going to make my dick raw if this keeps up. Jesus, I must be sixteen all over again."

I wasn't sure how long I stood there, the water running over my body, my eyes closed as I replayed every second of us in the living room. A smile grew, and I filed that memory away to bring out over and over, most likely in the shower or in my bed, with my hand on my dick again.

"Asshole," I mumbled as I turned off the water and stepped out of the shower. When I reached for the towel, I looked down to see Oreo sitting in the middle of the bathroom.

"I see you managed to stay out of the war zone."

She gave me a meow.

"Don't look at me with those judging cat eyes. Did you see her? She looked hot as hell, dripping in blue paint and dressed in practically nothing."

The cat stood, whisked her tail around and walked over to the small cabinet against the bathroom wall. She reached up and pawed at the door.

"Okay, go on. There is no food in there for you, Oreo. Go find Paige and stare at her with your judgmental eyes."

She stretched up again and pawed the handle, this time hitting just right and causing it to open.

I looked in and couldn't believe my eyes. A key was hanging in the small antique vanity.

With a quick look at Oreo, I asked, "Is this the key to the attic?"

Oreo meowed. Then I cursed.

"Holy shit, I'm talking to the cat like Paige does." *We've both lost our damn minds.*

I took out the key, holding it up. "I would bet my left nut that you open the attic door."

Oreo rubbed against my wet legs, leaving a trail of cat hair in her wake.

"Fine, I'll admit that you're a smart cat. There, I said it. Now go bother Paige." I watched as the cat walked out of my bedroom. I quickly shut the door and found some old jogging pants and my favorite Def Leppard T-shirt. I tossed my clothes in the trash and made my way into the living room, only to find Paige already cleaning up. I couldn't help but stop and watch her. If Milo hadn't interrupted us, I would have kissed her, and I'm glad he did. Because I knew we needed to talk before anything else happened between us. So far I'd acted like a freaking prick, touching and kissing her when I knew damn well I shouldn't.

I smiled when she started talking to Oreo. "The carpet is trashed, but maybe that's a good thing. I'm thinking we rip it up and see what the floors look like under here, what are your thoughts?"

Oreo answered, like always.

"Agreed. Now to get Lucas on board for ripping up this carpet."

"He's on board," I said, walking into the living room. Paige spun and smiled when she saw me, and the air from my lungs was sucked out. There wasn't anger, or hurt, or mistrust in her beautiful caramel eyes. She was looking at me like she used to. Like the sight of me made her happy. God, how I hoped I was reading it right.

"Hey, you clean up pretty good," she said softly, then chuckled when she looked around the room. "We made a mess."

I laughed as I did the same. "We certainly did."

"You agree to ripping up the carpet?"

With a nod, I walked over to her and stopped just short of her body. I could tell she was holding her breath.

"Yes, but I think we should keep it down until the painting is done. If the floors are decent underneath, it will protect them."

She smiled the most brilliant smile I'd ever seen. "I think they will be. I remember William talking about when he had the carpet put down, he told them not to destroy the original floors. May wanted the carpet. She was worried the grandkids would get hurt on the wood floors."

"How do you remember that, Paige? How do you remember all those conversations with Granddad?"

Paige shrugged. "I'm not sure. I've always loved this house, and I guess anytime William talked about it, I filed it away. Just in case we…"

Her voice trailed off, and she went to turn away from me, but I stopped her.

"Wait," I said, lifting my hand to her face. When her breath hitched, mine did as well.

I reached for a strand of her hair, pulling out the small bit of paint. "You still have paint in your hair."

Her cheeks flushed. "No thanks to you. I still can't believe you dumped that over my head."

"That was fun, I think we both needed it."

Chewing on her lip, she nodded.

"Mom sent me home with some chicken pot pie and salad. I'm starving. Early dinner?"

"That sounds amazing. What about all this?"

"We can clean it later."

Without thinking, I reached for her hand. She didn't attempt to pull it away, so I didn't drop it until we walked into the kitchen. I started to unpack the bag of food.

"I'll grab something to heat it up in," Paige said, taking out two bowls. "A bowl okay?"

"Grab two. She made a salad, too."

We worked in silence, moving around the kitchen like the last week hadn't even happened. All the tossed insults, the moments when we'd both let our weakness get the better of us. And then there were the words we'd spoken last night. That was what I wanted to talk to her about. To set her straight on a few things.

"Do you want to eat on the porch?" she asked, nodding toward the back door. "It's a beautiful day out."

"Yeah, that sounds nice. I'll grab the waters. Do you still like Ranch? Mom packed some."

She gave me a look that silently asked if I was being serious. "Seriously? Who doesn't like Ranch?"

I wanted to say Bianca but decided it was best not to bring her up, at least not right now.

Once we got settled, Paige pushed a forkful of potpie into her mouth and groaned. The noise went straight to my dick. And just like the asshole I was, I was instantly hard.

"Paige, I wanted to talk to you about what you said last night."

Her face fell, and she looked out over backyard and off into the trees. On the other side of the trees and pathway sat the greenhouse, and beyond that a wide-open pasture.

"I never meant to make you think I was comparing you to Bianca in any way. That morning when you made the muffins, it was fucking refreshing to see actual food. By the way, those muffins were amazing. Did you make them from a box?"

She gave me a soft smile. "No, from scratch."

I fell in love with her more.

"And your comment about your weight...I feel like everything I've been saying has been coming out wrong. You look amazing. You're beautiful, and I'm not saying that to try and make you feel better. When I walked up the pathway and saw you on this porch, talking and laughing with Milo, I couldn't even form words."

She looked at me. "You formed words. If I remember right, an insult or two."

I looked down, embarrassed. "I was trying hard to hide how I was feeling."

Her head tilted. "How were you feeling?"

My eyes met hers. "Confused. Excited to see you. Angry at myself for ever letting you go in the first place."

When her face morphed into shock, I let out an unsure chuckle and kept going. "My heart was pounding in my chest and I wasn't sure why. Seeing you brought back every single memory we shared, every dream we had, every touch we exchanged. And then that pissed me off."

"Why would that piss you off?"

"I don't really know how to explain it. I think it all just hit me. The guilt I felt for moving on after you."

"Lucas, I dated other guys, as well."

I shook my head. "That's not it, Paige. You asked me to trust you, to let you follow your own path, and I was so fucking scared you would pull away from me that I let you go before you could hurt me. I tried to hide the fact that I knew I had made a terrible mistake by being mad at you, even though I knew it had all been me. Then I sort of got lost for a while. Searched for someone to take away your memory, and that's when I met Bianca. She was the complete opposite of you. The only problem was, I still couldn't get over you. She knew it, too. Shortly after we started dating she found an engagement ring, and she got pretty damn excited. That was when she planned our first trip. Paris. I can't even begin to tell you the guilt I felt, going with her to Europe when it was you who had asked me to go with you first."

Paige's eyes glassed over, but she kept her tears at bay.

"Anyway, Bianca had a modeling gig there, we stayed for a week or so and then came home. She was in a foul mood when we got back, and when I asked her what was wrong, she asked about the ring. Let's just say it didn't go over well when I told her that I had bought it way before her and it had been meant for my old girlfriend. For you."

"What?" Paige asked, her hand coming up to her mouth. "No wonder she hates me."

I laughed. "Yeah. You were never her favorite person."

"You bought me a ring, Lucas?"

With a shrug, I answered her. "I did. The summer before we started college. I was going to ask you to marry me that Christmas. I had our life all planned out, Paige, and when you changed course, instead of being supportive, I freaked. It probably doesn't help to tell you that about a week after I broke up with you, I drove up to Arkansas."

"You did?" she asked, surprise laced in her voice.

"I was going to ask you to forgive me, *beg* you to forgive me, because I know I hurt you when I walked away from you."

"What happened? You never called me. I never saw you."

"I saw you purely by luck. You were walking from one of your classes and going through this park. You started to cry and leaned against a tree, then slid down to the ground. I started to walk toward you and stopped when I saw some guy lean down and ask you if you were okay. He pulled you into his arms. I stood there for what felt like forever as I watched another guy hold you. Then I left and drove back to Austin."

Paige stared at me, a blank expression on her face. Then she closed her eyes and slowly shook her head.

"Do you know who that guy was, Lucas?"

"Do I really need to know?"

Her eyes snapped open and anger moved across her face. "Yes, you do. It was Josh Miller."

I jerked my head back in confusion. "He has the same last name as you?"

She let out a strangled groan. "He's my cousin, you idiot! Josh is my cousin. He was a senior at the U of A when I was a freshman. I had sent him a text and told him I was having a bad day. I missed home, I missed you, I was sad we had broken up and I was on the verge of telling my parents I wanted to come home. He met me at the park. He talked me down from the ledge. Jesus Christ, you saw me hugging my own freakin' cousin!"

"Again, when did you start swearing so much?"

Her mouth fell open. "That's what you're going to say to that? Really?"

"Well, what do you want me to say? Am I pissed at myself? Hell yeah. Do I feel slightly sick? Yes. But I can't go back in time and change any of it."

She stood, knocking the chair over. "I don't know if I want to strangle you, or rip your balls off, or hug you because you're so stupid."

I squeezed my legs together, then stood. "Paige, I walked up on something that threw me. I had no idea your cousin went to school there, you never told me."

"You didn't want to hear anything about me going to the University of Arkansas. All you wanted was for me to go to school with you. You never once stopped to think what I wanted. You refused to listen to my plan."

"I did, Paige. I fucking did. And I made a mistake. A huge mistake that I have had to live with since I turned and walked away from you."

"Twice, apparently."

I scrubbed my hands down my face. "Listen, the past is the past, and I don't want to argue with you about it. I fucked up. Can we both just agree to that?"

Her arms crossed her chest. "We most certainly can."

"What I need you to know is that I don't want to hurt you, and maybe my motives for wanting to sell the house were off, but I never once wanted to take the house out from under you to hurt you or pay you back for something. I wouldn't do that to you, Paige."

Paige looked away from me.

"Please look at me."

She slowly met my gaze. "Then why were you so hellbent on buying me out, on selling this house? I know it once meant something to you."

I swallowed hard. "I did love this house, and I loved the idea of us being in it together. Maybe it had something to do with my pride and the fact that I messed up with us. All I know is the moment I saw you, I knew the life I had been living was a lie."

Her eyes narrowed in on me. "What do you mean?"

"I wasn't happy, and I haven't been happy for a long time. I let Bianca make all the decisions, I followed her around like a fucking puppy because I was trying to make up for the mistake I made with you. When you mentioned last night how much it hurt you to see me travel with her, I wanted to punch myself."

"I'm more than happy to do that for you."

We both smiled slightly. "I'm sorry I hurt you. I'm sorry I didn't just talk to you and tell you I was scared."

Paige wrapped her arms around her body and took a step back. "I wish you would have."

"Me too," I softly said.

"So, what are we going to do? About the house?"

I exhaled a deep breath. "We're going to find that chest and figure out what Granddad was thinking when he left us the house."

"Lucas, you don't think he did it as a way to force us back together? He always said we belonged together."

"I'm sure that was part of it, but I feel like there is something more. Something deeper that we're supposed to find. Together."

"Truce, then?" she asked, the sweetest smile on her face.

"Truce. And maybe we can, I don't know, start over again."

Paige dug her teeth into her bottom lip and stared up at me with the most innocent look I'd ever seen. A look that said she was just as unsure about our future as I was.

"Start over as what, friends?"

"Is that what you want?"

When she looked off into the distance, I couldn't ignore the instant ache in my chest, the feel of something heavy in the pit of my stomach. I wasn't sure if I could live with just being her friend for the rest of my life.

When she focused her attention back on me, she took in a slow, almost calming breath. "Why did you break up with Bianca? I want the truth, all of it."

"The truth?"

She nodded. "Yes."

"Um, well, I can tell you it was long overdue, but when I saw you I realized I didn't want to be with her anymore."

Paige let out a humorless laugh. "You didn't realize that when she was trying to keep you from attending your grandfather's funeral?"

My fingers sliced through my hair. "Of course, I did. I knew it maybe six months after I started dating her that she wasn't going to be the one, but I didn't want to admit I failed yet again."

"And seeing me changed your mind? Why?"

"Because I still love you, Paige."

The words slipped out so damn fast I couldn't have stopped them if I had tried.

"What?" she whispered, so low I barely heard it.

"Fuck," I said, scrubbing my hands down my face. "That was not what I meant to say."

"So you don't love me?" she asked, her voice shaking and unsure.

I faced her again. "I do, but I didn't want to blurt it out like that. I wanted to...start over, Paige. Be friends with you, date you, show you that I care about you and that I'm not trying to pull one over on you. I don't really know what in the hell I'm doing. I've been so out of sorts since I found out you owned half this house. I'm pissed at myself, I'm angry with Granddad, I'm fighting off the urge to kiss you every goddamn time I see you and then you go off and dress sexy and it's taking every ounce of strength not to ask to kiss you."

"You have kissed me, though."

"I know!" I said, throwing my hands up in the air. "I thought maybe if I acted drunk, I could make up for things."

Her lip snarled. "By kissing me and touching me? You thought you could make things better with sex?"

I stared at her. "Yes?"

"Is that your answer or a question, Lucas?"

"Can it be both?"

She rolled her eyes. "Us having sex isn't going to do anything but make this all more complicated, you know that, right?"

With a frustrated groan, I nodded. "Of course, I know that. It doesn't mean I'm not going to want you, because trust me, Paige. I want you. I've never stopped wanting you. I've never stopped loving you."

Paige turned and walked a few steps away, her hand over her mouth. For a moment I wondered if I should have kept my feelings to myself, but that moment came and went. I was tired of keeping it in.

"I'm sorry, Paige. I'm sorry for everything."

Chapter 15

Paige

I FOUGHT TO keep my body from shaking. Tears stung at the back of my eyes as I tried not to cry. Since the day Lucas walked away from us, I had been dreaming of hearing him tell me he was sorry. I even dreamed I'd hear him tell me he loved me. The truth was, I had never stopped loving him. That had been obvious to everyone who knew me, especially with my insane jealousy of his relationship with Bianca.

"Paige?"

"Give me a moment, please," I croaked, my voice shaky and unsure.

I felt his hands on my shoulders, and my breath caught in my throat. He turned me and placed his finger on my chin, lifting my gaze to meet his.

"I just want to be honest with you. I'm not asking you for anything. Well, maybe your forgiveness," he said with a slight smile. My heart drummed faster in my chest.

For the briefest of moments, I wanted him to kiss me. Then I snapped out of it and took a step back. Away from the heat of his body and the longing to feel his touch.

"I'm feeling a bit overwhelmed with all of this, Lucas."

He nodded. Sadness crept into his eyes and I knew I needed to be honest with him as well. "I never stopped loving you either."

A spark of hope flashed across his face.

"But I don't think we just tumble back into a relationship. I mean, every ounce of my body is begging me to let you touch me, to feel your lips against mine, to feel you between my legs again."

A low growl came from the back his throat and ignited a heat in my belly.

"And that's why we can't. We need to figure out some other things first, and the only way we can do that is with our heads clear. Sex is only going to complicate things."

"Or it could actually take some of the stress away, help clear our minds," he said with a wink.

Laughing, I shook my head. "I won't deny I ache for you, but we need to go slow. The intensity of our feelings could just be because we've been thrown together, and we are alone in this house. We've both had some major changes in our lives, and more to come. I'm looking at opening a new business, we're co-owners in this house, you work in Austin. What is our future going to look like? What is the future of this house? The ownership of it and the secrets it clearly holds?"

Lucas rubbed his neck, something he had always done when frustrated or thinking deeply.

"I'm not going to sell it. I'm not going to try and convince you to let me buy your half."

A lump formed in my throat. "Why did you change your mind?"

"I was motivated by the wrong emotions that first day. A part of me thinks Granddad knew I would be, and in his weird way to keep me from making another mistake, he made you part owner. He knew you'd never let this house go."

I smiled. "He was a wise man."

Lucas chuckled. "Yes, he was. I knew that same day I wouldn't sell it."

"So you've been, what? Torturing me?"

He shrugged. "It's been kind of fun seeing that fire in your eyes when you said you'd never leave."

I sighed, not wanting to admit it had been a little fun to go back and forth with him.

"So, what do we do from here?" he asked.

I walked back over to him and took his hand in mine. His eyes searched my face, and I slowly exhaled. "We get to know each other again by being friends."

"So, I probably shouldn't kiss you?"

My teeth dug into my lip, and I couldn't help the smile that spread across my face. "I don't think one little kiss would hurt. A friendly kiss. Like a peck."

"A peck?" he asked, moving closer to me.

I nodded. "*Mmm-hmm.* A peck." My voice was a whisper on the breeze while my eyes locked on his mouth.

He leaned down, inches from my lips. "I can do a peck."

"Okay," I softly said, reaching up on my toes to bridge the distance between our mouths.

The moment we made the connection, I was lost.

Lucas placed his hand on my lower back and drew me close while my hands moved up his body and wrapped around the back of his neck.

The kiss was soft and slow. Gentle. As if we were learning one another's kiss all over again. I moaned, then he moaned and deepened it, pulling me into him. His tongue moved in such an exploratory way that it nearly had my legs going out from under me. I wanted more. Needed more, but knew we'd already gone too far. Yet, neither of us stopped.

When his fingers pushed into my hair, I bit at his lip, causing him to growl again, this time in warning.

Lucas slowed the kiss, drew back and leaned his forehead against mine. Our chests rose and fell, each of us breathing like we had just run a marathon. And in a way, we had. Years of an emotional journey, not of miles but of moments, packed into our embrace, into that kiss.

"That...was some peck," he said as I smiled.

"We may have to define slow."

"I think so," he replied, giving me a soft *peck* on the forehead. "Maybe we should finish cleaning the living room, then explore the attic. I think I found the key."

Jumping back in surprise, I looked at him. "I thought you had the key! William gave it to you."

He shook his head. "Not that key. This morning when I went up to the attic, the upper door was locked. Your weird little cat helped me stumble upon a key earlier. I think it's the key to the attic. At least, I sure as hell hope it is."

"Oreo found it?" I asked, confused.

"It's a long story, but I kind of think that cat is a ghost or something. Hopefully not the *Pet Sematary* reincarnation kind but more like the *Casper* kind."

I furrowed my brows. "A ghost? Really?"

He took my hand and led me back to the table where he picked up my chair for me. We both sat down. Lucas met my gaze as he reached for his drink and held it up. "To our friendship."

A chill ran across my entire body before I picked up my glass and clinked it to his. "To exploring."

Lucas winked, then laughed. "To exploring."

Oreo had, of course, followed us upstairs and sat on the top step outside the attic door.

"Okay, let's see if this is the key." Lucas said.

Lucas pushed it into the lock, and before he turned it, I grabbed his hand.

"Wait."

He moved his hand and looked at me. One single bulb lit up the small hallway. My hands were shaking, and I quickly rubbed them together to calm my nerves.

"What if we find something that changes everything?"

With a frown, he asked, "Changes what?"

I shook my head frantically. "I don't know...this whole thing with the dates being wrong."

He closed his eyes and cursed under his breath. "I forgot to tell you. Dad sort of hinted that maybe Grams and Granddad might have broken up."

I was positive my eyes were about to bug out of my head. "What?"

"Yeah, he didn't really come out and say it, but he made it seem that way."

"And you forgot to tell me!"

He laughed. "Well, in my defense, a lot of messy shit has happened since I came back from my folks' place."

"That's true. So, you're not worried?"

Lucas took my hands in his. "Paige, I don't think Granddad would have us stumble on something that might hurt either of us in any way. I'm not worried."

I chewed on my lip. "Okay, I'm not worried either."

When he smiled, I felt my heart jump. I was going to ignore the urge to reach up and kiss him.

"Let's see what's up here."

Excitement bubbled inside of me. "I haven't been up here since I was a little girl."

"Same," Lucas said, turning the lock. We heard it click, and when he pushed the old wooden door open, it let out a creak — or was that a moan — that would give any scary movie a run for its money.

Oreo rushed inside.

"She doesn't seem to be worried. Come on," he said, taking my hand and stepping into the large attic. It took a moment for my eyes to adjust to the darkness.

"If I remember right, there is a light to your left," I said. Lucas kept a hold of my hand and walked a few feet.

"Here it is."

I heard the click of the switch, and light filled the attic as I took a long look around the giant space.

"Wow, I forgot how huge it was up here," I whispered.

"Why are you whispering?" Lucas asked.

I shrugged and laughed. "I don't know, just seems like the right thing to do."

Lucas walked toward the center of the attic. It ran from one side of the house to the other, both in length and width.

"Granddad told me he used to sleep up here when he was younger. He had his own area over in that corner in the front right."

I looked across the room and could make out a bed. "There's still a bed up here."

"That doesn't surprise me."

Doing a full circle, I took in the attic space. It was packed with boxes, old trunks, furniture. It was filled almost to capacity.

"Whose furniture is this?" I asked, making my way to an old chest. Sitting on top of it was a porcelain bowl and pitcher, the kind that would be placed in bedrooms for people to wash up with.

"This is my great grandparents' stuff."

I faced Lucas. "What? How do you know?"

Lucas was standing in front of a grandfather clock.

"I remember this clock. It used to be in the front hallway. God, I couldn't have been but maybe two or three. Granddaddy used to stand in front of it when it went off, the ringing of the bell used to make me laugh."

"But, I thought May and William lived in this house when you were born."

"They did. My great grandmother was still alive, she stayed in..." he stopped talking and quickly turned to look at me. "Your room. The room you're staying in now, it was her room."

I smiled. "How wonderful! William never told me that."

"He didn't talk a lot about his mom. My father used to tell me his grandmother was a troubled soul. She lost herself when her husband died. I remember she loved to knit. And read."

"That explains the bookshelf in that room. It's still filled with books," I said.

An odd look moved over his face, and he tried not to smile, but he did.

"What's so funny?" I asked.

"Ah well, I don't really know how to tell you this."

"What?" I asked, smiling. "Tell me! Is it something about the house?"

He laughed. "I'm sort of pissed I didn't remember this when we were attempting to run each other out of the house."

I tilted my head and gave him a questioning look. "Why? What is it?"

"My great-grandmother died in her room. In your room."

I was positive my jaw hit the floor. "Come again?"

"She died in there. In..." he started laughing.

"Oh God. No. Do not say it, Lucas."

He was laughing so hard, he could hardly speak.

My hand covered my mouth, and I shook my head.

Lucas nodded and said, "She died in the bed you're sleeping in!"

"You asshole! You let me take that room!"

Holding up his hands in defense, he attempted to talk while he laughed his ass off. "I forgot! I totally forgot!"

"You said the house was haunted! How did you not remember someone died in my room?"

He shrugged, then wiped his tears of laughter away. "I remembered Grams making a comment about how the house was haunted by her mother-in-law. It slipped my mind completely."

I jutted my chin out. "You are a terrible man! How did she die? Did it happen of natural causes?"

Once Lucas got himself in check, he took in a breath and let it out. "Sorry. Man, I must have needed that laugh."

I balled my fists. I didn't want to lose ground on the progress we had made with starting over as friends—friends who exchanged passionate kisses—but boy, did I want to kick him in his balls for keeping that little gem a secret.

"I'm sorry, babe. Honestly, I am. I really did forget."

His endearment sent a bolt straight through my body. I froze, staring at him like an idiot.

The smile on Lucas's face faded. "I really did forget, Paige."

With a jerky shake of my head, I forced myself to speak. "It's... okay. I may be moving rooms though."

He winked, sending yet another wave of electricity through my body. "You can bunk with me."

"Ha ha," I managed, while I pretended I didn't want to jump up and down and offer myself as tribute.

"Okay, we're looking for a chest," Lucas said, casting a glance about the room.

"What's that?" I asked, pointing to a large trunk set off to the corner. "I remember May telling us when we played up here that we were not allowed to open it."

Lucas made his way to the old trunk. "It's called a wardrobe steamer trunk. Granddad would tell me it was Grams' and that someday I could look through it."

I bent down and looked at it. The brown leather trunk had a domed top with brass cap feet on the bottom. It looked to be in great condition.

"Let's open it," Lucas said, reaching for the latch.

Grabbing his hand, I said, "Wait. What if we're not supposed to touch it."

He gave me the sweetest smile. "Actually, it's half yours, half mine. We're allowed to open it. Together."

Drawing in a deep breath, I gave a nod and Lucas opened it. The inside was in amazing shape, with a light and dark peach fabric lining. Five drawers were on one side, and the other contained a few wooden hangers with the most beautiful dress still hanging on one of them. It almost looked like a ball gown.

Lucas pulled the top drawer open. I gasped when I saw the inside.

"Holy crap."

"Well, no wonder Grams didn't want us playing with this," Lucas deadpanned.

My mouth opened and closed at least a dozen times as I stared at the drawer full of jewelry.

"Lucas, why in the world would May and William leave this all up here!"

"Costume jewelry?"

I laughed as I reached in and took out a necklace that held a princess cut ruby encased in diamonds.

"That is not costume jewelry."

"How do you know?"

I looked at him. "My grandmother had costume jewelry. Trust me, this is not the same."

"Okay, so Grams might have had a small fortune in jewelry. Why did she keep it in her travel trunk?"

"And why did May or William not touch it? Why wouldn't she have worn it? Why did your folks not look in here?"

"Same reason you didn't want to touch it. You were told not to."

The corner of my mouth rose into a slight smile. "Touché."

"I'm almost afraid to open the next drawer."

I reached for it and pulled gently. "I'm not! My curiosity is getting the best of me."

"What in the hell?" Lucas said, moving away from the articles of clothing in the drawer.

"Well, looks like May had a fetish for naughty knickers," I said with a giggle.

"Why is that crotchless? Oh God. Oh God."

"It was so they could use the restroom, you perv. But, by the time May used this chest, she wouldn't have needed these panties. These are old, maybe May's mom used it or something."

Lucas let out a gruff laugh. "Ha! Trust me, any man who knew a woman's underwear contained an opening like that took full advantage of it. I know I would."

I looked at him, heat hitting my cheeks as I pictured him doing just that. To me.

Ugh. Paige, you are taking it slow, just as friends, don't go there.

An evil smile spread over his face. "Want to try them on?"

Slapping him on the chest, I cried out, "Lucas Foster! That is gross!"

He raised a brow. "Why is that gross?"

"It just *is*! Those are your grandmother's, or great-grandmother's undergarments."

He snarled. "There goes that image in my mind. Thanks a lot for that cock block."

Laughing, I shut the drawer and pulled open the next one. It contained stockings.

The next drawer was empty, and the bottom contained a few journals, some books, a feather pen, and an empty jar of what had most likely been ink.

Lucas stood and looked down at the trunk. "If this was Grams', where did she take it? When did she use it? Or maybe it was her mother's and that's why they didn't want us touching it?"

I looked over some of the jewelry. "I think you need to have this all looked at, Lucas. For sure, show your father. These are family heirlooms."

"They're half yours."

With a quick glance at him, I shook my head. "No. They are not. They're yours."

Lucas looked at me and something passed over his face. I couldn't tell what he was thinking, but the way he stared made my insides go all crazy again as my stomach flipped.

"Do you have any idea what an incredible person you are?"

I stood and grinned. "I do. I'm a rare one, for sure."

His expression softened even more as he placed his hand on my cheek and smiled. "You most certainly are."

Chapter 16

Lucas

PAIGE AND I stood in front of the old trunk staring at one another. I wanted to kiss her again. Tell her I thought she was the most magnificent creature ever. Here she was, half owner to some pretty expensive-looking jewelry, and she was telling me it was mine. Most women wouldn't have reacted that way.

I closed my eyes and cursed. God, I wanted her so fucking badly. Snapping my eyes back open, I gave her one last look before I dropped my hand and looked about the attic.

"While this is all fun, looking in the forbidden wardrobe of crotchless bloomers, we need to find the chest."

"You don't find this so crazy, learning all these things about your family?"

With a shrug, I looked around the area where we were standing. There was so much shit in this attic, it would take us weeks to go through it.

"Sure, loads of fun, but I'm on a mission."

I heard Paige chuckle behind me.

"Well, I for one find it fascinating."

"Of course, you would. You're a woman."

"*Psh*, that has nothing to do with it, Lucas. This is your family's history up here. Who knows what else we'll find!"

"Earlier you were afraid to look."

Paige walked up next to me and looked down at an old sofa. "That was before we found what very well might be a ruby necklace in a vintage wardrobe trunk." She pulled the white sheet that was half-covering the sofa. "Do you remember this sofa?"

I smiled as I looked down at it. "Hell yes, I remember it. It was where I first kissed you."

Paige ran her fingers over the fabric and smiled. "I was so nervous." She looked up at me. "Were you nervous to kiss me that first time?"

"Yes," I answered honestly. "Mostly because I thought we would get caught making out and Grams would never leave us up here alone again."

She laughed and sat down on the sofa.

"Do you want me to kiss you again? For old time's sake?" I asked in a deep voice.

Her mouth parted, and her tongue darted out to wet her lips. If that wasn't a yes, I didn't know what was. I sat down next to her.

"A peck?" she asked, a smirk on her face.

Quickly grabbing her, I pulled her onto my lap so that she straddled me. If she sat down, her heat would be pressed on my ever-growing dick.

"Lucas."

My name on her mouth almost sounded pleading. I wasn't sure if she was asking me to not kiss her, or begging for me to kiss her. Either way, I was going with the best-case scenario.

I cupped her face in my hands and gently brought her mouth to mine. And we kissed.

Holy mother of all kisses. Paige deepened the kiss as she sank down, pressing herself against my cock.

Grabbing her hips, I lifted up, needing more contact. Her fingers jammed into my hair, and she gave it a tug, causing me to suck on her tongue and pull her closer to me.

"Yes," she whispered while she rocked against my hard-on.

"Fuck, this isn't slow, Paige. This is so not slow," I said forcing my mouth from hers.

Without a word, she pulled my mouth back to hers. Our first kiss was nothing like this. It was awkward, messy. Unexperienced tongues trying to figure out how to move together in a fluid motion. This kiss said a million unspoken things.

I love you. I've always loved you. I want you. I fucking need to be inside you.

"Son-of-a-bitch, Paige."

I pressed my cock to her as she wrapped her legs around me, a moan moving from her mouth to mine.

"Lucas."

"Stop saying my name like that or I'm going to fuck you right here. And then there goes slow right out the window."

She bit down on my lip. My hand slipped up her shirt and teased her nipple through the lace of her bra.

"Don't stop, Lucas. Please don't stop."

"We said slow."

"Just a little more. Please."

Who was I to deny her?

"I want to make you come, Paige."

"I won't argue with that," she panted, her hands moving over my hard cock and making their way to what I hoped was her hand in my pants.

"I will."

I froze, as did Paige.

We drew our mouths away from one another and turned to find Tom Miller standing in the middle of the attic.

Her fucking brother. Holy shit. I had stopped by the Miller ranch to talk to him, but he hadn't been there. And now he was here. Watching me dry hump his sister.

"*Oh my god!*" Paige whispered, pushing me off of her. "Tom!"

I stood, not even bothering to hide the raging hard-on. The way he was looking at me, I had no doubt my dick would shrink by the second.

Yep. There it was, the ultimate cause of a deflating cock. The brother. The father would do it, too.

Paige frantically looked at me, then to her brother.

"What, why are you, I didn't know you were coming over," she finally managed to say.

He stared at me with pure anger. Or maybe it was hatred. I wasn't sure. Either way, things were not looking good for me.

"After this dickhead stopped by the ranch to talk to me, I tried calling your cell, and I haven't heard from you. I got worried, so I came over."

"Sorry about that. I must have left my phone downstairs. Everything is fine."

"What are you doing up here?" he asked, his gaze and words directed solely to me.

"We were, uh, trying to find a chest."

He raised his brow. "Seems like you found it."

"Tom, please. Let's go back downstairs. I'll make you some tea."

"What is your game, Foster?" he asked.

"There is no game, Tom. I stopped by to talk to you. Tell you I was sorry about how things happened between me and Paige."

Paige looked at me with a stunned expression. "You did?"

I gave her a soft smile. "My dad told me Tom was angry with me."

"Ha," Tom said. "That's putting it lightly. If you think I'm mad, just be glad you didn't run into my father."

Walking toward her brother, Paige said, "Tom, let's go downstairs."

He turned to her. "He has a girlfriend, remember? Have you forgotten how he treated you? How he hurt you?"

Guilt clawed at my chest and into my throat.

"We've talked about things, and he doesn't have a girlfriend."

"Why is he here?"

Paige looked at me, utter panic in her eyes. Holy shit, she hadn't told her family yet.

"He lives here."

With that statement, I quickly looked for an escape because Tom Miller was fixin' to kick my ass.

I leaned against the counter in the kitchen and tried not to let my fear show. Tom was currently sitting at the table, shooting me death rays from his eyes.

"When were you going to tell us he's living here?"

"The next time I saw you and Daddy. You know he owns half of the house."

"Yes, just like I knew he lived in Austin with some fancy model in some fancy apartment and dressed like a damn hipster. I also knew he couldn't have been bothered to show up for his own granddaddy's funeral."

"That's enough, Tom. You don't know the whole story," Paige said in a matter-of-fact tone.

It felt like déjà vu. Except the last time I stood in a kitchen with a man staring at me like he hated me, I was much younger. Paige was trying then, like she was now, to convince her father I had only good intentions. The only problem was, I had been well on my way to stripping her naked and taking her, and if her father hadn't showed up, things would have gotten complicated. Now it was her brother in the role of her dad.

"Then tell me the story, Paige. Because what I just saw didn't look innocent."

"We got caught up in old memories," I said.

He glared at me, and Paige shot me a look that said *stop talking*.

"So the truth is, Lucas and I both live in the house. You know about the letter William left me, and he left one for Lucas too. We're trying to find a chest that William said contains answers as to why he left us both the house."

Tom laughed. "Ah, for Pete's sake. You're both smart enough. The only reason William left you both this house was to force the two of you to come together to work out a solution. Everyone knows that.

And his little plan is working, considering this dickhead just had his tongue down your throat and hands under your shirt."

I looked away and cleared my throat.

"Yes, I'm sure that was part of William's intention, but I think there's more. He wanted us to find something together."

"Paige, he didn't. Ever since you were a little girl you've been enamored with this house. Hell, you've been enamored with him."

He jerked his chin my way.

"William knew that. He forced the two of you together. That is not how you mend a relationship. He forced your hand and now you're letting another Foster take advantage of you."

"Wait one minute, Tom," I said, pushing off the counter.

"My granddad knew how much this house meant to Paige. He left it to her for that reason and that reason alone. No one can force Paige to do something she doesn't want to do, and I'm not taking advantage of anything."

"Then sell her your half of the house."

With a warning look, Paige said, "Tom, please stay out of this."

"No, Paige. If this jerk truly cares about you, truly wants to see you happy, then he should walk away."

"It's my family's house!" I protested.

"And word on the street is you want to sell it. Make a hefty profit and head back to Austin and probably take your model on another trip to Europe."

Paige groaned while she buried her face in her hands.

"Is that what people are saying about me?" I asked, dread settling in the pit of my stomach.

"Of course they are, Lucas. You left Johnson City and never looked back."

"Because the life I wanted here—"

"You let go. You made that choice. You. You gave up your chance."

"I made a mistake, which I'm trying to make up for."

He scoffed. "You want this house, plain and simple."

"Tom, I'm asking you to please stop," Paige begged.

I stared at Tom, then looked at Paige. Her brother's words hit me like a brick wall. Had I really lost my chance with Paige? Could we forget the past and figure out a future together? Or would everyone think I'd simply seduced her to get the house? Even if I never sold it, people would whisper behind my back.

"I'll let you and your brother talk."

Standing, Paige reached for my arm. "Lucas, wait."

With a quick step back, I forced a smile. "It was nice to see you, Tom. Please accept this as my apology to you for the way I treated your sister in the past. I truly do regret it."

"Lucas!"

Paige quickly followed me. I grabbed my keys and wallet from the small table in the foyer and headed out the front door.

"Please, don't go. Please."

I walked to my truck and opened the door.

"Stop!" she yelled. "You promised me."

Slowly, I faced her. "Everyone in this town is going to think exactly the way he does!" I said, pointing back toward the house. "I'll never be able to convince anyone any different."

"They don't matter. The only thing that matters should be me. What I think."

"What do you think, Paige? Because just last night I was the enemy."

She slowly shook her head. "Lucas, you've never been the enemy."

I swallowed hard. "I sure as fuck feel like it."

Paige stepped back as I slipped into the truck and started it.

"Where are you going?" she asked.

With a slight smile, because I really didn't want her to think I was upset with her, I said, "My folks' place. Maybe go for a ride. I just need to clear my head. I don't regret earlier, kissing you. And all."

She nodded. "Neither do I. Be careful, don't ride angry."

God, this woman. She was worried about me. I truly was a stupid idiot to ever let her go.

"I promise, and I'm not angry."

As I pulled away, I glanced in the rearview mirror to see her standing, watching me. We had taken two steps forward today, only to be pulled back three.

With a curse, I hit my steering wheel as I drove away from the woman I loved.

Chapter 17

Paige

LUCAS KICKED UP dirt as he drove down the driveway. That had been twice today we had been stopped before things got carried away. Even with a promise to each other that we'd go slow, I was beginning to wonder if that was really the smart thing to do.

Turning, I headed back into the house. I wanted to throttle my brother.

He stood in the middle of the living room, looking around.

"What in the heck happened in here?" he asked.

"It's a long story. Tom, I need you to understand something."

He faced me, concern etched on his face.

"You love him still," he said before I could utter another word.

"I've never stopped loving him. I don't honestly think it is possible for me to not love him. Lucas is a part of me, he owns a part of my heart, and I'm not sure what is going to happen. I don't know what the future holds for us."

"You have a future. The flower shop."

"Lucas would never stop that."

He let out a bark of laughter. "He tried to stop you before."

I threw up my hands and let them fall to my side. "That was the past. This is now. This is today. This is me and Lucas trying to find some common ground."

"And you think sleeping with him will help?"

My face heated. "We got carried away. We have a lot of memories between us, Tom. More good times than bad. Feelings that neither one of us really ever let go."

"He seemed to let them go. He was with that model long enough."

"I really wish people would stop bringing her up. He broke up with her. He said he never saw a future with her."

"You believe him?"

The corner of my mouth rose slightly. "Yeah, I really do."

He scrubbed his hands over his face and sighed. "Paige, I know he hurt you."

"Yes, he did."

"I'm just worried."

I walked up to my brother and wrapped my arms around him. "I'm a big girl. I know what I'm doing. Will you please trust me to handle this?"

"Will you promise you won't get back with him?"

My shoulders slumped, and I stared up at him. "I can't, and I won't promise you that."

"Fine, I won't ask you to. You know, I did like him at one time. So did Dad."

"I know you did, and Daddy adored him. And so did Momma. We got lost, and I don't know where this journey will lead us. On more than one occasion we've had divided interests, and I'm positive we will in the future, but I feel it in my heart that no matter what, I need to try harder this time. We *both* need to try harder. We're not eighteen anymore."

With a big inhale, my brother closed his eyes. "If he hurts you, so help me God."

"If he hurts me, you'll have to stand in line. I'm first."

With a chuckle, he wrapped me in his arms and kissed the top of my head. "I love you, sis."

"And I love you, too. So very much."

When he let go of me, I smiled. "Hey, you wouldn't happen to know a jeweler, would you?"

After my brother left, I changed and put on my running shoes. I had another hour or so before the sun went down, and I'd wanted to get in a run before it got dark. Tom had helped finish up the painting in the living room, then he cut around the carpet to make it easier for me and Lucas to pull it up.

I'd been gone almost an hour, with my feet pounding against the road, and I glanced down at my watch. I hadn't heard yet from Lucas; part of me was worried. Pushing my fear away, I ran faster toward the house. I slowed when I saw Milo parked behind me.

"Hey, what are you doing here?"

He smiled. "I got a call from Chuck."

With a frown, I asked, "Chuck Nelson? I thought he moved to Austin and opened up a club."

Milo rubbed his chin, a concerned look on his face. "He did, but he moved back to JC when Austin got a little too...weird. He opened up a bar right outside of JC."

I chuckled. "Okay, well, what does that have to do with me, and why do you look so stricken?"

"Well, he gave me a call. Lucas is at the bar; he's been there all afternoon. Said he's on his way to being two sheets to the wind."

My heart felt like it dropped to my stomach. "Is he okay?"

"I stopped by and talked to him. He's pretty down on himself. I thought maybe you could head on over there."

It didn't even take me a moment to make my decision. "Let me change. Will you text me the address to the bar?"

Milo grinned. "Sure. It's right outside of town, toward Fredericksburg."

Reaching up on my toes, I gave him a kiss on the cheek. "Thank you, Milo. I know you got dragged into all of this."

With a boyish grin that made me smile, he looked away for a brief moment, then back to me. "I lost my head for a minute or two when I thought about asking you out, but all it took was one time seeing Lucas look at you. He's never stopped loving you, Paige. I know that doesn't make what happened between y'all better, but it's true."

I placed my hand on his arm and gave it a squeeze. "Thank you, Milo. I'm going to go change."

Thirty minutes later, I walked into Chuck's Place. I couldn't help the grin that spread over my face when I saw Lucas. He sat at the bar, staring at a glass of beer. My heart hammered in my chest, and I had to focus on keeping my breathing even. He was so handsome. Even in this dark bar, he stood out. He always had. There had always been something so different about Lucas Foster. From the first moment we met, I knew my life would never be the same, even at such a young age. What started out as friendship didn't take long to morph into something more.

I slid onto the bar stool next to him and flashed a smile at Chuck.

"Well, if it isn't Paige Miller. I heard you were back in town."

"I see you are, too."

He nodded. "This town is my home. What can I do for you?"

After a quick glance at Lucas, who was staring at me, I focused back on Chuck. "Maybe a water with lemon?"

He winked. "Coming up."

"What are you doing here?" Lucas asked. He wasn't drunk; I could tell. But something was for sure weighing heavy on his mind.

"Milo told me you were here."

He rolled his eyes and let out a grunt before taking a long drink of his beer.

"Want to talk about it?" I asked, bumping his shoulder with mine.

Lucas looked directly into my eyes. "You know I love you. I've never stopped loving you, Paige. Even when I was with her, all I could see or think about was you. All I could do was curse myself for walking away from you."

"Why did you stand me up for dinner?" I asked, giving a quick nod to Chuck when he placed my water in front of me. "If you still loved me, Lucas, why would you hurt me again? Why would you stay in a relationship with another woman? Why travel with her and do all the things I wanted to do, but with her?"

His eyes glassed over, and he took another drink of his beer.

"Because I'm an asshole. That's why your brother is right, Paige. I don't deserve you. You deserve someone who is going to treat you like you are a princess. No, a fucking queen, because you are."

With a laugh, I shook my head. "I don't know about queen, but I'll take princess."

Lucas stared down at his beer. "I know Granddad was ashamed of me."

"He was not," I countered.

"He was. Look at the lengths he went to just to bring us together. I don't know if he wanted us to get back together, but I'm positive he wanted me to man up and tell you I'm sorry for what I did. For how I treated you. I wish I could go back in time. I'd do so many things differently."

It broke my heart to hear the hurt and regret in his voice. "He loved you very much."

He scoffed. "Yeah, he did, and I let her come between me and family. Even right up until the very end."

He grew quiet, and I let him be in his own thoughts for a moment or two.

"Lucas, can I ask you a question?"

Turning his whole body, Lucas looked at me. "Of course, you can. I don't want there to be anything unsaid between us anymore."

I chewed on my lip for a quick moment, then asked, "If you were so unhappy with her, why did you stay as long as you did? Why did you allow her to put a rift between you and your family?"

His eyes turned sad. "I don't know. I honestly don't know. Maybe because I was afraid of failing again, even though I knew it was never going to work out. She was a distraction from everything that reminded me of you. And Johnson City reminded me of you. Maybe deep down it was me avoiding home and all the ghosts of memories that I'd be forced to face, and I used her as an excuse."

"And one day you woke up and decided you were done?"

He laughed. "Nah, I decided I was done a long time ago. But seeing you, that day on the front porch of Granddad's house, of the house we once dreamed about owning, knowing that we both held a piece of it, I knew the charade was over. It wasn't fair to Bianca, and it wasn't fair to me. Truth be told, I knew on the plane ride back that I was going to end things. She caused me to miss my granddad's fucking funeral. I just didn't want to deal with it until after coming home and all of that."

I nodded. "If William hadn't left me the house, would you have sold it?"

A look of utter sorrow moved across his face. "I'd like to think I wouldn't. I might have gone down to the wire and come to my senses. It would have been the last thing that tied me to you. I don't think I could or would have let it go."

I let out a soft chuckle. "So, you're sitting in a bar, drinking because you're feeling like a worthless piece of shit who treated his family and friends like complete assholes."

His eyes widened. "Did I say all of that?"

With a shake of my head, I replied, "I filled in the blanks for you."

Lucas laughed. "Thanks for that."

I gave a half-shrug. "No problem. Are you ready to leave? How much have you had to drink?"

"Three beers."

My eyes widened in shock. "How long have you been here?"

"Since I left the house. Didn't make it to my folks' place."

I looked over at Chuck in confusion. "Milo said Chuck called because you had been here all afternoon and..." My voice trailed off. "*Milo.*"

Lucas lifted the corner of his mouth in a half smile and my insides clenched with desire.

"Seems like everyone is trying to help us along the way," I said.

Lucas pulled out a few twenty-dollar bills and tossed them onto the bar. "It seems like."

"Want to go back and play in the attic again?" I asked as I slid off the bar stool.

Lifting his eyes to meet mine, a slow, sexy smile spread over his face. "Can we please make sure to lock the damn doors?"

I laughed and took his hand as we walked out of the bar together.

"'Night, you two!" Chuck called out after us.

"'Night, Chuck!" we both called back.

Glancing around the bar, I noticed a few people watching us leave. Hand-in-hand, two old lovers who seemed to be picking up where they left off.

"Rumors are going to spread like wildfire, you know that, right?" I asked as we walked over to my SUV.

"So, let them."

I pressed my lips together and narrowed my gaze on him.

"What?" he asked with a bit of humor in his voice.

"You're okay with what people are saying, or possibly saying? Good or bad? True or false?" I asked, watching him carefully.

Lucas moved closer to me, causing me to lean against my car.

"Sitting in a bar for hours, thinking about all the things I've done wrong the last ten years of my life, I can honestly say I don't give two flying fucks what anyone says, what they think, or what they talk about. We aren't in high school anymore, Paige."

I swallowed hard as I stared into his beautiful green eyes. "What do you care about?"

"Finding that chest."

My heart sank.

"Learning your body all over again."

And my body came right back to life.

"Watching a sunset with you, seeing where life takes us next, and honestly not even caring, as long as I get to do it with you."

"Lucas," I whispered.

"I know, you said slow, and I'm going to try hard to go slow, but Paige, all I really want to do is kiss you."

With a quick lick of my lips, I placed my hands on his broad chest and softly said, "Then kiss me."

Lucas grinned from ear to ear and did just that.

Chapter 18

Lucas

AFTER KISSING PAIGE in the parking lot of Chuck's Place, I followed her back to the house. It was late and neither of us wanted to explore the attic. Truth be told, the idea of going up there at night sort of freaked me out.

I crawled into bed and spent an hour staring at the ceiling. The soft knock on my bedroom door had me lifting my head. "Paige?"

The door creaked as she peeked her head in. "Yeah, it's me."

"What's wrong?" I asked, sitting up.

"I can't sleep in that room."

I smiled. "Do you want to sleep in here? With me?"

She darted across the bedroom and climbed onto my bed. I groaned internally because she had on her sexy little pajamas. Thank God her hair wasn't in the damn pigtails.

Without hesitation, Paige climbed under the sheets, pulling them all the way up to her chin. We laid there in silence for a few minutes before I felt something on the bottom of the bed.

"Something is touching my foot," I whispered.

"What?" Paige whisper-shouted.

Pop.

Pop.

160

Pop.

"Holy shit, it's hitting my foot!" I said, sitting up quickly and reaching for the side light. When I turned it on, I stared at the little black-and-white beast at the bottom of my bed.

"It's Oreo!" Paige said in delight. "Come here, sweet girl. I'm so sorry I just left you up there!"

Oreo walked across the bed, her tail swishing back and forth as she moved. At one point, I was positive she shot me a *fuck you* look as she curled up between me and Paige.

"The cat cannot sleep in my bed."

"What? Why?" Paige asked in a mock shocked voice.

"I don't want her hair getting everywhere."

Paige pouted. "She's scared too, Lucas. Are you really going to kick her out?"

"Yes!"

Paige smiled and snuggled up next to the damn cat. "She won't bother you, I swear. You won't even know she's here. Will he, sweet baby girl?"

Oreo meowed and then proceeded to lick her ass. I snarled while Paige covered her mouth to hide her chuckle.

I turned off the light. "Now I'm really not going to be able to sleep."

"You can't sleep?" Paige asked softly.

"No, I can't."

"Do you need some warm milk? Or I could make some tea?"

"No, it's fine."

"Good night, Lucas," Paige said, reaching over and taking my hand in hers.

Her hand against mine instantly made me relax. Just one simple touch and within minutes, I was sound asleep.

I woke up the next morning with Paige snuggled next to my side, my arm around her and Oreo sleeping right on my chest. Her face inches from mine. As soon as I opened my eyes, the judgy cat was staring at me.

I watched Paige sleep. She was beautiful. I wanted to wake up like this every day.

My gaze went back to Oreo. "You can leave now," I said in a hushed voice. She stared at me. I jerked my body just enough to make the cat move but not enough to wake the sleeping beauty next to me.

The cat moved, but so did Paige. Her hand was on my chest, and it slowly made its way down my body.

"*Mmm*, Lucas."

My body froze. I had two options. Let her hand wander down to my stiff-as-a-rock cock or wake her up.

Oreo jumped back onto the bed. Her judgmental cat eyes glared at me.

"Fine!" I said.

"Paige? Baby? Are you awake?"

She nuzzled against my body more.

"You feel so good."

I swallowed hard. "Thank you?"

She giggled, and I knew she was awake.

"Your cat is staring at me like I'm about to ruin your virtue or something."

Paige lifted her head and rested her chin on the back of her hand, which was currently on my chest.

"Oreo, did you sleep good?"

I rolled my eyes.

"Seriously, Paige? You're against my body, I have a raging hard-on, and you're asking the cat if she slept good?"

Paige lifted her head and looked at me. "Did you sleep good?"

I smiled. "The best sleep I've had in years."

"Me too," she said, dropping her chin back on her hand. "I have to ask you something."

"If you're going to ask me something that requires thinking, don't."

She chuckled. "Why not?"

"I'm not sure if I have enough blood in my brain to think. It's all in my dick."

"Well, this is about your dick, so..."

I groaned. "This is mean. I just want you to know that."

"Noted. But that night you came home and pretended to be drunk…"

"I was sort of drunk."

"You still knew what was going on, though? Right?"

With a quick glance at her, I nodded. "Yes. I did."

Her teeth dug into her lip. "I heard you in the shower."

My breath stalled. "What did you hear?"

"You…making yourself come while saying my name."

I closed my eyes. Heat rushed into my cheeks, and my hard-on quickly lost his morning glory.

"Sorry about that. I guess I was a bit worked up."

She sat up and moved over me, then straddled my hips. My cock instantly woke back up, causing her to raise a brow.

"It was hot, hearing you. Seeing you."

My brows shot up. "You were watching me?"

"I heard a loud sound and thought you had fallen because you were drunk. Then I saw what you were doing and I…was too shocked to leave."

Laughing, I grabbed her hips and pushed my dick up into her warm heat. We both let out a moan of pleasure.

"Do you have any idea how fucking sexy you are, Paige?"

She shook her head.

"I've been jerking off to mental images of you since I first moved in."

Her tongue swept over her lip. "Do it now," she said, sliding off of me.

"What?" I asked in half-amusement, half-shock.

"Play with yourself. I want to watch you."

I was positive my face had one hell of a shocked look on it. "You want me to jerk myself off while you watch?"

She nodded.

"When in the hell did you get so kinky?"

Leaning down, she brushed her lips over mine gently. "I don't know. This is a new side of me and I sort of like her."

"I fucking love her."

"Then will you let me watch you?"

Tossing the covers off, I pulled my cock out of my pants and stroked myself. My eyes locked on Paige as she watched my every move.

She licked her lips, moaned, chewed on her lip, squirmed as she sat next to me. God, I was going to lose my load any moment, but I didn't want this to end. She was watching me like she'd never seen my dick before, and it was hot as hell.

Then her eyes flicked up to mine. We stared at each other for a moment before she opened her mouth slightly.

"Lucas, I want you."

"Thank you, Jesus." I let out a sigh of relief and took my pants off. I pulled the silk nightshirt over her head and took in the sight of pure perfection before me.

"I've missed you, for so damn long I've missed you, Paige," I whispered, leaning down and taking a nipple into my mouth. Her fingers went into my hair while she let out a long moan.

"Now. I need you now. I can't wait a second longer," Paige panted.

Pushing her down, I moved over her and in one movement, I pulled her pajama shorts and her panties off, tossing them to the side.

Paige spread herself open, and I wanted to taste her, but she grabbed at me, pulling me up to her while she wrapped her legs around me.

"Make love to me, Lucas. Please."

My cock was pressed against her entrance, ready to dive in when I remembered my wits. "I need a condom."

Paige nodded as I jumped out of bed and grabbed my wallet.

She stopped me before asking, "Have you ever slept with anyone without a condom on?"

"Of course not. Not ever."

"Same here."

The thought of Paige having sex with another man nearly drove me mad.

"How many guys have you been with?" I asked, not sure why I did.

Her brow raised. "Do you really want to have that conversation now?"

"No. Not really, but I want to know."

"Since you, only two."

I stared at her for a moment before I ripped the packet open and slipped the condom on.

"I'm on the pill since we're putting our business out there."

Moving to the bed, I settled between her legs, then pushed the tip of my cock inside her, causing her to suck in a breath.

"That's two too many."

She smiled, then dug her heel into my lower back, pushing me in deeper.

"Paige, are you sure?"

"Yes, I'm sure. I want this, Lucas. God, I want this."

"I love you. I've always loved you," I whispered against her lips before kissing her and pushing myself all the way in.

Her arms wrapped around mine, and she held me tight. For a few seconds, I didn't move, enjoying the tightness of her wrapped around me. Our hearts hammered, and I had never in my life felt such complete happiness. Such completeness.

Slowly, I moved in and out of her, our kisses soft and sweet as we moved in perfect harmony.

I leaned my forehead to hers as I drew almost all the way out, then pushed back in.

"Yes, Lucas. Faster."

I gave her what she asked for. Soon her hips were meeting me thrust for thrust. Her eyes met mine, and I knew she was close. The feel of her pussy squeezing around my cock nearly had me coming, but I held off. Waited for her. I'd waited this long for her, so I'd wait a little longer for this moment.

"I'm going to come," she whispered.

Our eyes locked and her body trembled, pulling me in even deeper.

"Lucas!" she cried out, her body arched up to mine as I hit the spot she needed for her release. She looked utterly breathtaking as she came. Never once did she take her eyes from mine.

"Paige, oh God."

And just like that, everything in my world fell back into place. The stars aligned. All was right in the world again.

We came together, and it felt like stars exploded behind my eyelids. Holy shit, I had never experienced an orgasm like that before. My body trembled and it took everything I had to hold my body over hers without crushing her.

Our breaths came fast and hard. I was still inside her when I leaned my forehead against hers.

"I don't want to move."

Her fingers moved slowly over my back. "Me either."

I chuckled. "I don't think we understand what slow means."

She laughed and wrapped her arms tightly around me. "That was the best sex I've ever had, not knocking all our other experiences, of course. Just the best sex I've had in my twenties."

I nuzzled my face into her neck and said, "Same for me."

"I know the right thing to do is say we need to pull back some, like we talked about, but the horse is now plainly out of the barn," Paige said, "So, when can we do that again?"

And just like that, I fell even more in love with her.

Chapter 19

Paige

MY GAZE DRIFTED across the attic to Lucas. I was pretty sure I'd be floating around on my orgasmic high for days. I felt different—like I had the first time Lucas and I had had sex. How crazy was it that I was comparing this morning to when I lost my virginity? But the past day with him had been so amazing, and I never wanted to forget it.

Lucas cursed and sneezed as he attempted to move a giant box from the corner where he'd been searching.

We'd been up in this attic for two hours. It was filled with antique furniture and dust, lots of dust. The thought was daunting, considering I had a storage shed also filled with furniture.

"I don't think the chest is up here. I can't find it anywhere," Lucas said.

Glancing around, I sighed. "What in the world are we going to do with all this furniture?"

Lucas shrugged. "I guess we could have an estate sale."

I walked up to the wardrobe chest and pulled open the top drawer that had all the jewelry in it. I had taken a picture of the ruby necklace, as well as a few other pieces, including a small diamond bracelet, and given it to my brother to take to his friend who was a mineralogist. I asked him to see if it was indeed costume jewelry or not. I still couldn't believe all of this was just thrown into a drawer in a wardrobe.

Shutting the wardrobe, I looked around and saw something by the window on the north side of the house. I carefully made my way over and bent down.

A small wooden box sat on top of an old wooden stool. It was no bigger than the size of a shoebox, but it required a key to open it. My heartbeat picked up, and I couldn't have wiped the smile off my face if I tried.

Carefully, I picked up the small box and walked to the sofa and sat. I stared at it while I ran my finger over the name carved on it.

William Lucas Foster.

"Lucas, I found something."

He quickly headed over and sat down. "What did you find?"

I held it up. "I believe this is the chest you have been looking for. It was sitting right on that stool, plain as day."

Lucas looked over at the window, then back down to the box. "You think this is it?"

I nodded and pointed to the keyhole. "It takes a key to open it."

Reaching into his pocket, Lucas said, "Only one way to find out."

He inserted the key, turned it and we both heard the *click*.

"Holy shit! You found it, Paige."

With a giggle, I handed the box to him. "You should open it. William meant for you to find it."

Lucas stared at the box. Then looked at me. "We don't need to open it."

My eyes widened in shock. "What? That's why we've been up here for the last few hours. Searching for this box. For the reason William left us this house."

He shook his head. "I don't care why he did it. All I care about is you. Helping you start your flower shop, going over to my folks' place each Sunday for dinner. Arguing with you on what color to paint our bedroom walls. Planning our wedding in the greenhouse. That's what I care about."

My eyes filled with tears and I tried, without success, to hold them back. When they slipped free, Lucas placed the box to his side and bent down in front of me, his hands on my face, his thumbs wiping away my tears.

"I love you, Paige. For whatever reason we've been given a second chance, and I don't want to question it anymore. The thought of wasting another minute makes me crazy. I want to spend the rest of my life with you, plain and simple."

My throat burned as I fought to hold back a sob. "You really don't know the meaning of slow, do you?"

He laughed and pulled my mouth to his, kissing me. When our foreheads met, we both let out a contented sigh. I drew back first.

"I want all of that, too, but I also want to honor William's wishes. He wanted you to find this chest. It must have been important to him."

Lucas closed his eyes and let my words sink in.

"Are you afraid of what you'll find?" I asked.

He opened his eyes and looked directly into mine. "No."

"Then let's do it together."

Lucas picked up the box, sat down next to me. I laced my fingers with his and smiled.

He opened the box, and we both looked inside it. We exchanged a quick glance, then Lucas picked up a stack full of envelopes.

"They're handwritten letters," he said as he opened the top letter and drew a deep breath. "It's from Grams to Granddad," he added in a barely-there voice.

I moved closer to him. "Do you want me to read them?"

He handed me the letter and nodded.

I cleared my throat, drew in a breath, and read.

Dear William,

Please do not be upset with me. I was confused and scared. I know today you asked me to be yours. I cannot, at least, not now. I do love you with all of my heart, though. Please never doubt that. Don't be angry with Lou, there is nothing inappropriate going on between us. He agreed to help me, to see that I got off safe. I knew if

I told you of my plans, you would stop me. I need to do this, William. I fear if I don't, I will forever wonder if my life was full or not.

This is my choice to leave Johnson City, to travel the world and..."

My voice trailed off. Lucas pulled me closer, his arm wrapped around my waist.

"Keep reading, Paige. Please."

I lifted my gaze to his. "The wardrobe trunk. She left him the day he asked her to marry him." When I looked back down at the date on the letter, tears filled my eyes. "It's dated almost a year before the letter we found in the observatory. Why would she have left him?"

Lucas looked just as confused as I felt. "I don't know. It sounds as if she declined his proposal, then he asked her again, but they didn't marry for another year? So two years after his original proposal is when they married. Why did they wait so long?"

"Because she wanted to travel, see the world," I said. I swallowed hard, trying to clear the heaviness in my throat. Lucas reached over and tucked a piece of hair behind my ear.

"Keep reading."

I focused back on the letter.

This is my choice to leave Johnson City, to travel the world and experience the things I have read about in my books. I wish when I had begged you to run away with me, you would have agreed. Instead, you called me a silly girl with big dreams. I guess that is what I am then, a foolish girl who wants to see the world. Who wants to visit the places she has dreamed about.

I will understand if you wish not to take me back. I know rumors will run wild, and I know what they will say about me. Please know it is not true. I will remain true to you and only you, William. You have my word.

I will write when I arrive in Paris. Lou is to accompany me on the ship, then he is going to England to visit his aunt and uncle and will return home ahead of me. I do have a schedule. I left it on your bed. Read it, my darling, and it will be as if you are with me. Or better yet, come join me, William! Come explore the world with me. Together!

Lucas let out a disbelieving laugh. "What in the hell? She left with Granddad's best friend, then asked him to meet her in Europe before they were even married? And here we were worried about rumors."

I gave him a soft smile. "Poor William. He must have been heartbroken. To read where she wanted to go and not be able to go with her. Why wouldn't he have gone with...?"

Lucas and I stared at each another. I set the letter in my lap and covered my mouth with my hands. It wasn't exactly our story, but suddenly it all felt too familiar.

Lucas closed his eyes and shook his head. "It makes so much more sense why Granddad was angry with me. Why he begged me to go after you...because he hadn't gone after Grams and he regretted his decision."

"Why did he not go after her, though? Or why didn't they travel after they married? Surely they could have compromised."

Lucas looked away. "Maybe stubbornness runs in the family."

Lucas flipped through the letters, finding another one and opening it.

"This one is dated six months later."

"Six months! How long was May gone?"

He shook his head and started to read.

My Dearest William,

I have not heard from you and I must be honest, I was hoping to see you in London. I waited at the restaurant I wrote to you about. I'm sure I don't have to tell you how heartbroken I was when you didn't arrive. I guess that is the silly romantic girl in me, thinking you would run after me and follow me on this journey. I feel so silly. I feel ashamed. I abandoned you and do not fault you for doing the same, if that is what you have done.

I've met some lovely people and have encountered a duke here in London. He is a distant cousin of a wonderful woman I have met and has gifted me with a beautiful necklace made of a ruby from what I suspect might be from a distant queen of England. He laughs when I ask him about it and tells me I should write books with an imagination like mine. It is a thought...write books about my travels. I could fill journal after journal with the tales. Oh, how I wish you were here with me. I cannot wait to show you the wonderful things I have found for our home when I return.

Love you always and forever,
May

Lucas set the letter to the side and searched for another. "This one is dated ten months after the first."

With a shake of my head, I looked at Lucas in disbelief. "She was traveling in Europe for a long time, I think."

"I don't know." Lucas started to read the letter.

My Dearest William,

I have received your letter. Words cannot even begin to describe the pain in my heart. I realize how selfish I have been with my travels, and I am to return home at once. I understand if I am too late.

Love you always and forever,
May

I turned the letter over.

"What did his letter say?" I asked.

"I don't think my father knows any of this."

"William or May never mentioned it to me, in all of our talks. Even when May passed, he always made it sound like they were so happy. He said she was always a carefree soul. Wait. He told me once she loved to travel. I just assumed he meant with him."

I reached into the box and pulled the very last letter out. "This one is dated only a month later."

"What does it say?" Lucas asked.

My Dearest William,

I am sorry I was unable to attend your wedding. I simply could not bring myself to watch you marry. I wish you all the happiness in the world. I won't pretend my heart is not broken, but I do not blame you. I left you no choice. We, my love, have not been given a second chance, and that is a permanent ache in my heart that I will live with until the day I die.

I love you...for always and forever.

Yours,

May

Lucas grabbed the letter from my hand and stared at it.

"What?" he asked, shaking his head in disbelief. "I'm so confused. Granddad was married before he married Grams?"

I didn't want to admit to Lucas that I was even more confused. William had said all the answers as to why he gave us shared ownership of this house could be found in this chest. But all that was in this chest was more confusion and heartache.

Standing, I attempted to figure it all out in my head. "Now the other letter makes sense. The one he wrote to 'M'. That date is only two days before this one, from May. So, was 'M' not May, but someone else?"

Lucas looked dumbfounded. He glanced back into the box. "Wait, there's one more letter."

I turned and watched him open it and read the first few lines. His eyes widened in disbelief.

"What! What is it? What does it say?"

He swallowed hard. "I think it's the answer we've been looking for."

Chapter 20

Lucas

THE PIECE OF paper was the reason my granddad had given both Paige and me ownership in this house. I just couldn't believe it. Everything I had always thought I knew about my grandfather and Grams was gone in an instant. It explained Paige's love of the house and why Granddad had given her a share in it. It was literally in her blood.

"Lucas, what does the letter say?"

"It's not a letter, it's a marriage certificate."

I handed it to Paige. She stared down at it in utter disbelief.

"Holy shit." Her eyes bounced back up to mine.

"This house is as much yours, as it is mine," I said.

Paige looked back down at the certificate, then up at me before she focused on the paper and read it. "I hereby declare the marriage of Lucas William Foster to Millie Rose Miller." She covered her mouth and stared at the paper.

Millie Rose Miller was Paige's grandmother. If my head was spinning, I knew for a fact, so was Paige's.

"William was married to my grandmother? Why would he never mention it?"

"If I remember right, you never met your grandmother."

"No," Paige said, looking utterly confused. "She died while giving birth to my ... father."

Paige's face turned white as a ghost. "Oh my God, are we...?"

"No. There's no way. There is no way Granddad would have ever have allowed that to happen. You and I were friends. I told him I had a crush on you; he wouldn't have allowed it. Not even to hide a secret."

"Wait, I need to sit down. None of this makes any sense. My father was raised by his dad, but was he his dad or was it William?" She looked up at me. "What is William trying to tell us, Lucas?"

I rubbed the back of my neck, wishing like hell we had just let all this bullshit go. But even I was starting to doubt everything. Was William Paige's grandfather also?

"The other letters we skipped over. We have to read all the letters!" Paige cried out.

Paige and I sat back down and started reading through the letters my granddad had kept.

"We must have skipped something," she said. "We have to keep looking."

I nodded, taking out the stack. "Let's look at the dates on the envelopes when they were mailed."

We opened each letter from Grams. We couldn't find anything else. Paige stood and wrapped her arms around her body.

"He wouldn't have let us date if we were related. He wouldn't have," she mumbled.

I stood and walked back to where Paige had found the chest. I lifted a blanket and nearly jumped for fucking joy. There was another chest, exactly like the one we had found. It was laid on its side; apparently it had fallen over at some point.

"There's another one. Another chest, Paige."

She rushed over to my side. "Does the key fit in there?"

With the chest in my hands, I walked back to the sofa, took the key and slipped it in. I almost let out a cry of joy when I heard it unclick.

Inside the chest were papers, along with a few letters. I pulled out the top paper.

"It's a birth certificate. It's got Granddad's name and Millie's name on it. They had a son, his name was ... Phillip Joseph Miller Foster."

"I'm going to get sick," Paige said, covering her mouth.

"The next paper is adoption papers."

"Adoption papers?" Paige asked.

"Joseph Miller, the brother of Millie Miller Foster adopted his nephew, Phillip Joseph Miller, one month after his birth." I kept reading. "It states in the paper that Phillip is not to ever know who his true father was, that both men agreed to keep it a secret."

"Why? Why would William not want to know his own son?"

I shook my head. "I don't know. But Granddad did know your father. He was friends with him. He did know his son, Paige, just not the way he should have."

"Yes. They talked often, and William was very fond of my father." Her voice trailed off again.

"It looks like Millie got pregnant almost right after their marriage. She died in childbirth. There is a note in here, a letter. It's from Granddad...to you."

Paige looked at me, fear etched in those beautiful eyes. Her hand shook when she took it.

Slowly, she opened it and read out loud.

Dear Paige,

You were but only a week old the first time I laid eyes on you. Oh, how I wish I could have held you. Time had healed my broken heart, but by then it was too late for the truth to come out. I wanted to tell you the truth tonight. As we decorated the Christmas tree outside. Oh, how I wanted to tell you how much you looked like your grandmother. Millie was beautiful. She was also my savior. She saved my life, Paige. She was there for me when I was broken in more ways than one. Wounded and sure I would never be able to love again. I was on my way to the train station in Austin, off to run after my first love, May. You see, May was a free spirit when she was younger. An adventurer, much like you. I asked her to marry me, and she got spooked. Ran off to Europe. It didn't take me long to figure out I needed to go after her. But fate had other plans, and I was in a car accident. In the hospital, I met and fell in love again, with a beautiful woman who had been my nurse. Your grandmother, Millie Miller. I used to tease her about her name. Soon, I realized I wanted to marry her. I asked her to move to Johnson City and be my wife. She agreed. When I got back to Johnson City, months after the accident, I had all of May's letters waiting for me, unopened. I couldn't bring myself to read them. I wrote to her and told her I had met someone and fallen in love and was to be married. May returned home right before the wedding, but she must have had second thoughts and never came to the wedding. She left for England a few days later. For the longest time I was so conflicted. You see, I had been in love with two women. I loved your grandmother with all of my heart. When she died giving birth to your father, I nearly lost my mind. No, I did lose my mind. I couldn't care for Phillip, and your great-uncle, whom you have known as your granddaddy, stepped in and raised his nephew as his own son. I took every piece of furniture that had been Millie's and put it in the barn after she passed. I couldn't bear to see it because it brought me such sadness. Eventually, I had it all put into a proper storage unit, but you will most likely know that before you ever find this letter. I saved it all for you, Paige. Of course for your brother too, but he never has been the one for those types of things. Those were pieces that meant something to her, family heirlooms, that belong to you. Please let Tom and your daddy look through it as well.

After Millie's death, I took to the bottle. That was when May appeared back in my life. I missed her, I truly did. She was the first woman I had ever given my heart to, and *she would always own a piece of it. When she heard about Millie's death during childbirth, she came back to America. I loved Millie, but Lord, I also loved May, and seeing her again sparked that love once more. May had her own demons, and she had fought them while we were apart. When she showed up on my doorstep, she was nearly three months pregnant. I knew in my heart I wasn't going to let her go again. I couldn't lose another love. We married as quickly as possible. The only person who ever knew the truth was your great uncle. I told him, explained to him that I needed to raise this child, that it was my second chance to get things right. The three of us agreed that we would keep it a secret. All of it. May had a son six months later. We told everyone the baby was premature, and he was little enough to make our lie believable. He was the spitting image of his mother. We named him after her father.*

Paige stopped reading and looked up at me. I instantly knew, but found myself asking, "What was his name?"

"Carl. Carl Lee Foster."

I sat there, dumbfounded. "Does he say if my father knows?"

Fumbling with the letter, Paige went on. "Um, let me keep reading." She took my hand in hers.

Carl Lee Foster is and will always be my son. Just like your father Phillip is my son. I loved them both, but I could only show one that love. Neither of them knows the truth, Paige. I would ask that you honor that wish. It is my hope that Lucas is there with you, if my plan works like I think it will. I know I don't have much time left on this Earth, and with how stubborn the two of you are, I know I will have to work magic to give you both the second chance you need. It's a little push, if you will. An idea I got a few months back when you were speaking about this house. I love you both, Paige. Lucas was my everything, and I do wish I could have told you and Tom how much you truly mean to me. When you were little and fell in love with the observatory, May told me someday you'd marry there, just like your grandmother had. It was why she held the teas in there with you and showed you all the flowers. She knew how much it had meant to Millie and that it was in your blood.

Do not be angry with me. Tell Lucas not to be angry. Everything worked out as it should have. Now, the journey continues on with you both.

Love always,
William

Paige dropped her hands to her lap and the letter fell to the floor as her eyes lifted to meet mine.

"I'm dreaming, right?" she whispered.

I shook my head, leaned down, and picked up the letter. I folded it and looked back at the chest. Another letter was in there, with my name on it. I picked it up and let out a sigh. We'd had enough letters for one day.

I pushed it into my back pocket, then shut the chest and pulled Paige into my arms.

"Lucas," she whispered, her arms wrapping around me. "I need a drink."

Laughing, I slid my arm around her waist and guided her toward the steps. "I need more than one drink."

After making a few phone calls, we had gathered up friends to meet at Luckenbach Dance Hall. Both Paige and I needed a night of distractions. No house, no letters, no adoption papers. Just friends. Something we both had needed more than we had realized.

When Paige met me at the front door, I couldn't drag my eyes off of her. Her hair was pulled up in one of those messy buns. A green dress hugged her body in all the right places, finished off with brown cowboy boots. She smiled when she saw me.

"Don't you look handsome, cowboy."

I winked and pulled her into my arms. To hell with slow.

"I've been itching to dance with you."

Her brows lifted. "Really? Just to dance with me?"

I nuzzled my mouth next to her ear. "If you'd rather I fuck you, I can do that first."

When her breath hitched, I couldn't help but grin.

"Such a mouth on you, Mr. Foster."

"Come on," I said, holding out my arm. "Let's go."

Paige and I had decided we were not going to talk about the discoveries we made earlier. The drive to Luckenbach was filled with small talk until it went silent.

I, for one, was still trying to wrap my head around the fact that Paige was Grandad's birth grandchild, not me. It wasn't that it bothered me; I knew Granddad had loved me, but all I could think about was all the time I'd wasted. I was sure Granddad and Grams were happy, but had Granddad really not wanted to know Phillip better? Anytime I saw William with my own father, he showed nothing but affection. He loved him, as he should have.

"You're thinking, Lucas. Stop," Paige said, reaching for my hand and squeezing it.

I forced a smile as we pulled into the parking lot of the dance hall.

Milo had pulled in right next to us, jumping out of his truck and making his way around the other side to let out his date. Jen and her husband Gene walked down the path toward the dance hall. Soon, a small group of our friends made their way in.

Milo looked back at the truck with a smile and a quick thumbs up. I gave him a head pop. I'd texted him earlier with an idea I'd need his help with. Turning, I looked at Paige. She was staring at me, a delicate smile on her face.

"The only dream I've ever had was marrying you, Paige. It doesn't matter to me where, when, or how, I just want to be with you, and I'm sorry I couldn't figure that out sooner."

Her lips parted slightly, then she looked down at her hands before she met my gaze again.

"So what you're telling me is you're not planning on selling me your half of the house?"

Laughing, I shook my head. "No. I'm not."

"And no chance you're moving out?"

"No chance at all."

Her teeth dug into her lip as a smile bloomed over her beautiful face. "I'm not selling you my half, and there is no way I'm moving out. So where does that leave us exactly?"

I opened the door to the truck and got out. As I walked around the front, Paige watched me. Opening her door, I reached for her hand and helped her out. She leaned against the truck and looked up at me. I pulled out my phone and sent a quick text to Milo. Paige gave me a confused look.

"We've handled so many things badly. I don't want to mess this up again."

"You won't. We won't," she whispered.

Music filtered from the dance hall as we looked into each other's eyes. A light breeze blew her curls, and I lifted my fingers to brush one from her face.

"Do you remember that night we danced in the parking lot of the football stadium after the game?"

With a small nod, she replied, "I remember."

My chest rumbled with thunder as the memory of that night came back in a rush.

"Do you remember the song?"

Before she had a chance to answer, the song started to play.

A single tear slipped free and moved slowly down her cheek. Leaning down, I kissed it away, then whispered, "'To Make You Feel My Love' by Garth Brooks."

"Oh, Lucas."

"I made a mistake, and I'll spend the rest of my life making it up to you, Paige."

I took her hand in mine and drew her against my body, slowly dancing while the song played. I was going to owe Milo big time for making that happen at the exact freaking moment I needed it to.

With the only woman I'd ever loved held tightly in my arms, I sang to her and we let everything but that moment slip away.

When the last note played, I pulled out the ring in my pocket and got down on one knee. Paige shook her head and looked at me in complete shock.

"Lucas."

"Don't say we need to move slow. Ten years is pretty damn slow, if you think about it. We are moving slow...just backwards. I've been carrying this ring with me for a long time. I think it's time I slipped it onto your finger."

Her soft brown eyes were lost in a sea of tears. She bent down and kissed me as she let out half a sob and half a laugh.

"Is that a yes? I need a firm, confirmed yes."

"Yes! That is a confirmed yes."

My cheeks burned with a wide smile as I slipped the ring on her finger. I stood, framed her face within my hands, and pressed my mouth to hers. After a soft moan, I deepened the kiss. I wanted to take her back to our house and make love to her all night, but I also wanted to shout to the world that this woman, this amazing, beautiful, loving woman was going to be mine.

We broke the kiss when we both needed to breathe. Paige gazed up at me, and I swore I saw the stars dancing in her eyes. I wished Granddad were here, so I could tell him thank you. If it hadn't been for him, none of this would be happening.

Meeting her gaze, I kissed her forehead and said, "Tell me what you're thinking, Paige."

She touched the side of my face and took in a slow breath before letting it out.

"How happy I am. How unimaginably happy I am."

Chapter 21

Paige

THE MOMENT WE walked into the dance hall, our friends erupted in cheers. Lucas wrapped his arm around me and pulled me to him. Milo walked up to us and shook his head.

"Jesus, Mary, and all the Josephs in Bethlehem. Only you two would go from enemies to engaged in what? A week's time?"

Lucas shot him the finger. "What are you talking about? This is us going slow."

Milo looked confused, and I laughed as I exchanged a look with Lucas. The private joke was just that, private. We didn't need to explain anything to anyone. I knew the only people who would worry would be our parents. My father, mostly, who would say we were moving entirely too fast. But that was a worry for later.

We spent the rest of the evening simply enjoying ourselves. We danced, we kissed, we made out in a back corner like two teenagers, then we danced some more. Jen was confused, especially when she saw the engagement ring on my finger. We hadn't told anyone, and even though Jen had caught a glimpse of it right off the bat, she didn't push the issue, and honestly, I was relieved. So many emotions had hit me in the last twenty-four hours. I wasn't sure I was able to take any more.

Our friends slowly started to bug out, one by one they said their goodbyes and we thanked them for coming. I had been worried at first about how it would go. Neither Lucas nor I had really hung out with our friends from Johnson City in ages. A few had gotten married, one or two had kids, but once we all got together, everything fell into place. When we had called our friends and told them we were going out to celebrate getting back together, they'd all been so supportive. I had missed this group of friends. The small talk between the years, the random texts or Christmas cards hadn't been nearly enough. Lucas made everyone take a vow we'd do this once a month.

When only Milo stood before us, the last of our friends, he picked up my hand, smiling at the ring. His eyes lifted, and he looked at me, then Lucas.

"Do I even want to know what happened between you two?"

Lucas and I exchanged a knowing look, then both said at the same time, "No."

"Fine, I'm going to just go with it. You're back together, you may or may not be engaged, and I'm going to guess there is no more talk of buying anyone out?"

"You would be correct," Lucas said.

"On which part?" Milo asked.

"All of it," Lucas said with a slap on Milo's arm.

He rolled his eyes. "You two were always so weird."

I stood in the middle of the large, open room. "I can see it now! The brick walls will be painted white. Maybe some cabinets over here, in a light shade of pink or even white and grey."

Lucas leaned against the opposite wall with a wide grin. It had been four days since we had stumbled onto the two chests. Two weeks since he had moved in. And everything had been perfect.

"You know, the furniture in the storage shed...there might be some pieces you could use for the flower shop."

I smiled. "Lucas, that's an amazing idea."

We had yet to make our way to the storage unit. I knew we were afraid of digging up any more secrets.

"Will you sell other things, besides flowers?" Jen asked.

"I think so! It would be so fun going to market. You could come and help me pick out some things."

"What is market?" Lucas asked.

"It's a trade show where you can go and look for items to carry in your stores," I answered.

Jen walked around tapping her finger to her chin. "You know, there is a girl here locally who makes soaps and lotions using goat milk. You could talk to her about carrying her items here. She even does soap petals to put into baths. They are amazing."

Excitement bubbled up. "I love that idea! And the apiary that's right outside of town has products from their honey bees. We could stock their stuff, as well."

Jen nodded in excitement.

"What about baskets?" Lucas said out of the blue.

Jen and I turned to look at Lucas. So far, he had remained quiet, asking a question here or there.

"Baskets?" I asked.

He looked unsure of what he was going to say. "Never mind. I was thinking out loud."

"Please tell me what you were going to say. I want your input too, Lucas."

His smile seemed uneasy. "This one time I saw this flower shop, and it reminded me of you. On the outside, the owner had wicker baskets that were filled with flowers. It reminded me of you when you would walk the flower garden with your mom and Grams. You'd cut the flowers and lay them in the baskets. I always thought it looked nice. Might look cute outside your little flower shop."

My jaw fell open, and I rushed over to Lucas, throwing myself into his arms.

"It was a cute idea, but don't you think you're giving him a little too much credit?" Jen asked.

Lucas chuckled and wrapped his arms around me. "Not that I'm complaining, but what was that for?"

I kissed him. Lucas pushed his fingers in my hair, drawing me even closer as he deepened the kiss.

"Okay, seriously, I know you're making up for lost time, but no one falls into a romantic kiss like that for the hell of it!" Jen stated.

Smiling against Lucas's lips, I whispered, "You just named the shop."

His brows pinched in. "What?"

"When I was in France, right outside of Paris, there was this little flower shop, it was called The Little Green Shop. I thought at the time that it was a cute name. You said the little flower shop, instead of green, but it's the perfect name."

I took a step back and tilted my head as I regarded him. "As a matter of fact, there were baskets outside, with flowers in them."

Lucas let his smile slip, and I realized why he had acted so indifferent. "You've seen that shop, haven't you?"

"I've seen hundreds of flower shops, Paige."

I shook my head, and a rush of sadness swept over me that I couldn't stop, even if I had wanted to. Lucas and I had been living in a bubble the last four days, so much so that we still hadn't talked. About anything. It had been easier to push it all aside and be in the moment.

"Was it in Paris? With Bianca?"

He looked away and over to Jen. I followed his gaze and saw my friend give him an expression that might have been a warning to tread lightly. She lifted her brows and took a few steps back. "I'm going to step outside, take a look at the exterior and see what your dad is thinking, Lucas."

Lucas nodded, then met my hard stare.

"Yes, I think we saw the same flower shop," he finally said.

I turned away and walked into the middle of the store. I knew I was feeling childish, but I couldn't help it. No matter how happy we were in this moment, it still hurt knowing he had traveled to so many places with Bianca. Places he should have gone with me. I had wanted to experience those places with him. I couldn't help but think of May. She had to have felt the same way when William never came after her.

186

"If I could go back in time, Paige, I'd be there with you. I wasn't even with Bianca that day. She was at a photoshoot, and I was walking around Paris. I saw the shop and walked into it."

I gasped and turned around. "Were you in a blue coat?"

With a befuddled expression, he asked, "What? When?"

"Were you in a blue coat? The day you walked around Paris? I saw the flower shop and stopped to admire the flowers. When I glanced into the shop, I thought I saw you. Dressed in a blue coat. I berated myself for thinking it could be you, but I knew you had gone to France before with Bianca. I went to step into the shop but was too nervous about how you would react if you saw me. Then I realized how stupid I was and went back the next day. I vowed I wasn't going to do it, but I asked the shop owner if she remembered a man from the day before. She said yes, he was American, but that was all she could remember. It was you! Wasn't it?"

"Honestly, Bianca always had me dressing in the stupidest of clothes, but it could have very well been me."

I nodded, then looked away. I didn't want the excitement of only a few moments ago to slip away, but it did.

Lucas wrapped his arms around me, holding my back tightly against his chest.

"We can't change the past, but I promise I'll do whatever I can to make your future—our future—beautiful."

My eyes closed as I dropped my head against his sturdy body.

"I'm sorry," I whispered. "I'm sorry for reacting that way. It was childish, and I don't know what came over me."

He leaned his chin on the top of my head and let out a long breath of air.

"We need to talk, Paige. We're playing pretend, and we need to talk about it. All of it."

I let out my own exasperated sigh. "I know. Let's go home."

I turned in his arms, and Lucas lifted my chin until our eyes met. There was so much emotion in his look. Love, regret, anger, sadness. Both of us had a whirlwind inside and pretending like the past had never happened was only causing the whirlwind to turn into a hurricane.

He leaned down and kissed me gently. My arms instinctively wrapped around his neck, and he held me tighter, lifting me off the ground as he sucked on my tongue, then nipped at my bottom lip.

"I love you," we said together.

We laughed and quickly stepped apart when Lucas's dad cleared his throat.

"When did this happen?" he asked.

Lucas and I exchanged a look and then focused back on his father.

"A few days back," Lucas answered.

Carl nodded. "Your granddad always said it was fate that the two of you would end up together. When he told me about leaving the house to both of you, I wasn't so sure it would work. I would have rather he told you the truth."

I swallowed hard and looked at him.

"What do you mean by that, Dad?"

With a laugh, Carl walked into the room. He glanced over his shoulder, making sure we were alone before he spoke.

"I know the truth. That William wasn't my father by blood."

My hand came up to my mouth as I tried to hide the quick intake of breath. "How do you know? Did he tell you?"

Carl glanced sadly down at the floor before looking back over to Lucas to give him a slight smile.

"No, he didn't tell me. About six years ago a gentleman from England came to see me. He claimed he was my brother and that I had been named in the will of his father. Apparently, my biological father had a guilty conscience about abandoning your grams."

Lucas ran his hand over his face and let out a mumbled curse. "Dad, I just found out only a few days ago. Granddad said you didn't know and asked us not to tell you."

"I know. I never told him about the visit. I had been willed some land in Scotland. Apparently dear ol' Dad was a lord or a duke or some bullshit. I informed them that I didn't want anything and that it belonged to their family. We went about having it legally turned over to my half-brother. He's a nice guy. We've kept in touch over the years, as friends. I didn't tell your granddad. I figured he and Grams had their reasons. But it was never lost on me how much you looked like William, Paige. The connection the two of you shared. It's a small town, rumors still got around. No one will say it, but everyone knows Dad gave up his son that his first wife had the night she passed way."

A tear ran down my cheek. "Does my father know?" I asked.

Carl rubbed the back of his neck. "He's heard the rumors. We grew up together and people talked, but we both ignored it. I think deep down your granddad knew we both knew. Phillip adored William, and William adored him. Just like he adored you, Paige."

Lucas paced across the room. "This is so fucked up. Why didn't Paige and I hear any of these rumors? Y'all didn't think to say anything to us? If you and Phillip knew why William left the house to us like he did, why the hell didn't you say anything? Why make us find out like that?"

He shrugged and gave us a half-smirk. "I think your granddad wanted you both to go on that adventure together, the one you never got to go on with each other. He's probably laughing as we speak."

I could see that Lucas didn't find any of this funny. He shook his head and walked out of the store.

Carl looked at me, and I pulled in a deep breath before letting it go. "It's been an emotional rollercoaster the last few days."

He chuckled. "I can only imagine. May I give you a piece of advice, Paige?"

I nodded. "Yes, please."

"Let the past go. None of what happened two years ago, or even ten, is going to change your future. You decide the path you're going to take. I see the way the two of you look at each other. Everyone has seen it from the first time you walked hand in hand up the pathway to that house. Be there for each other. Stop and listen to your concerns, fears, dreams. And most important of all, follow your heart. It will always lead you home."

My chin trembled as I attempted not to release my sobs. The words of two different Foster men felt like they had pierced into my soul and instantly grounded me.

Nothing else in this world mattered but being home. And home wasn't a house. Or a job. It was him.

Lucas was and would forever be...home.

Chapter 22

Paige

I LOCKED THE store and turned to face Carl and Jen. "He left?" I asked Jen. She gave me a sympathetic smile and nodded.

"He said he was heading to the ranch to fix a fence for you, Carl."

With a hearty laugh, Carl pulled me in for a hug, then kissed me on the forehead. "The boy always did take to hard labor to work out his anger."

I echoed his smile with one of my own. "I remember."

"Stop by. I'll have Lynn make us some dinner."

"I will after I run home and change. Can you get me your estimate for the front of the shop if I draw up some ideas?"

He nodded. "The building is in great shape. I think if you purchase it, you'd be making a wise investment."

"I agree," Jen said.

There was no way I could contain my smile. "I'm going to put in an offer, but I know the bank will want to see a business plan. I can have one written up quickly once I get the bids in."

"We can chat at dinner, maybe then you can give me your vision."

Reaching up on my toes, I kissed his cheek. "Thank you."

He winked, then turned to Jen. "I'll see you girls around. I need to run a few other errands."

We watched as Carl made his way to his truck. Once he was in and pulled out, I faced Jen. "Am I crazy?"

"Do you really want me to answer that?"

"Yes," I said, wrapping my arm around hers as we made our way to the car.

"Well, what exactly are you asking me about? Your relationship with Lucas, which I might add happened rather quickly, even if no one was surprised. Everyone always thought the two of you belonged together."

"I always knew I was crazy in love with him. He makes me stop thinking straight. That's a whole other 'night out with drinks' conversation. What I mean is, am I crazy for opening a flower shop?"

She stopped walking and faced me. "You're asking me if I think it's crazy that you're following a dream? No, I think it's amazing. I envy you, Paige. And no matter what, you know I'll always support you."

"Why are you such a good friend?"

With a half shrug, she replied, "I have to be. You know some of my darkest secrets from when we were younger. If I don't keep you happy, you could let them out."

Laughing, I held her closer to me. "I would never."

"Ha! That's the difference between you and me. If you don't give me free flowers and let me help run this little shop, I'm going to tell Lucas how you described his cock to all of us that one night you got drunk at my sixteenth slumber party."

Gasping, I jerked away. "I never did any such thing!"

She raised a brow.

My cheeks heated, and I covered my mouth to hide my giggle.

"It was rather descriptive, wasn't it?"

"Yes, and I had nightmares about cocks for weeks. I'm pretty sure your detailed description of it and how it worked made Annie Mason ask her mother about it, and that was why she was never allowed to hang out with us again."

We both fell into a fit of laughter, and it felt amazing to laugh like only best friends could.

The moment I pulled down the driveway and saw the BMW, my heart raced. Lucas's truck was parked in front of it. My hands shook. *Weird.* He said he was going to his parents' ranch.

Pulling up next to the BMW, I turned off my car. I slipped out and walked toward the front porch.

He wouldn't. He wouldn't hurt me again. I knew it with every ounce of my being.

I turned the handle of the front door and walked in.

Male voices could be heard coming from the kitchen. I walked in and found Lou Howard sitting at the kitchen table with Lucas. They were both looking at papers.

"What's going on? Lucas, I thought you were going to your folks' place?"

Lucas looked up and gave me a smile. "Lou needed to meet with me, so we met here."

I looked from Lucas to Lou and back again. "What's going on?"

Lou cleared his throat. "Lucas asked me to draw up some papers for him a few days ago. I'm getting him to sign them."

My stomach clenched. "What kind of papers?"

Lucas smiled as he made his way over to me. "I've asked Lou to bequest my half of the house back to you."

"What?" I asked in a shocked voice. "Why would you do that? When did you do that?"

"The other morning, before we found the chest."

I was stunned into silence. "I don't want you to. Why would you do that?"

He smiled, and my knees felt weak. "Because I wanted you to know none of it mattered anymore."

"But you never said—"

"I honestly never thought we'd find anything."

"This house belongs to you as much as me. It's ours. Both of ours. We're going to get married here, raise a family, pour a crazy amount of money into making it amazing. All together. Not because we each own a share of it, but because it's ours."

I shook my head, almost violently.

Lucas placed his hand on the side of my face and whispered, "Shhh, don't get upset."

"I am upset."

I stepped around him and walked to Lou. Glancing down, I saw the papers Lucas was about to sign. I picked them up and ripped them in half.

"Christ, Paige!" Lucas shouted as he rushed over to me.

"This is insane!"

Lou sat back in the chair, smiling. "Lord, the two of you remind me so much of William and May. It's unbelievable. It really is."

Lucas and I faced Lou. "What?" I asked in a disbelieving voice.

"Holy shit, you know the truth, too?" Lucas asked.

Lou let out a roar of laughter as he gathered up his things. "Of course I know. I was his best friend. William told me everything. My father was the one who drew up the adoption papers for both boys."

I stared at Lou, my shock growing.

"I was wondering when you came in and asked me to refuse your bequest, if you had both found your answers yet. I see that you have."

"Why didn't you just tell us, Lou?" I asked.

He picked up his briefcase, looked at me, then Lucas, and then roared with laughter again. "Now, what would be the fun in that?"

Lucas and I stood in the kitchen and watched Lou walk away.

"Enjoy your evening," he called out as Oreo came bounding into the kitchen.

Once we heard the front door shut, I faced Lucas and smacked him on the chest. "You ass!"

"What?"

"Why did you think I would want to take this house from you?"

He smirked. "To be fair, only weeks ago you were *trying* to take the house from me."

I rolled my eyes and tossed my hands up. "I need a drink."

Drawing me into his arms, Lucas pressed his mouth to mine. "First, we're talking."

He grabbed two beers from the refrigerator and walked us out onto the back porch. We sat down, and I took a long drink before looking out over the landscape.

"First, we need to tell our parents we're engaged," he said.

"You know they're going to lecture us. Tell us we're moving too fast."

"Let them," he said. "Second, nothing about what we found out changes anything in my eyes."

With a smile, I reached for his hand. "It doesn't change anything for me either."

"Good. Next thing, and probably the most important, I hate the color of paint you picked for the office."

My mouth dropped open. "What is wrong with the color?"

"It's pink."

"It is not pink! It's a very light peach and it was the color of that room when it was first built. I found a strip of the original paint in the closet and took a picture of it. They matched the color."

"The office is mine, you even said so. I don't want that color. Maybe a blue."

"Ugh, blue?"

"What's wrong with blue?"

I shrugged and took another pull from the beer. "I guess I can find a blue shade that was used during that timeframe."

"Next, I want to go somewhere neither of us has been before for our honeymoon."

"Honeymoon? We're restoring a house, I'm opening a new business, you're going to be driving back and forth to Austin. Life is crazy. I think we need to push the idea of a wedding back some. At least until things settle."

He shook his head. "Nope."

With narrowed eyes, I asked, "No...to what?"

"The house only needs paint and some furniture changed around. The kitchen is the biggest renovation, and we can handle that. Milo is taking care of the outside reno. Between the two of us, we can take care of the interior painting."

"Yes, but eventually you'll be returning back to work full time."

Lucas looked at me with a serious expression. "About that. I've decided to take a job offer I received earlier today."

"From who?" I asked.

"My father. We always wanted to work together, so I'm going to take it."

A warmth spread through my entire body. "Lucas, this is amazing news!"

He smiled, then let it fade some. "I won't make as much money as I was making, but it'll still be a decent amount. Plus, I'll be helping on the ranch more. Dad really needs it. Your father could also use an extra hand to give Tom some time off every now and then."

I sat down in his lap. The way he held me, his hand on my waist, sent a bolt of excitement and lust racing straight to my core.

"I know Daddy would love that, and Tom will appreciate it."

He set his beer down, then pushed a stray strand of hair behind my ear. "As far as marrying you, Paige, I feel like I have wasted so much time, and I know it's only a piece of paper, but I've wanted to marry you for as long as I could remember. I don't want to wait. Can we go *slow* on the wedding, too?"

Smiling, I wrapped my arms around his neck, then kissed him gently. "Six months. Let's let everything settle for that long, which will give us time to get the greenhouse in order for our wedding."

The way he smiled made my breath catch in my throat. "You still want to get married in there?"

"Yes, I do."

He frowned and let out a breath. "I'm going to have to think of a wedding present to match Granddad's present to Millie."

I turned and straddled him in the chair. "The only thing I want is you."

"That I can give you as freely and as frequently as you want."

I pressed against his hard-on. "How about now?"

Lucas groaned. "Here? Right now?"

"Yes." I lifted my shirt over my head and tossed it to the side. Lucas let out a guttural growl from the back of his throat as he ran his thumb over the peak of my nipple. I gasped when he sucked it through the lace fabric.

"More," I panted, reaching down to unfasten the button and zipper on his jeans. "I want more."

"I don't have a condom," Lucas replied, unclasping my bra strap with expert fingers.

"I want to feel you, Lucas. All of you."

He paused and stared at me. "What?"

"I don't want you to wear condom."

When his brows pulled in, I hated the look on his face.

"But if you don't want—"

He placed his hand on the back of my neck and pulled my mouth to his, cutting my words off with the most passionate kiss I'd ever experienced.

"Get undressed," he said gruffly, lifting me to stand. We quickly discarded the rest of our clothes. Lucas sat back down in the chair, his eyes sweeping greedily over my body.

"The idea of being inside you bare...I'm not going to last long, babe."

I smiled and straddled him in the chair. "That makes two of us."

His fingers slipped into my body first, and we both moaned. "Fucking hell, you're so wet."

I rolled my hips. "I want you so much."

When he withdrew his fingers, I let out a whimper of protest. His hands went to my hips and guided me down onto him. My eyes closed as he filled every inch of me.

"God, yes," I hissed when I was fully seated on him. I rolled my hips instinctively, but he dug his fingers into them.

"Wait, don't move."

"Is something wrong?" I asked, watching the pained expression on his face.

"It feels... God, it feels... I need a second, Paige. If you move, I think I'm going to come."

With a giggle, I placed soft kisses along his jawline, then down his neck. "You feel so good inside me."

He moaned when I moved slightly.

"Lucas, I have to move. I'm dying to move."

"I can't think straight. I've never had sex without a condom, this is big."

My fingers sliced through his dark brown hair before I grabbed a handful and pulled his head back, causing him to look into my eyes.

"I want to fuck you," I said.

"Oh God, I think I might have just come a little."

I moved my body up and down, slowly at first, rolling my hips and loving the way his body rubbed against mine. It wasn't going to take me long to come, and judging by how hard Lucas was, I had a feeling it wouldn't take him much longer.

"It feels so good," I whispered, moving faster, rolling my hips as I felt him inside me. "Lucas."

His name sounded more like a plea than anything. I was aching to come. Needing to feel him deeper inside. The idea that he was going to come inside me left me nearly panting with lust and desire.

"Fuck me faster, Paige. Harder."

I gripped my hands onto his shoulders and moved faster. The sound of my body hitting his filled the air, mixing with the sounds of nature. It was one of the most amazing moments of my life.

"I'm so close," I gasped.

Lucas moved his hand down between us and pressed against my clit, causing me to buck even harder.

"Fuck, I'm not going to last. Paige. *God.*"

His voice was strained, and I loved that I was bringing this out in him.

The buildup of my orgasm came fast and raced through my entire body, causing me to cry out his name while I dropped my head back. I instantly felt him swell bigger inside of me.

"Christ, it feels so good. I'm coming."

Lucas let out a string of curses mixed with moans of pleasure, and my body trembled again. I didn't know if it was another orgasm, or if my first one hadn't settled down yet. All I knew was my body had never felt anything so amazing.

Feeling spent, I leaned against him while he wrapped his arms around me. Our breathing stayed fast and hard. My heart pounded against his. I loved that we were connected to one another like this. If I thought I could crawl into his body, I would have.

"Holy hell, that was the most amazing moment of my life. I'm never wearing a condom ever, ever again."

I laughed and drew my body back. Still sitting on him, I moved my hips some. He raised a brow and then cupped my face.

"I wish like hell he'd come back up that fast, but I need about thirty minutes after that mind-blowing orgasm."

With a pout, I moved again, feeling the sticky wetness where our bodies were joined.

Lucas moaned and cupped my breasts with his hands. "Okay, ten minutes. I think I only need ten minutes."

"That's more like it, babe, *slow* and steady."

Chapter 23

Lucas

THE NEXT MORNING, I rolled over and smiled when I felt Paige next to me. We had moved from the back porch to the shower, where I fucked her against the shower wall, breaking two of the tiles, which made us laugh hysterically because the whole bathroom needed to be redone anyway.

We moved to the bed, and after an hour of talking about our future, her flower shop, the kitchen remodel, and the fact that we needed to figure out what to do with all the furniture in her storage unit and the attic, I made love to her again. We didn't rush. We just moved slowly. Even our kisses settled down to a softer, deeper level. When I came inside her again, she wrapped her arms and legs around me tightly, whispering in my ear how much she loved me.

No other woman had ever made me feel the things I felt with Paige. As a matter of fact, I could only remember being with her before and now. Every other woman in between faded into the darkness.

I moved my fingertip softly down her arm, watching her breathe. Her body was facing me, and she looked like an angel sleeping. I was about to lean down and kiss her, push her onto her back and make love to her again, when my phone buzzed on the side table.

When I rolled over, I saw that my mother was calling. I thought about not answering but decided I'd better.

"Hey, Mom."

"When were you going to tell us you're engaged!"

I sat up quickly, causing Paige to stir.

"What?"

"I had to find out from someone else that you and Paige are engaged."

"Who told you?"

"Lucy, the checker down at Super S. Do you want to know how shocked I was? So, it's true?"

I frowned, then rubbed my hand over my face.

How in the hell did people find out I had asked Paige to marry me? She had taken off the ring after our night out. We'd agreed she wouldn't wear it until we told our parents.

"Is it true, Lucas? You've only been back in each other's lives for a few weeks. Tell me you didn't do something so insane. Good Lord, it must be in your blood. Your father asked after dating me for two weeks. Look at William and May, they rushed to the altar, too."

Smiling, I kissed Paige on the forehead, eliciting a soft moan from her.

"What was that?"

"Oreo the cat," I replied as I slipped out of bed. "You haven't said anything to Dad yet, have you?"

"Oh my goodness, it's true!"

Walking into the bathroom, I grabbed a pair of shorts and slipped them on. Something about being naked and talking to my mother on the phone felt wrong.

"Yes, I asked her to marry me. We wanted to tell you, Dad, and Phillip together. I was going to call about inviting Paige's dad, Tom, and Katy over for dinner this week."

"Married. Are you sure you both want to rush into this?"

With a sigh, I made my way quietly out of the bedroom and into the kitchen. "Let's see, we own a house and live together. We dated for years before the big fuck up."

"Language, Lucas Foster."

"Sorry. It may seem like we are rushing, but we are taking our time, Mom. We're in love and have never stopped loving one another."

She let out one of those girly sighs that women do when they're watching romantic movies or reading romance novels. "You two always did love each other. Are you sleeping together?"

I groaned. "Mom, I'm really not going to answer that."

"That's a yes. Now, don't think I'm not happy. I'm overjoyed! Thrilled beyond belief. Everyone knew the two of you belonged together, and that horrible Bianca was nothing but a mistake."

"Thanks for that."

"Don't act like you're surprised I couldn't stand the girl."

"More like loathed her, but okay."

"Those were your words just now, not mine. No one knew what you were thinking when you started dating her. You were out of your damn mind, that's for sure."

"Gee, Mom, language. And don't hold back. Can we please stop talking about her? She's in the past."

"Amen to that. Are you using protection? A baby right now would only add stress to the situation."

"Again, I'm not going to answer that question."

"I'm just saying, the two of you have made some serious life changes in the last month. Both of you leaving your jobs, starting new ones, living together."

"I'm working for Dad. I hardly think it will be stressful."

"You must not remember how your dad does things. And what about Paige? She's opening a flower shop! If she got pregnant now..."

"Mom! Paige is not going to get pregnant. Please stop saying that."

"Well, the two of you aren't getting any younger, you know. I wouldn't hold off too long on having kids."

I pulled the phone away from me and dropped my hand to my side. Looking up, I prayed to the heavens for strength and patience.

"What's going on?" Paige asked, walking into the kitchen.

I held up the phone. "My mom. Talking about us having a baby."

Her eyes went wide. "A baby? Does she know something we don't?"

Chuckling, I walked over and kissed her then brought the phone back up to my ear.

"...She was thirty-six when she had her baby, and Lord, the complications."

"Mom, you literally just said we shouldn't have a baby, now you're saying we shouldn't wait."

"That was not what I said, clearly you were not listening to me, Lucas."

"You're right. I wasn't."

Paige shook her head and made her way to the oven and turned it on.

With a deep, calming breath, I said, "Mom, call Phillip. Invite him, Tom, and the girls to dinner this week. We'll announce the engagement then."

Paige spun with a horrified look on her face. I held up my finger in a *wait a moment* gesture.

"In the meantime, please don't say anything to anyone, and if someone like the cashier at Super S mentions it, debunk it for the time being. For me and Paige, okay?"

"I can do that. Do you want me to find out where the rumor generated from? You know I have my ways."

"No," I replied with a chuckle. "It won't matter soon enough. Everyone in town who shops at the Super S will know."

Paige slumped against the counter.

"Your father said you were coming over later, I'll see you then?"

"Yep, see you then."

Hitting End on the phone, I met Paige's gaze.

"Tell me she didn't find out about our engagement from a cashier at the grocery store," Paige said.

"Okay, I won't tell you that."

She rolled her eyes. "Milo or Jen?"

"I'm going with Milo."

Her brow raised. "Really? You think he'd say something to someone?"

"Yes. The new girl he's dating probably told someone else, who then told someone else, who then told the cashier at Super S, who eventually asked my mother about it."

Paige tried to hide her smile, but the corners of her mouth rose slightly. "Gotta love a small town."

"Do you? Because sometimes it's quite annoying." I let out a frustrated sigh. "Were you wanting to go to the storage unit today? I've got to meet Dad to help him with the ranch, then go to a job site in Fredericksburg. I can skip if you want me to go with you."

She shook her head. "No, I'll take a peek around in there. I'm curious to learn more about my grandmother. I'm secretly hoping to find some pieces for the flower shop. Oh, speaking of, we never made it over to your folks' last night. I need to get your dad a rough sketch of what I want the front of the shop to look like."

I smiled. "I sort of already did that for you."

"You designed it for me?" she asked, her eyes lighting up.

"Yeah, last night I got up when you were exhausted from all the incredible orgasms I gave you."

Her cheeks turned a beautiful pink. "You're a stronger human than I am, dear sir. I needed rest after all those. May I see?"

"Of course." I pointed behind her. "My sketchbook is right there."

"You actually drew it? You didn't do it on the computer?"

Warmth spread though my chest at her smile. If anyone knew how much I loved putting pencil to paper and drawing, it was this woman. "It felt good to get back to basics."

Paige took the sketchbook off the counter. She opened it and gasped.

"Lucas, this is exactly how I pictured it in my head." Her eyes met mine. "It's like you stepped into my mind and pulled this out. How did you know this was what I wanted?"

I shrugged. "It's how you described it when we were younger, when you used to dream about owning your own flower shop."

Her eyes pooled with tears. "You remembered that?"

"I remember everything, Paige."

Her hand came up to her mouth, and she glanced back down to the drawing. She looked like she was becoming overwhelmed with emotion, so I made my way over to her. I took the sketchbook from her hands, set it on the counter, and pulled her into my embrace.

"Are you okay?" I asked softly against her hair.

She sniffled, then wrapped her arms around me. "I couldn't imagine doing this without you. I hate that we had to lose William in order to find our way back to one another."

"Me too," I replied, running my hand gently over her back.

Oreo rubbed at our legs, meowing and standing up to paw at me and then Paige.

We both laughed. "Your cat wants food."

Paige reached down to pick up Oreo. She snuggled her face into the cat's neck, and I instantly heard Oreo start purring.

"Good morning, sweetheart. Are you hungry? Did we forget to feed you last night?"

As she made her way to the pantry where she kept the cat's food, I couldn't help but take in the sight in front of me. It felt like everything was exactly how it should be. I was incredibly happy for the first time in a long time.

And in my experience, that meant the shit was surely about to hit the fan.

Chapter 24

Paige - One month later

ISTOOD IN the middle of the flower shop and looked around. Everything was coming along faster than I'd dreamed it would. The interior brick walls had been painted a creamy white. Lucas had measured out how long I wanted the counter and was making it out of reclaimed barn wood he'd found on one of the job sites he was working on with his father.

With a paintbrush in hand, I stared at the antique desk in front of me. It came from the storage unit filled with antique furniture that had been Millie's. I had asked my grandfather if anyone in the family would like to look at the furniture, as well. A few cousins of mine had come and picked out a few pieces. Some Lucas and I brought back to the house, some would be displayed here in the flower shop, and the rest would remain in storage until I figured out what to do. The thought of selling any of the pieces wasn't even an option. The small wooden crib that had been in the house for my father was currently in the flower shop, waiting for a coat of paint. I envisioned filling it with blankets and pillows.

The door chimed, and I turned to see my father. "Daddy, what brings you here?"

He made his way over to me, giving me a kiss on the cheek.

"I ran into Linda May Hacker."

With a roll of my eyes, I replied, "Oh Lord, what did she have to say?"

"Nothing worth repeating. The woman is vile. No wonder your momma couldn't stand her."

"Daddy, be nice." I warned, pointing the paintbrush at him. "Even momma didn't talk ill of her."

"Ha. You just never heard it. And besides, I'm only speaking the truth."

With a smile, I dipped the brush into the can and then started to paint. "Have you talked to Lucas?"

He let out a grunt and picked up a brush, joining in. My father hadn't been all that pleased to find out Lucas and I were engaged. He was still harboring bad feelings about how we had broken up. We'd told him, Tom, Kate, Carl, and Lynn about a month ago at dinner. Lynn, of course, already knew. Carl was happy. My father, yeah, he was still having a hard time with it. Tom and Kate weren't the least bit surprised. Callie and Tom Jr hadn't been there, so we had told them a few days later. The only thing they cared about was being a part of the wedding, which we promised them.

I stopped painting and looked at him. "Daddy, I love him."

"He hurt you. Broke up with you for a stupid-ass reason and then never came back to Johnson City. Took up with some model and traveled all over with her. Why couldn't he have done that with you?"

"It's in the past. I've left it there, why can't you?"

Giving me a hard stare, he shook his head. "Because I'm your father, Paige. I swore on the day you were born I would never let anyone hurt you. And he hurt you, deeply. I hate that he just walked back into your life and you let him without a fuss."

I was positive my jaw dropped to the floor. "Without a fuss? Dad, you don't know what happened between me and Lucas. And I won't apologize for loving him. Yes, he hurt me, but I never stopped loving him. I'm almost positive that if I settled down with someone else, a good portion of my heart would still belong to Lucas until the day I died. A love like that doesn't come along often."

He scoffed. "He doesn't deserve you."

With a sigh, I closed my eyes. I could feel my heartbeat pick up. I hated that I had to defend Lucas. I knew I couldn't have my father hating Lucas for the rest of our lives. It would make everything more difficult. I drew in a few deep breaths and was ready to tell him he had to talk to Lucas and come to some sort of truce. When I opened my eyes again, my father was staring at me. The corner of his mouth rose the slightest bit, and he nodded.

"I'm sorry. I'll talk to him, sweetheart," he said softly, then gave me a slight smile.

"Thank you, Daddy. It would mean a lot to me if you forgave him."

"I know. But if he ever hurts you again, I'm having his legs broken. Slowly."

I tried not to smile, but I lost. "Deal."

"Did you ever find what William wanted the two of you to find?" he asked after a few minutes of us painting in silence. I froze, and he noticed.

"I'll take that as a yes. What was it?"

"Well, it was... um..."

I cursed inwardly. Lucas and I had never come up with a plan on how or what to tell people that we'd found. Lou already knew the truth. So did Carl and Lynn. But my father, as far as I could tell, didn't know.

He frowned as he looked at me. A heavy feeling settled over my chest, and I my hand trembled slightly. Why had I not been prepared for this?

"We...did...find something. He pretty much just wanted us to get our heads out of our asses and get back together."

Daddy narrowed his eyes at me. "Okay. That's what you're going with?"

"It's the truth," I said in a defensive tone.

"Right. You're about as naïve as William, Paige, if you really think I don't know the truth."

I swallowed hard. *Good Lord. Does everyone in this town know?*

Clearing my throat, I said, "I don't know what you mean."

He laughed, then went back to painting. He remained silent for the longest time until I finally couldn't take it.

"Did everyone in this town know William was my grandfather?"

His head snapped up, and he stared at me, in complete shock. *Oh. Shit.*

My father stood there with a paintbrush full of white paint now dripping down his hand, staring at me like I'd lost my damn mind.

"What did you say?"

"Nothing," I quickly replied.

"Paige, what made you say that William was your grandfather?"

I rubbed my lips together, trying to think of a way to get out of what I had just said. A part of me wanted to tell him the truth. Carl had known; how could my father not know?

"Is that your phone ringing?" I asked, glancing down to his pocket where he always kept his cell phone.

"No."

"Lucas went to Paris with Bianca, did I tell you that? The one city I really wanted to go to with him."

Now my father put the brush down, grabbed a paper towel and wiped off his hands. He folded his arms across his chest and glared at me.

"You're trying to change the subject, and it won't work."

I squeezed my eyes shut and blew out a defeated groan before focusing back on my father.

"We found a marriage certificate. William was married to Millie, your mom. Granddaddy was really your uncle by blood, not your father."

He looked at me with a blank expression.

"We found the adoption papers. When May came back from England, which is a long story in and of itself, she was pregnant by some earl or duke or something. William and May married quickly, then she had Carl. William adopted Carl legally. So, you see, William felt obligated to leave me half the house and half of it to Lucas. I know this is a load full of information, and well, when you brought up the truth, I figured you knew because Carl knew."

That made his brow raise even more.

"Oh, I'm making this worse. You didn't know, did you?"

He rubbed his neck and looked away for a few moments. "I had my suspicions. Heard talk around town when I was younger. Asked William about it once, and he just smiled and placed his hand on my shoulder and gave it a squeeze, but he never actually answered the question. I found out a couple of years after your momma and I got married that someone had paid off our ranch. Did some digging and all roads pointed to William. Never did ask him about it, though. I figured he had a reason. I knew I looked just like him, a hell of lot more than Carl did."

I smiled.

"So, to answer your question, I guess I knew, just never admitted it out loud."

"How was something like that kept such a secret?" I asked.

He shrugged. "Country folks know when to keep certain things private and when not to."

"Linda May certainly didn't know."

Daddy laughed. "No, probably because she moved in so late. The old timers knew."

"I didn't know. I had no idea."

"You had an amazing bond with William. I'm glad."

With a smile, I replied, "Me too. I'm sorry you didn't."

"I did. He was a good friend. I loved your grandfather. He was a good man and loved me fiercely. That was probably one of the reasons I chose not to believe the rumors, even though deep down I guess I knew."

"I found William's wedding pictures with Millie. You looked exactly like him when you were younger. Do you want one? I can have some copies made?"

"I'd love one."

"I'll get them right away. There's also a family photo album. I'll bring it by tomorrow. I wasn't sure if maybe we had some cousins or something who might like the pictures. Millie and Grandpa were the only two siblings. I haven't been able to find out if there were any cousins."

"Daddy never had any other kids, so it's just me. All his cousins were from the Austin area. He moved here after I was born."

"To take care of you, because William wasn't emotionally able to."

"So, William left you the house because you are his granddaughter. How did Lucas take that?"

I half-shrugged. "Fine. William adopted Carl, so Lucas was his grandson also."

"He's not bothered that he isn't blood-related?"

"Not at all," I said, giving him a look that asked where he was going with all of this. I placed my hands on my hips and shot him a look that should have bolted him to the floor.

"Do not think for a moment that Lucas is trying to get his hands on the house. Daddy, he asked Lou to bequest his inheritance to me before we even found out."

"He did what?" my father asked, clearly taken aback.

"He tried to give me the whole house. It's just as much his as it is mine. We both want to see it fixed up and raise our own family there, just like we talked about when we were younger."

He walked over to me, pulling me into his arms. "I am happy, sweetheart. I really am. As long as the little prick treats you right and makes you happy, I'm okay with him."

With a giggle, I kissed him on the cheek. "What were you talking about when you said you knew the truth?"

He laughed. "Hell, mine was so much simpler. That William was trying to get the two of you together. I never dreamed it would be all of that."

I shook my head. "It was a shock, to say the least. Are you okay, Daddy? Knowing the truth?"

"I am, princess. Like I said, I always knew it deep down."

With a smile, I motioned back to the desk. "Come on. Let's finish painting this desk, then you can take me for ice cream."

"I like the sound of that plan."

Chapter 25

Paige

PULLING UP TO the barn, I saw Lucas in the corral working a horse. My stomach flipped with desire and a memory flooded in.

Lucas stood in the barn, his cowboy hat tipped low, his green eyes a stark contrast to the black of his hat. He smiled, and it was so mind-blowing that it left me unable to breathe. His boyish looks contrasted his large frame. My fingers itched to trace every inch of his body. To explore how he was built. To feel the way his muscles moved when we finally had sex.

"Are you sure, Paige? We don't have to do this. I'd wait forever for you."

I returned his smile and pulled the dress over my head, leaving only my bra and panties, along with my favorite pair of red cowboy boots. Lucas swept his eyes over my body in a greedy fashion: fast, then slower. The look on his face would forever be etched into my memory. He licked his lips, and I heard myself moan ever so slightly. A pulse between my legs grew faster, harder. God, I couldn't wait for him to be inside me.

"I want this Lucas. I've been wanting this."

After putting my car into park, I made my way over to the fence. I climbed up and sat there, watching him work the whip. The way his muscles moved through his tight T-shirt had my body humming with pure lust.

The horse was just as beautiful a creature as Lucas. The horse's muscles flexed as he ran around the circle, exerting hardly any effort as he seemed to dance over the dirt.

When Lucas lowered the whip, the horse slowed. He came to a stop, then made his way over to him. I watched in awe as he bent his head and Lucas leaned his forehead to the horse's. He whispered something to the horse while he stroked the side of his neck gently.

It was official. I was insanely jealous of the horse.

After watching them for a few minutes, I decided it was time to let them know they had company.

"I hate interrupting this bromance, but I sure wouldn't mind some of that attention."

Lucas faced me. My stomach flipped when he broke into a wide smile, the one he seemed to save for me. I felt my body tremble ever so slightly as he walked toward me.

"This is a nice surprise."

He reached up and helped me jump off the fence, then wrapped me into his arms. The horse came up and bumped Lucas on the back, causing us both to stumble into the corral fence.

"Goodness, looks like I have to fight for your attention," I said with a chuckle as I stroked the horse gently on the neck.

"Ranger remembers you," Lucas said with a bit of mischief in his voice. "Or at least he remembers what you did to me in his stall."

My cheeks heated as the horse snickered. "Sharing is caring, Ranger. I've already told you that once."

"I still feel that hay up my ass."

I laughed harder and took the horse's reins as I walked alongside Lucas. My eyes did a quick sweep of his body.

Wrangler jeans. Tight and sexy.

Stetson cowboy hat. Hot as hell.

Tight T-shirt that left nothing to my imagination. Swoon city.

Cowboy boots, old and well-worn. *Yes, please.*

"If you keep looking at me like that, Paige, Ranger is going to have to watch me take you against his stall."

My body hummed with excitement.

"Then let me look a little harder."

Lucas let out a growl and picked up his pace. "Let me take care of the horse, then I'll take care of you."

I felt my lower lip go numb as I realized I was biting down on it.

Thirty minutes later, Lucas had me up against the wall of Ranger's stall. "Take off your pants."

"It's not that easy. I have on boots," I said with a giggle.

"I only need one boot off, one leg out of your pants."

I gave him a mock expression of surprise. "You'd take me half-dressed?"

"Yes, seven ways to Sunday if given the opportunity."

Moving with lightning speed, I pulled my boot off and dropped it to the side, then slipped my leg out of my jeans. I went to pull my panties down when Lucas grabbed my hand.

"Don't bother." He lifted me, pushed my panties to the side and entered me in one quick movement. I gasped at the sudden fullness.

"Shit, are you okay?" he asked, his breathing ragged.

"Yes. I'm okay. Don't stop."

Lucas moved again. The feel of him inside me, so fast and hard, had my body building faster than ever before. I could feel my orgasm at the beginning stages already as he hit the exact spot I needed him to. I was so close. Adjusting my hips, I gasped. My orgasm was about to hit.

Then everything changed. We weren't alone, and I didn't just mean the horses.

"Lucas was in the corral earlier. They have to be around here somewhere."

With eyes as wide as saucers, Lucas stopped moving the moment he heard his father's voice.

"I tried to call her cell and leave a message."

I closed my eyes. Both of our fathers were in the barn.

Before I could move, Lucas spun and dropped us both to the stall floor.

"So much for no hay in our asses," I whispered.

Lucas threw his hand over my mouth as he rushed to help me get my pants back on. I, on the other hand, started to laugh uncontrollably.

"Stop!" Lucas whisper-shouted.

When we finally managed to get my jeans back on, Lucas crawled and got my boot, then grabbed my hand and moved to the back corner of the stall.

"Ranger's in his stall, so maybe they're outside," Carl said.

Ranger started fussing, clearly not liking how close we were. Lucas looked up at him, pleading eyes and all. Which made me start laughing all over again. I covered my mouth with both hands and closed my eyes. Maybe if I willed it hard enough, both men would walk out of the barn.

That's when I heard Lucas.

"Shit."

I opened one eye and saw my father standing in the stall, looking down at us. Thank God I had my jeans on, although they were still unbuttoned, and I was missing my boot.

"Hey there, Daddy," I said with a wide smile. "What brings you here?"

"Jesus," Lucas groaned, scrubbing his hand over his face.

"Paige. What are you doing on the floor of a stall, half dressed?" The way my father turned and glared at Lucas made me jump up.

"I'm dressed, Daddy."

He lifted a brow.

"I'm also going to be marrying Lucas, so let's not pretend that we're not sleeping together."

"For the love of all things holy, Paige, you're making it worse!" Lucas said.

Now my father was standing with his fists in tight balls. "Foster, you better run if you know what is good for you."

"Phillip," Carl said, a slight bit of humor in his voice. "Leave the boy alone."

"Dad! Are you laughing?" Lucas asked as he hid behind me.

My dad took a step forward. "Hiding behind my daughter is not going to help you, coward."

"For fuck's sake, Lucas. I raised you better than that. Don't hide behind your fiancée. At least get behind the horse."

I started to laugh all over again.

"It's not funny!" Lucas and my father said simultaneously.

"What's everyone doing in here?" Lynn said as she walked up. "Paige! I'm so glad you're here. I found a girl who makes the most amazing wedding cakes."

"Really?" I said, slipping my boot back on.

"What happened?" Lynn asked.

"Your son is what happened. He was... They were...in the stall!" my father managed to say.

As I walked by, I tapped him on the chest. "Oh, Daddy. This isn't the first time in the barn."

"Holy shit! You threw me under the bus, Paige!" Lucas said.

"Son, now would probably be the best time to run," Carl said, laughing again.

With that, Lucas rushed past me and my father and hightailed it out of the barn, my father hot on his tail.

"I didn't realize my dad could still move like that," I said, giggling.

"Well, he's only fifty-three, he still has a lot of get up and go in him," Lynn said as we walked out of the barn.

Carl removed his cowboy hat, ran his fingers through his hair and sighed. "I really should go save my one and only son. I need him alive to help with the courthouse renovation."

Lynn waved her hand in dismissal. "He can surely outrun Phillip. Now, let's talk wedding cakes."

Chapter 26

Lucas

THE MOMENT THE cold bag of corn touched my eye, I hissed.

"Sorry." Paige looked at me with a sympathetic smile. "How did he catch you?'

"The old man is fast! Really fast. I should have remembered that from when he coached football in middle school."

She pressed her lips tightly in an attempt not to laugh. Again.

"Then, after he hit me, do you know what he said?"

Paige shook her head.

"He laughed, first of all, then he told me that was for taking your virginity. I know he knows that wasn't the first time, especially after you told him."

This time she did laugh. Hard.

I rolled my eyes, then groaned when my right eye ached.

"I think he's been waiting to do that for a number of years. The whole hitting you for ruining his little girl thing."

I scoffed. "Little does he know it was all your idea."

"Like you were against it."

"I was! I didn't want to have sex with you for the first time in a stall."

"You didn't complain. Besides, I thought it was romantic. You even put a blanket down for us."

"Only because Milo told me to do it. Experience from when he and Jen did it in the barn."

Paige's mouth dropped open. "Jen and Milo slept together?"

"I thought you knew that."

She shook her head and made a weird sound. "Wait until I see her again. She's always going on about how I never tell her everything. Ugh. How could she not tell me Milo was her first?"

"He wasn't," I replied, drawing a gasp from Paige.

"That little whore!"

I laughed, then gently pulled her hand down. "How's it look? I have a meeting tomorrow with some clients in Austin I'm still trying to finish up with."

She chewed nervously on her lip. "Is it outside? If it is, you might want to keep your sunglasses on."

My shoulders slumped. "Why would it be outside?"

Paige shrugged. "Wishful thinking."

"Shit." I picked up the bag of frozen corn and put it back on my eye.

"I'm probably going to get a hotel in Austin tomorrow, since I'll be out late. They always like to do dinner and drinks afterwards."

Paige brushed a piece of my hair back.

"Okay, I'm meeting with a florist in Fredericksburg to go over the flowers for the wedding. Are you still okay with me meeting her alone?"

"Totally. I know nothing about flowers, and I want you to pick what you want to have."

She smiled. "I found an old picture of the greenhouse, Millie standing in there in her wedding gown. She was holding a bouquet of beautiful white chrysanthemums. I thought a few of those in the arrangements might be nice."

"What about for your bouquet? What do you want?"

The way she smiled made my heart feel like it skipped a beat. "Pink daisies."

In that moment, I fell in love with her a little more, if that was at all possible. "The first flowers I ever gave you."

She nodded. "I think I might add in a white rose or two."

Smiling, I placed my finger on her chin, drawing her mouth to mine. "God, I love you."

Our mouths met in a sweet kiss when I heard the porch planks protest with someone walking on it.

"You want your other eye black and blue, son?" Phillip said, causing me and Paige to smile against our lips.

"No, sir."

"Then get your mouth off my baby girl."

"Daddy, that's enough. You got your shot in, Lucas is now off limits for any future injuries."

Phillip crossed his arms over his massive chest. Why hadn't I ever noticed how freaking built he was? He honestly didn't look a day older than forty, and he sure as hell didn't run like he was in his fifties.

He huffed and gave me an incredulous look. "We'll see about that. One mess up, and I will tear you apart."

I swallowed hard, then cleared my throat. "I have no intentions of messing up anything, sir, ever again."

"Holy hell, Foster. Where did you get the shiner?" Pete Mulligan asked as we all took a seat around the large conference table.

"My future father-in-law, Phillip Miller."

Timothy, my old boss and the guy in charge of this venture, laughed. "I still can't believe you're engaged."

I smiled as I glanced around the table. Luckily, Bianca wasn't here. She was an investor in this apartment building being built in downtown Austin. I had recently learned about her involvement. I was positive she did it because she heard Timothy had asked me to stay on as the lead designer.

"I'm thinking the dad doesn't approve of you," Pete stated with a chuckle. More light laughter trickled around the table.

"Well, considering I dated his daughter in high school and then broke up with her before we left for college, he has a few issues with me. Anyway, we're not here to talk about me, we're here to go over my design."

I pulled up my CAD design and hit the play button, then directed everyone's attention to the large screen behind me.

After thirty-five minutes of describing the building, the projected timeframe, and a rough estimate of costs, I leaned back in my chair and waited. Pete made a few notes, leaned over and spoke quietly with his business partner, Roger. Then he looked up at me and smiled.

"I like the design, a lot. It's in keeping with the feel of Austin, to appeal to the locals, but the inside amenities will appeal to the investors who want to live downtown."

With a brief glimpse at Timothy, I smiled at Pete. "I'm glad you like it."

"You're pretty confident about the timeframe?" he asked.

"As with any project, things could come up to slow us down. You have to take that into consideration, as well as dealing with the city. Something as simple as pulling a permit can turn into a long, drawn-out process."

The door to the conference room opened and a young woman walked in. She leaned down and said something to Pete. He rolled his eyes and nodded. "Tell her she'll have to wait. The meeting is almost over."

Lifting a brow, I watched Pete look down at his notes, then he stared directly at me. "I have an investor who is dumping a lot of money into this project. When I say a lot, I mean *a lot*. Her social presence alone will sell units. From what I understand, you are... familiar with her."

My heart raced.

"Her name is Bianca Williams. She was late getting into Austin from Rome. Fashion show or something."

I cleared my throat and said, "I'm sure she'll be able to watch the presentation and get caught up."

Pete gave me a shit-eating grin. "She has requested that you fill her in. I'm going to ask that you do this as a personal favor to me, since she is the largest investor we have on the project. I'd like to keep her...happy."

I moved uncomfortably in my seat and shot a look at Timothy. "What exactly are you asking me to do here, Pete?"

"Lucas," Timothy scolded.

Pete laughed and held up his hands. "I'm not asking you to fuck her."

A few people moved in their seats, clearly put off by Pete. It pissed me off even more, considering there were two women in the room.

"Is that really how you talk in business meetings?" I asked, anger laced in my voice.

"I need this woman to be kept content. I don't give a fuck why she ended up wanting to invest in this project, but it has something to do with the lead designer. So, what I'm asking you to do is go to the bar in the hotel lobby with the rest of us, have a drink with her and play nice."

"He can most certainly do that," Timothy said. "Lucas is a professional, and he knows Bianca. He can handle her, isn't that right, Lucas?"

I shook my head and stared down at the table. I needed this fucking job to build up a nice nest egg for me and Paige. Working for my dad would pay pretty well, but it wouldn't pay what I was previously making.

"Sure, no problem," I said. When I looked up, one of the women was staring at me. She looked familiar, and I tried like hell to place her. Her jaw muscles flexed, and she looked at me with pure disgust. She picked up her phone and started to type on it.

What the hell is that all about?

"Okay, let's all go down to the bar now that we've gotten the boring stuff out of the way," Timothy said, clapping his hands while he stood.

I gathered up my computer and put it into my bag. Timothy stayed back, waiting to talk to me.

"Lucas, I need you to be civil with her."

"I'm not fucking sleeping with her, Tim. I'm engaged. I'm in love with another woman."

He nodded as he let out a frustrated breath. "I know, I know. I also know how unhappy you were with Bianca, and we both know the only reason she invested in this is to be near you."

"Why can't Pete see that?"

"All he sees are dollar signs. Have a drink with her, then slip away and head back to the country."

I rubbed the back of my neck. "I'm staying at the hotel tonight. I didn't want to drive back late, and I knew we'd be drinking."

"Smart move. Just be nice to her, we'll get through this." He gave me a slap on the back and headed toward the elevator.

"Tim, wait. The woman sitting to the left of Pete. Who was that?"

He thought for a moment. "Harper, she is Pete's VP in marketing."

"She looks familiar to me."

Tim shrugged. "Maybe y'all met before in one of the beginning meetings."

I nodded. "Yeah, must be."

Twenty minutes later, I was at the bar, on my second drink while Bianca told me all about her trip to Rome. It wasn't lost on me how Harper kept looking at us. She was shooting daggers, and I wasn't sure if they were aimed at me, or Bianca. Or both of us.

Another thirty minutes went by, and I had had enough. I pulled my phone out and saw I had a text message from Paige. With a smile, I opened it up to read it.

Paige: How is it going?

Me: I'm about to head up to my room. They loved the design, so looks like we are a go.

Paige: That's great! I'm happy for you.

Me: Thank you, babe. What are you doing?

Paige: Oreo and I just put on a movie and are snuggled up on the sofa. I finished painting the upstairs bathroom. It looks great!

Me: I can't wait to see it. How did the appointment with the florist go?

Paige: Amazing. All flowers are ordered and she even gave me some pointers for my own shop.

Me: That's awesome.

"It's rude to be texting, Lucas," Bianca said, trying to place her hand on my arm. I moved it away and glared at her.

Paige: Anyone interesting you're talking to?

I stared at her text. The right thing to do would be to tell her Bianca was here. I sighed and pushed my phone into my pocket. I'd tell her about Bianca once I got up to the room.

When I looked across the table, Harper took a picture of me. I frowned, but then she moved her phone to the side and took another picture of Timothy and Pete talking. Maybe she was taking them for marketing reasons. Although, why take photos of us all drinking at a bar?

With a shake of my head, I called for Timothy. "Tim, I'm going to call it an evening."

He nodded. "Good work today, Lucas."

I shook his hand. Standing, I grabbed my bag and waved to everyone at the table.

"Calling it a night. Y'all enjoy yourselves."

Chancing a look at Harper as I walked by, I saw she was laughing with Lou Hansen, the marketing manager for Timothy's company.

Quickly, I headed out of the restaurant to the elevator.

"You weren't even going to say goodbye?" Bianca said from behind me. She moved next to me in front of the elevator.

"No, I wasn't. I didn't even want to see you." It was harsh, but truer words had never been spoken.

She jutted out her lower lip. "That's rather mean of you. We were close for a long time. Lovers."

I rolled my eyes and let out a frustrated noise. "We were nothing but two people who used each other. A distraction."

With a humorless laugh, she said, "Ouch. That's all I was to you?"

"Yes."

She let out a soft whimper of displeasure. "I wanted more. I couldn't help it if you were stuck in the past. I heard you're marrying the little dimwit."

I sent her a look that would have pinned any man in his place. "Don't utter a word about her. Don't even say her name."

Her eyes widened in mock shock. "Wow. Okay, seems like she's got her claws into you pretty good."

Another man walked up and stood next to us. The elevator opened, and he walked in first, not even allowing Bianca to walk in. I might have not been able to stand her, but I was still a gentleman. I motioned for her to walk in, and she reached up and laced her arm with mine.

"Why thank you, Lucas."

I jerked my arm from hers. She pushed the button for her floor, then looked at me. "What floor are you on?"

With a smirk, I replied, "I think I'll wait for you to get off before I push the button for my floor."

With an evil laugh, she shook her head. "You really think highly of yourself, Lucas. Do you honestly think I'll try to sneak into your room? You weren't that good of a fuck."

"If that's the case, why do you keep coming after me?"

The man in the elevator let out a soft chuckle. When his floor came up, I stepped out with him so I wouldn't have to be alone with the vulture. She shot me the finger as the elevator doors closed.

The guy turned and faced me. "Dude, she was hot, but I can totally see why you're worried. She has a bit of crazy in those eyes."

"You have no idea. Besides, I'm engaged, very happily engaged."

He nodded. "Got ya. Good luck." He headed down the hall. I went to the stairs and climbed the three flights to my floor. By the time I got to my room, my head was pounding.

When I walked into my room, I pulled out my phone and cursed. I only had one percent left on my battery.

"Fucking hell."

I quickly sent Paige a text that I was in my room and my phone was about to die. I hit send and the phone went black. I threw my bag onto the bed, sat down and looked through it for my phone charger. Once I plugged it in, I got undressed and took a shower. I'd call Paige when I was out.

After standing in the shower for a few minutes, letting hot water run over my body, I got out, dried off, and walked over to my phone. Paige hadn't texted back.

I typed out a text to her.

Me: You still up? Was going to call.

She didn't reply so I figured she had fallen asleep.

Me: Sorry, it was a bit crazy at the bar. Unfortunately, I ended up having to talk to Bianca tonight. She's one of the investors on this project and the president of the company building the condos found out we had a history. He wanted me to make nice with her. I'm in my room now, if you wake up, call me. I love you.

After setting my phone on the table, I sat down on the bed, propped up the pillows, and turned the TV on. My phone buzzed on the nightstand, and I smiled when I saw it was from Paige.

Paige: I already knew you were there with Bianca. You made good on making nice.

"What the fuck?" I mumbled as I looked at the screen shot Paige had sent me. Bianca was leaning over, saying something to me as I looked down at my phone. That's when it hit me. The picture Harper had taken. She had sent it to Paige. But how?

My fingers jerked through my wet hair. Holy hell. Harper was Paige's roommate her freshman and sophomore year of college! I suddenly remembered seeing pictures of her on Paige's Facebook and Instagram.

I hit Paige's number.

"Can't sleep?" she said instead of saying hello.

"Seriously? Is this what we're going to do? Play games?"

Paige remained quiet for a moment. "I'm not playing any games, Lucas. You're the one who neglected to tell me you were spending the evening with your ex-girlfriend. I simply was caught off guard when an old friend sent me a text. Needless to say, I would rather you had told me, that's all."

"I didn't know I was going to be seeing her."

"You knew she was an investor. You didn't think that was something you should have told me? I wouldn't have cared, Lucas, but when you keep things from me, of course it gives me a moment of pause."

"Usually investors don't show up for shit like that. She wasn't there for the meeting and only showed up afterwards because she knew we'd all head to the bar. So how was it you had a little spy in the fold?"

She laughed. "Spy? Hardly. You mentioned my father's name and then mine, Harper put two and two together and realized you were the same Lucas who broke up with me in college. That's all."

"That explains all the dirty looks coming my way. If you knew Bianca was there, why didn't you just say so?"

"I didn't know until Harper sent the picture a few minutes ago. Earlier she texted to tell me she finally got to meet you."

"Funny, she didn't introduce herself to me. Too busy giving you a play by play of my moves? Would you maybe like to FaceTime so you can see that my room is empty?"

She remained silent, then I heard a slow exhale. "Believe it or not, I actually trust you, Lucas. Even when Harper sent me the picture of you stepping into the elevator with Bianca. I texted her back and asked her to stop and said that I trusted you a hundred percent."

Anger boiled in my veins, and I had no fucking idea why.

That was a lie. I did. I hadn't stood my ground and said no. Bianca had tried to play a game tonight and here I was blaming Paige for playing games instead.

Paige didn't say anything for a few moments. She mistook my silence for anger. "Did the pictures throw me? Yes, but I'm smart enough not to believe everything I see. Honestly, what makes me more upset right now is how angry you are with me. I'm tired, and I'm going to bed. I'll see you in the morning, Lucas. I love you."

The phone went silent, a clear sign she'd hung up. I drew back and stared at it. She had every right to be pissed at me. I quickly got dressed, packed up my things and made my way to the front desk to check out. There was only one place I wanted to be, and the quicker I got there, the better.

Chapter 27

Paige

THE SOUND OF the bedroom door opening made me freeze. Oreo lifted her head and looked toward the door.

I swallowed hard. "I don't mind if you want to co-exist in the house. But a ghost in my bedroom when I'm home alone is not going to sit well with me."

A soft male chuckle made me sit up.

"Lucas, what on Earth are you doing here?"

He dropped his things on the floor, then pulled his shirt over his head. I watched him come to a stop next to the bed and kick off his shoes, then his pants and boxers. He climbed into the bed, drawing my body flush against his.

"I'm sorry I acted like an idiot. I was pissed at myself for not telling Pete that I wasn't going to make nice with Bianca. Timothy and Pete were still at the bar when I checked out of my room. I told Timothy that I was done, one hundred percent finished with all projects."

"What?" I said, sitting up to look down at him. "Lucas, you said you were going to be paid really well for that job. If you leave the company, you're out of work completely."

"Not true, I'm working for my father. And besides, they signed off on the final design. I'll still be paid."

With an disbelieving laugh, I shook my head. "You do realize the pay cut you just took."

"We can afford it, don't worry. We can still have the wedding and fix up the house. I've got some money put aside."

I rolled my eyes. "I don't care about that. Are you sure you want to walk away from your job? I thought you loved it."

He pulled me down to him. "I love you more. I love the life we're starting for ourselves, and honestly, I want to be here for the house remodel and helping you start your store. That's what I love."

Resting my chin on the back of my hand, I gazed at him for a few moments. "Talk to me."

Lucas sighed. "I'm pissed at myself for letting them bully me into sitting with her tonight. I think in a way, Pete actually wanted me to sleep with her. He's so worried about securing her investment. But Harper probably told you that."

"No, she didn't say anything like that. She told me you looked like you wanted to be sick the entire time you were sitting there. She also wanted to tell you she was sorry she didn't trust you. She'd only ever heard about you after you broke my heart in two."

Lucas rolled me over so fast I let out a small scream. He was on top of me, his body between my legs, his hard length against my instantly throbbing core.

"Did you tell her I've changed? That I do things *slow?*" he asked, kissing me softly on the neck and along my collarbone.

"Mmm," I whispered, wrapping my legs around him and lifting my hips to get better contact. He was naked, but I had on a pair of cotton sleeping pants. "I didn't have to. She figured you'd changed since we were engaged, which she told me you announced to everyone."

He gazed down at me. "I'd rent a plane and write it across the sky if I could."

I smiled. "You didn't have to come home tonight. I wasn't mad."

Lucas rubbed his nose against mine. "I know, but the moment I realized what an ass I had been, I needed to be here. Needed to tell you how much you mean to me and how much I love you."

My heart filled with love as Lucas placed gentle kisses over my face and finally pressed his mouth to mine.

Before I knew what was happening, Lucas had pulled my sleeping pants down, and I was kicking them off my body.

The moment he slipped inside me, I let out a long moan of pleasure. Lucas moved slowly, filling me completely, then withdrawing painstakingly slow before entering me again.

"Lucas, faster," I whispered, wrapping my legs around him.

"I want to make love to you slowly. Feel every single movement."

My fingertips moved lazily over his back.

"Do you have your dress?" he asked.

Between the pounding of my heart in my ears, the thrumming of my body, and the way his whispered voice left me dizzy, I managed, "Yes."

"Then marry me...now."

I froze, but he kept moving.

"What?" I asked, thinking I hadn't heard him right, or maybe had misunderstood.

"I want to make you mine, now."

Pressing my hand to his chest, I pushed him back until his eyes met mine. "I am yours, Lucas. No marriage certificate will ever change that or make it more believable. I've always been yours and I will be forever."

"I know everything is changing for you, and you're finally making your dreams come true, but I want you to be my wife and I want... I want..."

He sounded so unsure, as if he was worried to tell me. I placed my hand on the side of his face and smiled. "Tell me what you want. This isn't only about my wishes and dreams. It's about yours, as well."

The way his eyes glistened made my heart feel like it dropped in my chest.

"I want a baby. I want to marry you and try for a baby and fill this house with as many little ones as you want. If you only want one, I'm fine with that. If you want ten, I'll gladly keep you knocked up or die trying."

A mix between a sob and a laugh slipped between my lips. "Have you lost your mind? Lucas, we've only been back together for a few months. Everything in our world is upside down. I'm starting a new business..."

"And you will kick ass at it. You can work. You don't have to give that up. Once you go back to the flower shop, I'll take care of the baby. It will be easier for me since I'll be working for Dad."

"You're serious?" I asked, searching his face and feeling my heart nearly explode with love for this man. "You want to try for a baby right away?"

"If you want to. If you don't, I understand."

My head should have been swimming with confusion. I had to be crazy thinking of getting pregnant while opening up a new business. But, something deep inside knew I wanted this as much as Lucas did. We had wasted so many years, I didn't want to waste another single moment.

"I can probably move the wedding up. It's really just family and friends, and it's not a big affair. I'll call the florist tomorrow and ask the earliest we can get all the arrangements finished."

"Your dress?"

"It was nearly a perfect fit. I did want to lose maybe ten pounds or so."

Lucas frowned. "Why the fuck would you want to do that?"

I laughed. "I'm carrying a good extra ten pounds, at least."

Lucas was still inside of me. Now he withdrew completely, leaving me instantly feeling empty.

He stared intently. So much so that I felt heat move up from my neck to my cheeks.

"What are you doing? Why did you pull out?"

Lucas slowly shook his head, stood, and reached for my hands, pulling me out of the bed.

"Lift your arms," he whispered as he pulled my tank top off my head. He tossed it to the side and then let his eyes move ever so slowly over my body.

"You are the most beautiful woman I have ever laid my eyes on. Every single thing about you is perfect. Everything."

I could feel my blush grow hotter.

"Lucas, I—"

He pressed his finger to my lips. "I don't want you to change and I never want to hear you say you have weight to drop. When I look at you, Paige... God, when I look at you, my breath is stolen from my lungs. You have no idea how you make my body feel so alive. The way I want you is unlike anything. If I could spend the rest of my life exploring your body like it was the first time, I'd do it day in and day out. Don't ever try to change. Not for me, not anyone."

I felt one tear, then another, trail down my cheeks. Lucas cupped my face in his hands and swept his thumbs over my skin.

"You are the most precious thing. You are rare, and beautiful, and perfect. I knew the moment I walked away from you that it was the biggest mistake of my life. Never again will I go a day without telling you how fucking lucky I am that you're mine."

I tried with all my might not to cry. After rubbing my lips back and forth in an attempt to settle my emotions, I looked up and met his gaze.

"I'm not perfect, by any means, but to know that's what you see when you look at me makes me almost the happiest woman on Earth."

He smiled, then frowned. "Almost?"

I nodded. "If you let me paint your office the color I picked out, I'll be beyond crazy happy."

Lucas stared in utter disbelief. A small smile tugged at the corners of his mouth before he lost control and started to laugh.

"You are impossible. How about this. I'll let you paint it pink—"

"Light peach."

"Whatever you want to call it," he said with an eye roll. "If you marry me this weekend."

"This weekend!" I gasped.

"Take it or leave it."

"You know, I learned the art of negotiation from some of the best. I could attempt to sweeten the deal."

His brow lifted.

"Fine. I'll marry you this weekend."

I screamed when Lucas picked me up and tossed me over his shoulder. He dropped me onto the bed and we both laughed. The moment he slipped inside me, everything felt exactly as it should. And I was indeed, the happiest woman on Earth.

Chapter 28

Lucas

ICAUGHT SIGHT of my father as I rode up on Ranger. It was a beautiful, cool fall day, something Texas didn't have a whole lot of. It was always either damn hot or damn cold.

Ranger came to a stop, and I jumped off the side of him, adjusted my hat and made my way over to the fence.

"I told you I would fix this, Dad."

He looked up at me and smiled. I knew it still meant a lot to him to have me back home, working alongside him, both here on the ranch and with Foster construction company.

"It was such a cool morning, I wanted to get it taken care of. What are you doing here?"

"Wanted to talk to you about a few things."

He nodded. "Grab those pullers. We'll talk and work."

Smiling, I picked up the fence pullers. My father had always been the type of person who didn't believe in wasting a single moment. If he could do something more efficiently, he did. I couldn't help but wonder if he got that from his English father. I pushed the thought away and spoke.

"First, I wanted to talk to you about bringing Ranger to Granddad's place. I've been working on the barn, not that it needed much work. Granddad made sure it stayed in good condition, even though he stopped keeping animals there years ago."

My father twisted the wire and looked at me. "You need to start calling it your place, son. It's your property. Your ranch. And yes, Ranger is your horse. As a matter of fact, if you want to take more of these beasts off of my hands, I'm more than happy to let you."

With a chuckle, I said, "I'm sure Paige would love a horse, as well. We've both missed riding like we used to."

"The two of you used to ride every day, pretty much. She always did like Princess."

"You don't think Mom would mind? She adores Princess."

"She adores Paige more. Trust me, your mother hasn't ridden in six months. She's been keeping herself busy with other things. I think that fall she had last year might have scared her."

I nodded as the memory of last year came back. My father had called me in a state of utter panic. Mom had been out riding and had been thrown from a horse. She broke her arm and had to have surgery to get it back in place. She had climbed up onto a horse a few times after, purely to prove to herself that she wasn't afraid. After that, she had stopped riding altogether. I couldn't blame her. The few times I'd been thrown from a horse, it had scared me, too. Horses were both so damn powerful and so damn gentle.

Glancing over to me, my dad smiled. "You don't know how good it is to see you in real clothes."

With a frown, I looked down at my clothes. "Real clothes? When have I not worn real clothes?"

He huffed. "Those damn collared shirts and khaki pants that woman always had you in. Let's not even talk about the preppy shoes."

I laughed. "I used to wear that to work, Dad. Not everyone wears jeans, cowboy boots, and Stetson hats to their jobs."

"I do. My daddy did before me."

I wanted to point out that his biological father had probably never slid a cowboy boot on in his entire life. I didn't, though; I let that one go.

"I missed the ranch. The smell of it out here makes me happy."

"Manure and grass." He took in a deep breath and let it out. "Ahh, nothing like it. I could roll in it."

"I wouldn't go that far," I said, snarling.

"What else did you want to talk about?"

"Do you have plans this weekend?"

Already knowing the answer, I watched as he seemed to go through the internal calendar he kept in his head. He was the only person I knew who never wrote a damn thing down. Something I had not been gifted with.

I smiled. "Dad, you don't ever work on the weekend. It's always been your golden rule. Why are you thinking so hard about this?"

He huffed again. "How do you know I don't have plans? I was going to play golf with Lou this Sunday after church. Then your momma talked about going into Fredericksburg for the Octoberfest on Saturday."

I gave him a thoughtful look as I rubbed the back of my neck. "Damn shame you've got such amazing plans. I was sort of hoping you might be free Saturday night, around six."

"Six? I'm sure your mother and I will be back by then. You thinking dinner with you and Paige?"

"Something like that. More along the lines of a wedding, then a small dinner after."

He twisted the last tie around the repaired fence. "I think we can make that..."

I laughed when his head whipped around, and he stared at me, his mouth damn near to the ground.

"Did you say a wedding? This Saturday? That's in three days, Lucas."

"Yes, sir, I know. My bride-to-be is in a bit of a panic. You see, we negotiated last night. I said I'd let her paint my office pink in exchange for a wedding this weekend."

He rubbed the stubble on his chin. "Why in the hell would you agree to let her paint your office pink?"

I loved that that was what he wondered about. "I believe it was you who told me once, after Paige and I had an argument, to pick my battles."

He grinned and pointed to me. "That is why you're my favorite son."

"I'm your only son."

"Minor thing. So, care to tell me why the rush?"

We started to gather up the tools and walked them over to the ranch truck.

"I'm tired of waiting. I've wasted too much time being an ass. I want to start a family."

That caused him to pause. "How does Paige feel about that? She's starting her shop... Does she want to start a family this soon?"

I smiled. "Yes. I told her I'd stay home with the baby. I figured I could work something out with a nanny."

A roar of laughter came from his mouth. "A nanny. Your mother would smack you upside your head if she heard you say that. Just yesterday she had me clearing out your old room. It's going to be the nursery, she said."

"Huh?" I said, not believing what I heard.

"Lucas, women have a way of knowing things before we do. Your mother is the best in the world with this little gift. She probably already knows the wedding is Saturday at six. I learned, as will you, that often you will say two words to your wife followed up most times by four more words."

I could feel myself grinning. "What words would those be?"

My father looked me dead in the eyes. "'Yes, dear.' And 'whatever you want, sweetheart.'"

After spending the morning with my father on the ranch, we drove to the courthouse and checked on the renovations. Then we swung by and checked on Paige's shop. It was moving along faster than either of us could have hoped. The outside was nearly complete, and I couldn't wait to see the sign I had made hung up.

I parted ways with my dad, but not before making arrangements to pick up Ranger, Princess, and two other horses my father insisted would be happier with me and Paige. I then swung by the grocery store and picked up a bouquet of flowers for Paige. As I drove down the driveway, I frowned at the number of cars and trucks parked outside the house. I saw Milo's truck, Jen's car, Gene's truck, as well as my folks' car. I pulled off to the side and got out, flowers in hand as I made my way to the house. I could hear everyone outside.

When I rounded the house, I stopped.

"Holy shit," I said, looking around the backyard at the sight before me. Paige turned and waved, standing on top of a ladder. She was hanging up Edison lights.

"It's about time you showed up. I need your help in the greenhouse," Milo said, motioning for me to follow him. I walked over to Paige and looked up at her.

"What's going on?" I asked.

She laughed as if I had just asked her the most insane question.

"We are getting married in three days! I had a ton of things to do to get ready. The ceremony will be in the greenhouse, then we will have the reception here in the backyard. I already looked at three different news stations for the weather. It's going to be a beautiful day!"

The way she was smiling made me feel like I was floating on a cloud. "Baby, why didn't you tell me you were doing all of this? I would have been here to help."

Paige took a few steps down on the ladder, then leaned over to kiss me. "You wanted to talk to your dad. I called your mom and invited her over for breakfast. The moment she found out the wedding was this weekend, plans were put in motion."

I laughed. "Sounds like my mom. Your dad?"

She looked past me, and I followed her gaze. Phillip was sitting at a table doing something with Jen.

"He's making decorations for the greenhouse with Jen. He did ask if I was pregnant, and if that was why we were rushing."

"God, I wish I had been there because I would have loved to have said yes, just to see what he would do."

Paige frowned. "Was one black eye not enough? Or you feeling spry enough to do another 5k running away from him?"

"Now that I know the old man can run, he won't be able to catch me next time."

With another peek over my shoulder, Paige pressed her mouth shut and looked back at me.

"He heard me, didn't he?"

She nodded. "You might want to run."

Chapter 29

Paige

ISTOOD ON the front porch and took in a deep breath. It was the morning of my wedding. The day I had dreamed about since I was twelve years old, when I realized I liked Lucas as more than a friend. It was the first time he held his hand out for me when I was getting off a horse. He hadn't even realized he'd winked at me when I jumped down and stumbled. He had caught me, asked if I was okay, then winked at me. At twelve, I vowed to marry him someday.

At fourteen, I realized I had more than a crush: I had fallen in love with him. At sixteen, I gave him not only my heart, but my body. At eighteen, he crushed my heart. Now, at twenty-nine he promised me the moon and stars, and I was madly in love with him.

I sat down in one of the white iron chairs I had found in the storage shed, along with a beautiful white iron table. From pictures I had found in Millie's photo album, I knew this table set had once adorned this front porch. And it was back in its original spot. The large white columns that went across the porch had to be one of my favorite things about the house. It gave it a grand appearance, while still leaving it to look like a country house. I looked up at the chandeliers that my father and Lucas had hung last night. The two of them, spending the night before our wedding hanging light fixtures and drinking beer. Lucas had said it was probably the best bachelor party he'd ever had. I loved that my father secretly made Lucas think he was teetering on the edge of liking and hating him. In truth, my father had always adored Lucas. He had been angry with him, like I had, but he loved him like a son. Last night, when I heard the two of them laughing, it warmed my heart, filling me with so much happiness that I had broken down and cried.

Oreo came up and rubbed against my legs.

"Good morning, sweetie."

When she jumped on my lap, I noticed she had a ribbon tied around her neck. I untied it, and the key to the attic fell on my lap. I looked around, then picked up the key.

"You want to go up into the attic?" I asked as she purred so loudly I couldn't help but giggle.

"Actually, it was me who wanted to go up there."

Turning, I smiled at Lucas. "You know, we're not supposed to see each other until the wedding."

"Do you really want to start doing things by the book now?"

Laughing, I shook my head and picked up the cat, then made my way over to him.

"You want to go exploring...now?"

"Yes. Tom gave me this last night."

He held up the necklace that had been in May's trunk.

"Tom told me they were real diamonds in the bracelet, so I gave him the ruby necklace. It is a ruby. A very expensive ruby."

I lifted my brows. "Your grandfather?" I asked.

"That's what I'm thinking. He probably showered her with jewelry when he was dating her."

"And she left it all up in the attic."

"Tom brought his friend over, the jeweler. He offered to buy a few of the pieces."

"Really? Wow. Are you going to sell them to him?"

Lucas laughed. "Your father would really kick my ass. Paige, they're worth a lot of money. A lot of money."

"Okay. Well, that's good, I guess."

He placed his hands on my shoulders and smiled. "I'm talking about enough money to pay off the mortgage on the flower shop. Enough money to pay for that kitchen reno you want, and enough money to put away for ten kids to go to college at any university they want."

"What exactly are you saying?" I asked, my voice stumbling.

"Let's head up there really quick."

I followed Lucas. Once in the attic, he winked at me before opening up the chest. He pulled open the drawer and shook his head as he gazed down at the jewels.

"So...I'm saying, Grams casually kept thousands of dollars' worth of jewelry in her traveling trunk for years. Okay, not just thousands of dollars. That piece you're holding is a five-and-a-half-carat ruby that is worth twenty-thousand dollars. According to your brother's friend, there might be over a million dollars' worth of jewelry up there."

I gasped. "Wh-what!"

He nodded. "I called my father this morning, asked him if he could contact his family in England, alert them to all that we found. He just called me back, and they don't want any of it returned. As far as they are concerned, my father's dad would have wanted the family to have it. He gave it to Grams as a gift."

My hands shook. "Lucas, I can't even think right now. Why in the world would William and May leave all that up in that trunk?"

He shrugged. "I don't know. Maybe May didn't want it as a reminder of what she had done. Out of respect for Granddad? Maybe she didn't even realize what she had in there."

"We need to put it in a safe, you know that."

I laughed. "Yeah, I know. The family did ask a favor...from you."

"Me?" I asked in surprise.

"We sent pictures of the jewelry to them. There is a brooch in there, one that has been in the family for a while. My grandfather gave it to Grams when she told him she was pregnant. He was married at the time, that's why he left her alone, plus I guess she told him she was in love with another man."

"William," I whispered.

"Yes. Anyway, they asked if you would wear it at our wedding."

Lucas reached into the chest and pulled out a black brooch with a woman's picture painted in the middle of it. Pearls lined the outside of the piece. It was stunning.

"Apparently, this is my great, great—there might be one more great in there—grandmother. Her name was Lady Elizabeth Davers."

"Lady? I still can't believe you have nobility in your blood."

Lucas cleared his throat and spoke in a terrible English accent. "My lady, I come from one of the finer peerage families of the mother land."

Laughing, I pushed him lightly on the chest. "I'd love to wear the brooch. I found the pearl earrings Millie wore in her wedding to William. Isn't it terribly romantic that I will be wearing something from both women?"

"It's simply perfect. I love you, you know that, right?"

"Of course," I said softly, reaching up on my toes and kissing him. "And I love you."

"So, do you want to go fool around up in the attic?"

"I would, but everyone will be showing up soon."

His brow lifted. "Who is everyone?"

"Your mom, Jen, the makeup and hair girl Jen found at the last minute. They'll all be here soon."

Lucas looked stunned. "The wedding isn't until tonight. Why is everyone coming over now?"

I placed my hand on the side of his face, then gave it a few light slaps. "You better hope we don't have ten little girls, Lucas, because you have no idea what it takes for women to get married."

He groaned, then kissed me on the tip of my nose. A small box in the corner of the attic moved and fell to the floor. Lucas and I both looked at the box, then back to one another. A moment later, we were pushing each other out of the way to get the hell out of the attic.

"Something has to be done about the freaking ghost!" Lucas called as he nearly fell down the steps.

Once we were out, the door locked and both of us breathed like we had run a marathon. I let out a long breath. "Married first. Honeymoon second. Ghost third."

Lucas nodded. "Maybe Oreo can talk her into leaving."

"You look beautiful," Lynn said.

"Lucas is going to shit his pants. Sorry, Mrs. Foster."

Lynn chuckled. "It's true, he will. If he doesn't go weak in the knees first. I'm glad the veil isn't over your face. You're too beautiful to cover it."

I felt my cheeks blush. "My heart feels like it is going to beat right out of my chest."

"I felt the same way," Jen said. "Except I also felt sick to my stomach. And for a good fifteen minutes, my mother had to talk me into not running from the church."

Lynn and I looked at Jen with shocked expressions. "You didn't want to marry Gene?"

"I did. But in a few brief moments of hysteria, I didn't."

Turning back to the mirror, I drew in a slow, steady breath. "I have no doubt in my mind I'm ready to marry Lucas. I'm afraid the moment I see him I'll try to bolt out of my father's arms to get to him."

Jen and Lynn both let out soft chuckles. Lynn took a step closer to me. "I have been trying to decide when is the best time to do this, and there doesn't seem to be any time that probably won't make us both cry our makeup off."

My hands reached for hers. "What is it?" I could hear the concern in my voice.

"Everything it okay. I didn't mean to scare you. Oh sweet, sweet Paige. The day your momma passed away, she called for me that morning."

"I remember," I said softly.

"We spoke and she..." Lynn let out a tender laugh as she recalled the memory. "She told me that she knew someday you and Lucas would marry. I told her I hoped like hell she was right."

My hand came up to my mouth as a laugh and sob slipped free.

"Your momma was always right. Here is another example. You're about to marry Lucas."

I wiped a tear.

Lynn pulled out a box that was in her purse. She handed it to me. "Your mother told me that when you got married, I was to give you this."

I gathered up my dress and walked over to the bench in the room where I was getting ready. It was one of the upstairs rooms. The whole upstairs had been turned upside down to get me ready. The wedding prep was the most fun I'd ever had. I had been treated like a princess. Manicure, pedicure, a facial, massage—that one was from Lucas—and endless primping and laughing.

With a deep breath to calm myself, I untied the ribbon on the box and slid the lid off. I was greeted with the smell of my mother's favorite perfume and pink tissue paper. Carefully opening the tissue, I smiled at the sight.

"Her handkerchief," I whispered. "I used to play with it when I was little. She told me it was a wedding gift from her mother."

I ran my fingers over the embroidered initials. My heart pained at the thought of my mother not here. I had been trying all day not to think about it, but at times, the sadness had been so overwhelming that I knew I could burst into tears any moment. But this, this gift made me feel like she was here with me.

"It's beautiful," Jen said, her hand on my shoulder. "You should wrap it around your bouquet."

I quickly stood. "The brooch. We can pin it to the handkerchief."

Lynn smiled brightly. "That's an amazing idea, Paige."

Jen walked over and got the bouquet. "It's almost time to go down, so let's let the stems dry a bit before we wrap it. Let's touch up your makeup, give you hair one more spray, then you'll be ready to go."

I nodded.

As I stood in the mirror, I let my eyes wander down my dress. The white satin mermaid gown hugged my body in the most delicious way. I loved that it showed off my curves and knew Lucas would appreciate it even more. The delicate crystal belt added the perfect touch. The halter top was satin and gave way to lace and a stunning pattern of crystals, beads, and sequins that made an intricate, yet delicate, open pattern down my back. Most of my back was exposed, making the dress feel sophisticated and sexy.

My hair had been put into a low bun with only a few hanging curls. Jen stood on a stepstool and pinned on the simple veil. I didn't want one that covered my face, yet it felt like I was missing something if I didn't have it.

Lynn handed me the pearl drop earrings I had found in Millie's things in the storage shed. I put them on and took another look at myself.

"You're going to steal the air from the room," Lynn said, kissing me and then turning to Jen. "I'm leaving her in your hands. I'd like to see my son, and then I think I need to get to my seat."

I squeezed her hand. "Thank you for everything."

She gave me a soft smile. "Of course, my sweet girl."

After Lynn left, Jen looked at me and then we both took another glance at my reflection in the mirror.

"I hope he shits his pants," I said with a silly giggle.

"Trust me. He will," Jen said, giving me a quick kiss on the cheek.

Karen, the makeup artist from Fredericksburg, handed me the bouquet of pink daisies and white roses. "I've dried off the stems and carefully wrapped the handkerchief your mother gave you around the stems and secured it with the brooch."

She wrapped it, so the initials could be seen. "You did a beautiful job. On everything," I said.

"My God, you look like your mother."

Turning, I smiled at my father. He was dressed in a black tux.

"You look handsome as all get out!" I exclaimed, making my way over to him. I kissed him on the cheek, and he took a step back, giving me a once-over.

"The bastard doesn't deserve you. No man does."

"I would bet Granddad told Momma the same thing about you."

He laughed. "He did, and he was right. I was nowhere good enough for her, but I loved her so much."

I smiled. "She loved you too, Daddy."

He nodded and cleared his throat. "I happen to know that undeserving—"

"Daddy, be nice."

With a roll of his eyes, he said, "I happen to know that Lucas loves you very much. I just saw him."

"How does he look?"

He gave me a wicked smile. "Nervous as hell. I offered him some whiskey, but he declined."

"You did not!" I said, slapping him playfully on the chest.

He sighed liked he had amused the hell out of himself. Taking my hands in his, he said, "It's time. Are you ready?"

I nodded. "I've waited for this day for a long time."

He held out his arm to me, and I slipped my arm through his.

"Let's go get you married."

Chapter 30

Lucas

A SMALL HANDFUL of people sat in chairs in the greenhouse. Paige had kept the decorations surprisingly minimal. A few bouquets of flowers were scattered around the room, and the altar was an arch covered in light pink and white roses. Preacher Smith stood there, a smile on his face as we waited. The music started, and my heart nearly jumped to my throat.

I had asked Milo to stand in as my best friend, which had made the bastard start crying. It happened the day we had all been decorating the backyard until one in the morning. He was drunk as all get out and nearly passed out on the sofa. I walked in and saw him watching *Top Gun* for some unknown reason. When I asked him to be my best man, he broke down and hugged me. Yeah, awkward, but I was glad he agreed.

I smiled as I let my eyes sweep over the friends and family we'd invited to the ceremony. In all, it was only twenty-four people, most of whom were friends of ours growing up. The reception, on the other hand? We had sent out a text three days before the wedding and had invited over a hundred-and-fifty people. Some were former colleagues of Paige's, some mine. A lot were our folks' friends, people we'd known growing up, and one or two of our college friends.

Callie and Tom Jr. walked down the aisle, each of them nodding and saying hello as they made their way. Callie went off to the side with Jen, and Tom Jr. stood next to me. He had the very important job of holding the rings. I gave his hair a quick rub and winked at him.

"Good job, Junior."

He beamed with pride.

The air changed the moment I saw Paige walking down the path. I couldn't get a good look at her through the greenhouse windows, but the moment she stepped inside, my breath caught in my throat, and I swayed.

"Do you need me to hold you up there, Lucas?" Milo asked in a hushed tone.

I watched as Paige and her father started down the aisle. "Maybe."

He chuckled and gave me a pat on the back.

As Paige walked slowly toward me, our eyes met. A million things ran through my mind. Things I wanted to tell her.

She looked absolutely beautiful. Too stunning for me to form proper words. Her eyes seemed to sparkle, and for the briefest moment, I knew Millie, May, and William were here with us.

Paige and Phillip stopped in front of me, and Paige turned to her father.

"I love you, Daddy."

He wiped a tear from his eye. "I love you more, my sweet girl."

I reached out, and Phillip placed Paige's hand in mine.

"She is precious and means the world to me," he said, his voice cracking. "I couldn't give her to you unless I knew deep in my heart that she meant the same to you."

A heavy soreness built inside as I squeezed her hand gently.

"I'm not giving her away, Lucas. You don't give away something you love. But you can share her with me."

Paige let a sob slip free. "Daddy," she whispered.

"Thank you, sir. And I swear, I will treasure and love her with everything I have for the rest of my life and beyond."

He nodded, wiped his tears, and then went to his seat.

Paige and I took a few steps closer to Preacher Smith. I turned to her and our eyes met.

"You are breathtaking. Beyond beautiful."

She smiled, a slightly pink tint to her cheeks. The preacher started to talk, but all I could do was look at her. When we faced one another to say our vows, I wasn't even positive I was talking, but the way she was smiling at me, I knew I must have been. We exchanged rings, and when it came time for me to kiss her, I summoned up every ounce of strength I had not to ravish her with kisses and take her back to the house.

The kiss was soft, sweet, and slow. When we pulled away, we both laughed because everyone was cheering like a bunch a crazy people. I leaned my forehead to hers and stared into her soft brown eyes.

"Hello, Mrs. Foster."

A tear slipped from her eye and made a slow trail down her cheek. "Hello, Mr. Foster."

"Thank you," I whispered.

"For?" she asked with a giggle.

"For taking this *slow* and making me the happiest man on Earth."

Paige smiled, wrapped her arms around my neck and kissed me once more. This time, the kiss was indeed a bit naughtier.

Epilogue

Three years later

A S I WALKED up to The Little Flower Shop, Paige stood outside. She was talking to an older woman, a smile on her face and one of the baskets she kept outside the shop in hand. It was filled with flowers that looked like small bundles of wheat. At her feet, a basket filled with mums, and next to that, even more flowers. The façade of her shop looked exactly how Paige had described years ago. The grey, wood-framed large windows gave it a rustic look. One of the windows opened and gave way to a small window box filled with Gerber daisies, one of Paige's favorite flowers. Over the last three years, Paige had also turned the greenhouse at our place into one of the most impressive sights I'd ever seen. Half of the greenhouse held some of her favorite flowers, the other half was a play area for our daughter, Zoey.

Inside the flower shop was just as amazing as the outside. It was exactly how Paige had always described it. She had even picked up a few items for the shop when we went to Italy for our honeymoon. It had been two weeks of pure bliss. Exploring small villages, eating some of the most amazing food I'd ever tasted, and trying wine after wine, until I vowed to never drink wine again.

Paige stopped taking her birth control pills right after the wedding. We thought for sure we'd end up pregnant sooner rather than later. We certainly tried hard enough, and right when we resolved to stop pushing it, Paige got pregnant. By the time Zoey was born, a year and two months after our wedding, the flower shop had opened and was thriving. The house remodel had been finished, my office had been set up, with a nursery right off of it, with a door for me to walk straight through in case Zoey needed me. I'd started my own consulting firm, which allowed me to take on a very few clients. I spent most of my time helping my dad run the ranch and working a few constructions projects. Yeah, safe to say that we were very busy.

Paige had decided that we needed a small nursery in the back of the flower shop, as well, for the days she really wanted to have Zoey with her.

Zoey pulled at my hand as she tried her best to get to her momma. She squealed in delight, and Paige looked our way. A brilliant smile erupted on her face when she saw me and our almost two-year-old daughter heading toward her. She turned to the woman, said something, then set the basket down and held her arms open for Zoey. She ran right into them.

"Be careful, Zoey, don't knock mommy over," I warned. Paige gave me a smile and scooped our little girl up in her arms.

"Hello, my darling girl. Did you have fun today?"

Zoey laughed and squirmed to get out of Paige's arms. I took her from Paige and then kissed my wife softly.

"We missed you today."

Paige looked at me and laughed. "You say that every day."

"That's because we do, don't we, squirt?"

Zoey nodded. "Yes! Miss you, Mommy! And baby bwother."

My eyes glanced at the round, eight-month pregnant belly of my stunningly beautiful wife.

"How is my boy today?" I asked, running my hand over her stomach and feeling a swift kick.

With a raised brow, Paige replied, "Does that answer your question? He didn't get the memo that Mom doesn't like the idea of him playing soccer with my insides."

I laughed and set Zoey down. She ran into the shop, calling out to Lauren, a young woman Paige had hired. She'd worked for Paige in Austin and was only a couple years younger than us and had been looking for a change and to get out of the city. Paige offered her the position of manager of the flower shop, and she had taken it without a second thought. Everyone had fallen in love with her from the get go. Including my daughter, but especially Milo, who had been smitten with her from the first time he met her. After a couple of months of friendship, then a few more months of dating, Milo and Lauren were engaged and planning a wedding for June.

"Would you mind setting that basket over there?" Paige asked, pointing.

"You about ready to head home?" I asked, walking up to her and placing my finger under her chin, lifting her gaze to me. "The doctor told you to take it easy, you know. You're on your feet too much."

Paige sighed. "I'm so bored when Zoey is in preschool and I'm not working. I'd lose my mind if I had to just sit at home all day."

"Fair enough, but I want you to be sitting more. This son of ours is giving you a run for your money with this pregnancy."

She huffed. "That's putting it mildly."

We walked into the flower shop and saw Zoey sitting on a small chair, watching as Lauren put together a flower arrangement. Lauren would point to a flower, and Zoey would call out the name, then clap at herself for getting it right. She was a lover of flowers, just like her mommy.

Paige and I walked through the store and into her office. I called back to Lauren, "Yell if she gets to be too much."

"Too much, ha! Please!" Lauren replied.

Paige leaned against her desk and gave me that smile. The one that said she was wanting something. Needing something.

"You have a naughty look in your eye, sweetheart," I said, walking up to her.

The corners of her mouth twitched as she attempted to hold back a smile. "I called your mom earlier. Told her I needed a night off. She offered to take Zoey for the night."

My brows raised. "What did you have in mind?"

"First, I thought maybe you could make me some of your amazing chicken salad. The kind on the walnut and cranberry bread. I bought some earlier."

"Consider it done."

"Then, I thought maybe we could have popcorn drizzled with caramel sauce and peanut butter while we watch a movie."

I snarled. "I'll make a batch for you and a batch for me, minus the sauces." I made a fake gagging motion and Paige grinned.

"Then, I thought maybe you could work magic with that mouth of yours."

That got my attention even more. "Someone needs to orgasm?" I asked as I leaned in and kissed her neck.

"More than you know. The moment I saw you just now it took everything I had not to jump on you and ask you to..." she lowered her voice, "fuck me in the back cooler."

"We've done that before. We could do it again. We wouldn't even get sweaty."

She laughed. "I'd rather have you at home. Does that sound like a plan?"

We heard the bell ring on the door and Zoey cried out. "Grammy!"

"That sounds like an amazing plan," I said. "Grab your stuff, I'll take you home."

Paige let out a sigh as if all was suddenly right in her world.

We walked out into the main flower shop and watched as my father carried Zoey around like she was an airplane.

"Grandpa Phillip is coming over for dinner tonight," my mother said, turning and grinning when she saw me and Paige. Her eyes went down to Paige's stomach, and she made an O shape with her mouth.

"Sweetheart, that boy is growing by leaps and bounds."

Paige rested her hand on her stomach. "Tell me about it."

After saying goodbye to Lauren, we all headed out to our vehicles. Paige must have kissed Zoey goodbye ten times.

"She's going to Mom and Dad's for the night, Paige. Let her go," I finally said, taking her hand and pulling her to the truck.

"Bye, baby girl! Be good for Grammy and Grandpa!"

Zoey lifted her hand but didn't look back at us. "Bye!"

Paige gasped. "Did you see that? She didn't even look back at us!"

"Probably because she knows she is about to be treated like a princess. Let's go. I need to feed you, then give you sexual favors."

Three hours later, Paige and I lay in our bed, Paige satisfied with not only one, but three orgasms, and me exhausted from showering her with attention and trying to have sex in the latest position: on our sides. My ass had never cramped so hard in my life. It was still sore laying there as I wondered how in the hell one got a Charlie horse in their ass cheek.

I watched as Will did a tumble in Paige's stomach. Something that looked like his heel made a trail from one side, to the other. Paige smiled as she touched her stomach with one hand and shoveled her nasty concoction of popcorn in the other.

"I've been thinking," she said out of the blue.

"About?"

"Future little Fosters."

I laughed. "What about them?"

Paige looked at me, another handful of popcorn headed for her mouth. She looked so beautiful, lying there, completely naked, my baby in her swollen stomach. If she had told me she wanted eight more kids immediately, I would have said yes. Paige was even sexier pregnant. I had walked around with a hard-on during both pregnancies. Both of which had made Paige as horny as all get out. Especially the last three months of each pregnancy.

"I think I want to stop after Will."

Sitting up, I set my popcorn to the side. "Really? You want to stop at two?"

She nodded. "Are you okay with that? We have the magical pairing. A boy and a girl."

"I'm happy as long as you're happy. A family of four sounds nice."

With a smile, she nodded. "I think so, too. And they're close enough in age that it will be fun watching them grow up together."

"It will make vacations easier. You chase one, I chase the other. Besides, I heard that when the kids outnumber the parents, life gets messy."

She laughed. "Totally."

"I have something for you," I said, leaning over and pulling out an old wooden box.

"What's this?" she asked, attempting to sit up more in bed. I reached over and helped her, then slid a pillow behind her back.

"I was up in the attic a few days ago, looking through stuff, and found this."

Paige gave the box and then me an inquisitive look. Even after three years, we still hadn't looked through everything in the attic. Of course, once Paige got too big with Zoey, we stopped going up there, and then life just got busier. We'd taken all the jewelry out of Gram's travel wardrobe. Some we had sold; some we kept for Zoey for when she got older.

"I miss going up there," Paige said, running her finger along the F that was engraved on the box. "Have you checked what's in here?"

I nodded. Excitement bubbled, and it was everything I could do to not act like Zoey and jump around the bed and beg Paige to open the box.

"What's in it?" she asked.

"Open it and see."

With a smile that reminded me of Paige when she was a little girl, she opened the box. She frowned and pulled out the neatly folded letter. Her eyes swept over the paper and her mouth dropped open in utter shock.

When she looked up at me, she asked, "Is this for real?"

I nodded. "Yes. I had Lou look into it, and he got back with me today. It's legally ours."

Paige covered her mouth and stared at the paper. She slowly shook her head and faced me again. "He gifted May...a castle?"

I laughed, and in my best Scottish accent, I replied, "Ay, it looks like we own a wee castle in Scotland, m'lady."

Paige sat speechless.

"A castle? Is it in ruin?"

"Only way to find out is to take a trip to Scotland, when you and the wee lad are up for traveling."

Her eyes lit up like Christmas morning as she said, "I'm now the happiest woman on Earth!"

I lifted a brow. "Even though my office is blue...after I begged you to let me paint over the pink?"

She threw her arms around me and laughed. "It was peach!"

The End

Kelly Elliott is a *New York Times* and *USA Today* bestselling contemporary romance author. Since finishing her bestselling Wanted series, Kelly continues to spread her wings while remaining true to her roots and giving readers stories rich with hot protective men, strong women and beautiful surroundings.

Her bestselling works include, *Wanted, Broken, The Playbook, and Lost Love*, to name a few.

Kelly lives in central Texas with her husband, daughter, two pups, four cats, and endless wildlife creatures. When she's not writing, Kelly enjoys reading and spending time with her family.

To find out more about Kelly and her books, you can find her through her website.

www.kellyelliottauthor.com

Other Books by Kelly Elliott

Stand Alones
The Journey Home
*Who We Were**
*The Playbook**
*Made for You**
*Available on audiobook
Take Me Away (Coming 2020)

Cowboys and Angels Series
Lost Love
Love Profound
Tempting Love
Love Again
Blind Love
This Love
Reckless Love
*Series available on audiobook

Wanted Series
*Wanted**
*Saved**
*Faithful**
Believe
*Cherished**
*A Forever Love**
The Wanted Short Stories
All They Wanted
*Available on audiobook

Love Wanted in Texas Series
Spin-off series to the WANTED Series
Without You
Saving You

Holding You
Finding You
Chasing You
Loving You
Entire series available on audiobook
*Please note *Loving You* combines the last book of the Broken and Love Wanted in Texas series.

Broken Series
Broken*
Broken Dreams*
Broken Promises*
Broken Love
*Available on audiobook

The Journey of Love Series
Unconditional Love
Undeniable Love
Unforgettable Love
*Entire series available on audiobook

With Me Series
Stay With Me
Only With Me
*Series on audiobook

Speed Series
Ignite
Adrenaline

Boston Love Series
Searching for Harmony
Fighting for Love
*Series available on audiobook

Austin Singles Series
Seduce Me
Entice Me
Adore Me
*Series available on audiobook

YA Novels written under the pen name Ella Bordeaux
Beautiful
Forever Beautiful

Historical
Predestined Hearts by Kelly Elliott and Kristin Mayer

COMING SOON
Never Enough (Book one in the Meet Me in Montana series)
December 10, 2019

Southern Bride Series
Love at First Sight
Delicate Promises
Divided Interests February 2020

COLLABORATIONS
Predestined Hearts (co-written with Kristin Mayer)
Play Me (co-written with Kristin Mayer)
Dangerous Temptations (co-written with Kristin Mayer)

www.ingramcontent.com/pod-product-compliance
Lightning Source LLC
Chambersburg PA
CBHW070925260626
47162CB00007B/2790